FOR THE VICTIMS AND FAMILIES
OF THE 2021 BOULDER KING SOOPERS TRAGEDY

TRALONA BARTKOWIAK, 49   RIKKI OLDS, 25
SUZANNE FOUNTAIN, 59   NEVEN STANISIC, 23
TERI LEIKER, 51   DENNY STONG, 20
KEVIN MAHONEY, 61   OFFICER ERIC TALLEY, 51
LYNN MURRAY, 62   JODY WATERS, 65

SOUVENIR ANTHOLOGY

StokerCon™

THE **PHANTOM DENVER** EDITION

2021

Horror Writers ASSOCIATION

HEX PUBLISHERS

COVID COMPLICATIONS

Y OU KNOW WHAT THEY SAY about the best laid plans of mice and men? Well, the same holds true for publishers and convention planners. StokerCon™ 2021 wasn't just going to be a showcase of great horror talent; we also intended to shine a big, bold spotlight on Colorado's thriving horror community, demonstrating why it's the perfect host state for the genre's most important literary convention. This souvenir book, containing works from several notable Colorado horror writers and themed around a most striking and curious local landmark, was intended to cap off an unforgettable visit to the Mile High City. Unfortunately, the ongoing pandemic requires StokerCon™ 2021 to go virtual, denying you the physical thrills and chills Colorado has to offer.

But fret not! The change just means this souvenir book's original aim is more important than ever. Since you cannot experience a delicious bite of horror in our state, we're happy to deliver it right to your door, a memento of a phantom convention thwarted by real world horrors. We can't wait to see you in cyberspace. In the meanwhile, saddle up and see what this book's pages have in store for you. We hope you enjoy it, and we hope you'll come away with one important message:

Colorado just loves you to death.

This is a work of fiction. All characters, organizations, and events portrayed in this book are products of the authors' imaginations and/or are used fictitiously.

STOKERCON™ 2021 SOUVENIR ANTHOLOGY
THE PHANTOM DENVER EDITION

Edited by Joshua Viola
Copyedits by Alec Ferrell, Bret Smith, Jeanni Smith, and Emily Wismer
Cover illustration by Aaron Lovett
Cover layout by Damonza.com and Joshua Viola
Portrait art by Aaron Lovett
Story illustrations by Aaron Lovett
Header art by Aaron Lovett
Art direction by Joshua Viola
Typesets and formatting by Alec Ferrell

A Hex Publishers Book

Published & Distributed by Hex Publishers, LLC
PO BOX 298 Erie, CO 80516

www.HexPublishers.com

Joshua Viola, Publisher

Print ISBN-13: 978-1-7365964-0-1
First Edition: May 2021
10 9 8 7 6 5 4 3 2 1
Printed in the U.S.A.

TABLE OF CONTENTS

A LETTER FROM THE EDITOR

I MAGINE YOURSELF LANDING AT Denver International Airport, eager to get a drink and mingle with friends at StokerCon™ 2021, the threat of the coronavirus a distant memory. Luggage in hand, you've just left Baggage Claim and you're on your way to your hotel, sure to catch a glimpse of a towering, disconcerting statue of a blue mustang with blazing red eyes situated just beyond the airstrip.

If this was your first trip to Denver, you'd probably be thinking, *What the hell is* that *all about?*

There's no guarantee you'd see the statue, of course. Maybe you'd get a Lyft and fall asleep in the backseat. Maybe you're the type who is constantly absorbed in your smart phone. Or perhaps you're simply the least observant person in the world and oblivious to a bright blue 32-foot-tall horse leering down at the puny humans below.

But no, you didn't see it for other reasons...

2020 happened.

So, to make sure we're on the same page, take a moment to consult the Internet for a few photos. Google "Blucifer."

Unveiled at the Denver International Airport in 2008, two years after its creator, Luis Jiménez, was killed while working on it, the fiberglass statue is officially titled *Blue Mustang*. The locals call it Blucifer because of its demonic appearance and unfortunate history regarding Mr. Jiménez. The statue is sort of a mascot around these parts, and I thought it'd be a fine subject for the collection of (mostly) original fiction I curated for this book.

I could have chosen the Stanley Hotel, the brooding Rocky Mountains, one of the many ghost towns, a Native American legend, or any number of things that could create a horrifying, authentically *Colorado* storytelling experience.

But I chose *Blucifer*.

After all, if you're going to ride into the apocalyptic sunset of 2020, what better way to do it than saddling up on a monstrous blue steed?

Work on this anthology began as the world descended into several well-worn horror tropes. On television, we saw hallways filled with dying patients who swamped the ICU capacities of many hospitals. We saw refrigerated trucks lining up to store corpses from overflowing morgues. Loved ones died in isolation, their last words gasped out over Skype. In places like China and Iran, we saw satellite evidence of unceremonious mass graves dug by governments who refused to acknowledge the dead. In the United States, simple scientific and medical principles became political weapons, grist for the mill of old cultural grudges. Those of us who write always knew that successful dystopian fiction requires the hard work of detailed world-building. We didn't realize a dystopian reality just means watching the world around us fall apart and pondering what, if anything, can be done about it.

Which brings us to a philosophical point. Does horror fiction maintain its vitality during dark times? Who desires the great god Pan in the face of a pandemic? Do despair and disease blunt the appetite for ghosts and vampires? Or is there something about the genre's roots that thrive even when the soil is over-fertilized by the nightly news? Vexed by scientific terror, isn't there an escape hatch to be found in stories about the supernatural? Strange times call for stranger stories, stranger situations, stranger gods.

This certainly is my hope and belief. Horror writers try to imagine dreadful possibilities and weave them into gripping tales. A terrible year may make horror fiction unpalatable for a while, but I believe even dark

realities afford unique opportunities to study the human condition, to examine the nature of terror, grace, doubt, and faith. As a result, stories strengthen, psychological insight deepens, and the writer matures.

Every year brings forth events reminding us of the adage that reality is stranger than fiction. Many of us have felt like we've been trapped in a fever dream these last few years, culminating in 2020 with COVID-19, murder hornets, terrible natural disasters, social upheaval, and, of course, *Tiger King*. The writer must take all the horrors of 2020, meditate upon them, and use them to fuel their art. I hope this book is an example of that.

Intense gratitude exists in the heart of every storyteller, and gratitude is the strangest of creatures. It has the ability to feed on the smallest scrap of light and blaze forth stronger than ever. In 2020, President Trump's lack of leadership was a constant source of anxiety for me. My childhood best friend was hospitalized and almost died from COVID-19, bringing me tremendous stress and worry. I also endured the death of my mentor, the great writer Keith Ferrell. There was family stress I cannot even begin to describe. Even cracks of light seemed hard to come by some days.

But my gratitude found them all the same. Authoritarianism was voted out; sick friends survived; my wonderful memories of Keith sharpened, and his lessons, wisdom, and generosity of spirit will always stay with me. I got to collaborate with the wonderful talent included in this book, many of whom have become good friends. I edited two other anthologies and had my work published in a third, right alongside one of my personal heroes, Stephen King.

Best of all, I was able to work with my favorite collaborator of all time—my partner, Aaron Lovett. Together, we painted a variant cover for Aftershock Comics' new Lovecraft-inspired comic book series, *Miskatonic*, which you'll see in the gallery section. You'll also notice Aaron created this souvenir book's cover illustration, the flipbook animation in the header, and most of the interior art. To top it all off, in late 2020, Aaron and I got married (on Halloween, no less) and we started the adoption process.

By the end of the year, my gratitude didn't have to go scrounging for glimmers of light. The little guy was gorging himself, and I'm very glad to keep him well-fed in the safety of the Rocky Mountains. Not even Blucifer's enormous size can blot out the glow.

Denver would have been fortunate to host StokerCon™ 2021, honoring the very best writers, artists, and enthusiasts the horror genre can offer. Even though we can't gather together in the dark heart of the Mile High City this year, I hope this souvenir book provides a taste of what could have been, and perhaps a look at what's to come when the worst of the pandemic is behind us. Nevertheless, I'm proud that my company, Hex Publishers, participated alongside the Horror Writers Association in what promises to be a memorable virtual event. I cannot thank HWA President John Palisano enough for making the opportunity a reality, and I hope the quality of this book justifies his faith in me.

I believe you're in for a tremendous treat. This year's Guests of Honor require little in the way of introduction and include the gifted Steve Rasnic Tem, Lisa Morton, Maurice Broaddus, Seanan McGuire, Silvia Moreno-Garcia, and Joe R. Lansdale. Among them, these writers have many pages of exciting stories that have terrified thousands upon thousands of readers.

This StokerCon™ anthology took a slightly different path than books of the past. While it still highlights guests and award-winners, it has a genuine Colorado flavor with the addition of stories and poetry themed around Blucifer. These tales offer a glimpse of the literary brilliance the state has to offer. All of the stories fall under the umbrella of horror, but we haven't forgotten sub-genres. You'll find a bit of science fiction, a dash of adventure, and a pinch of absurdism. In addition to the original short fiction and art, there are interviews, anecdotes and essays on the writing and publishing process from local masters in the industry.

None of this would have been possible without the contributions of my many talented friends who helped make this book so very special. Thank

you, Mario Acevedo, Meghan Arcuri, Carina Bissett, James Chambers, JoAnn Chaney, Hillary Dodge, Warren Hammond, Jason Heller, Travis Heermann, Angie Hodapp, Stephen Graham Jones, Sam Knight, Aaron Lovett, Jonathan Maberry, Brian Matthews, Josh Schlossberg, Jeanne Stein, Molly Tanzer, John Wenzel, Jeamus Wilkes, Carter Wilson, Dean Wyant, and Alvaro Zinos-Amaro.

I especially want to thank Sean Eads, Alec Ferrell, Bret Smith, and Jeanni Smith, whose passion, dedication and camaraderie helped carry this project past the finish line.

So, turn the page and behold the light that arose from the darkness of 2020.

Joshua Viola, Editor

ANTI-HARASSMENT POLICY

What are the aims of this harassment policy?

- To help all attendees and staff feel welcome, valued, and as safe as possible.
- To define and discourage harassing, abusive behavior.
- To make it as safe and simple as possible for people to report harassment, if necessary.
- To clearly establish for staff and attendees how reports of harassment will be handled.
- To set fair consequences for such behavior.

Why does StokerCon™ need an anti-harassment policy?

We've implemented an anti-harassment policy in response to widespread reports of harassment at conventions and in order to meet our goal of providing a safe and comfortable convention experience for everyone.

StokerCon™ is dedicated to providing a safe and comfortable convention experience for everyone, regardless of gender, sexuality, ability, physical appearance, body size, actual or perceived race, national origin, family or marital status, socio-economic class or religion. In order to offer a welcoming and safe space for everyone, we require participants to be respectful of all others and their space, be it physical or social.

What is harassment?

Harassment includes:

Offensive verbal comments about gender, sexuality, impairment, physical appearance, body size, race or religion. Racist behavior, including: attendees being expected to be an authority on corresponding characters in various genre and media settings; and/or being talked down to or assumed to be less knowledgeable about topics being discussed because of ethnic origin showing sexual images in public spaces. Discussion or images related to sex, pornography, discriminatory language or similar is permitted if it meets all of the following criteria:

Organizers have specifically granted permission in writing; it is necessary to the topic of discussion and no alternative exists; it is presented in a respectful manner, especially towards women and LGBTQIA people; and attendees are warned in advance in the program and respectfully given ample warning and opportunity to leave beforehand. This exception does not allow use of gratuitous sexual images as attention-getting devices (such as clothing or costumes in the dealers' room) or unnecessary presentation or panel examples. Intimidation, stalking or following, photographing or recording someone without their permission, sustained disruption of talks or other events, uninvited physical contact including uninvited sexual attention. Participants asked to stop any harassing behavior are expected to comply immediately. This includes not only anyone involved in the incident, but any onlookers contributing to the disruption.

What are some examples?

As a general rule, practicing common sense in physical and social interactions with strangers will ensure everyone has a comfortable convention experience. Here are some guidelines for types of behavior that may make others uncomfortable or be considered harassment:

Physically touching or endangering other people without an express invitation is never acceptable. Touching other people's personal effects without an express invitation. This includes clothing, assistive devices, bags, and on-duty service animals. If physical contact is wished, do so verbally or with a friendly gesture. Holding a hand out for a handshake is a good example. Sharing space with other people requires active demonstra-

tions of respect and empathy. Good examples can be: leaving other people a clear path to an exit, moderating the volume of your voice, limiting the expansiveness of your gestures as well as maintaining an appropriate physical distance.

Please respect the desires of a person or persons who have expressed their wish for no further contact. Do not contact them, either by your own agency or through an intermediary.

StokerCon™ welcomes vigorous debate, but that do not verbally attack people.

Be aware of consent to continue interaction with another person, observing non-verbal and verbal clues. Pay attention if the other party wishes to end the interaction. If there is any question if the other party wants to end the interaction, end the interaction yourself.

When in doubt, don't make assumptions: ask.

Who can report a problem?

Anyone who was directly affected by or witnessed harassment can file a report, and is encouraged to do so.

What should I do if I am being harassed?

In some cases, you may find the harassment stops if you clearly say 'no' or 'please leave me alone', or simply walk away. We would appreciate it if a volunteer was still informed to help us identify any repeat offenders.

If you continue to be harassed or notice someone else being harassed, please contact a convention volunteer immediately. The volunteers will help participants contact venue security or law enforcement, provide escorts, or otherwise assist those experiencing harassment to feel safe during the con. The first convention volunteer or organizer you report to will take whatever steps they can to assist you in feeling safe, and will put you in contact with or bring you to an appropriate senior staff member. We value your attendance.

You do not have to give us details of the harassment, and can choose whether or not to take a formal report. If you wish to report, we will take details of the harassment and work with you to respond to the issue in a way that assists you in feeling safe and maintains the safety of the wider convention environment, as well as enforcing our anti-harassment policy. If you report a serious criminal matter, please be aware that we may be obliged to contact the police. We would however take into account any concerns you may have around involving them.

If you would like to discuss the harassment without making a report, we will help you meet with the designated on-call senior staff member. Please bear in mind that this is for informal emotional support only: our volunteers don't have counselling training, and we can't promise confidentiality. You can access this service by contacting any convention volunteer.

What sort of problem can I report?

Any behavior or pattern of behavior that you feel comes under the definition of harassment. If you feel someone's behavior is dangerous or harmful to you or others, if someone's behavior makes you feel afraid or very uncomfortable, or if someone is actively making it difficult for you or others to enjoy or fully participate in the convention, we would like to know about it.

Who can I make a report about?

Anyone whose behavior causes you concern. We will give all reports equal consideration. Our handling of reports will not be influenced by factors such as the social status or convention role of anyone involved in the situation.

When can I report a problem?

At any time; however, we request that reporting take place as soon as possible during or after an incident, especially if you believe that someone may be causing problems for multiple people at the convention. Reports

will be taken seriously and handled appropriately regardless of when they are made.

How do I find a convention volunteer?

Our convention volunteers are called Red Shirts, and can be easily identified by their red T-shirts. Any one of them can be your first point of contact. The volunteer may need to involve a more senior staff member to assist with your issue.

What actions can StokerCon™ convention staff take to a harassment incident?

Senior staff reserve the right to take any action they deem appropriate, including:

Issuing the offender with a warning if, in the determination of senior staff and/or the person reporting the incident, the incident is considered accidental or minor;

making an internal note of the incident to document repeat offending;

making a formal report of the incident available to volunteers, senior staff or all convention participants at the discretion of senior staff; contacting hotel security; contacting law enforcement; removing the offender from the convention with no refund; and

reporting the offender's behavior to other convention or regulatory organizations.

If you email a report after the convention, the Chair of StokerCon™ will receive your report. They will explain in detail what the possible outcomes are and what will be asked of you, read your report, and interview other people (witnesses, the person the report is about) as necessary. The Chair will determine whether any action needs to be taken. You will be informed of any action that StokerCon™ takes in connection with your report.

StokerCon™ representatives will follow this policy and the internal procedures of the hotel/venue with the safety of all the convention's attendees in mind, which may require us to take certain actions without the consent of the person making the report. We will do our very best to balance the needs of all involved parties and the needs of the convention when they conflict.

What won't happen if I make a report?

We will not reveal your identity or the substance of your report unless it is absolutely necessary to obtain information about the incident or take action related to the incident.

We will not take any sort of retaliatory action against you for reporting or not reporting a problem.

We will not provide mediation or intermediary communication services.

While we will always err on the side of safety and treat all reports as true, we will not assume that a report being made automatically means that action needs to be taken.

What will happen if someone says I caused a problem?

If someone tells us that you have violated the code of conduct, two convention representatives will ask to speak with you about it in a private place.

If you decline to be interviewed, we may ask you to leave the convention. If, after speaking with you, we believe that you have acted in a manner deemed as harassment then we may ask you to change your behavior or leave the convention, or take other actions.

We will not take action until we've spoken with you and anyone else involved and done our best to get a clear picture of what happened.

If we believe that no violation occurred, you are welcome to go about the convention as usual. We will not attempt to mediate or carry messages between you and the person who made the StokerCon™ report. If someone deliberately makes a false report about you, that is itself harassment and we will take appropriate action in response.

How can I help make StokerCon™ safer?

Be aware of this harassment policy, of using non-oppressive language, and of boundaries.

Back up others—if you see someone being harassed or appearing uncomfortable, ask if they're okay.

WHAT IS THE HORROR WRITERS ASSOCIATION?

THE HORROR WRITERS ASSOCIATION (HWA) is a nonprofit organization of writers and publishing professionals around the world, dedicated to promoting dark literature and the interests of those who write it. HWA was formed in the late 1980's with the help of many of the field's greats, including Dean Koontz, Robert McCammon, and Joe R. Lansdale. Today—with over 1,700 members in countries such as Australia, Belgium, Brazil, Canada, Costa Rica, Denmark, Germany, Honduras, India, Ireland, Israel, Italy, Japan, Netherlands, New Zealand, Nicaragua, Russia, Spain, South Africa, Sweden, Taiwan, Thailand, Trinidad, United Kingdom and the United States—it is the oldest and most respected professional organization for the much-loved writers who have brought you the most enjoyable sleepless nights of your life.

One of HWA's missions is to encourage public interest in and foster an appreciation of good Horror and Dark Fantasy literature. To that end, we offer the public areas of our website, we sponsor or take part in occasional public readings and lectures, we publish a blog and produce other materials for booksellers and librarians, we facilitate readings and signings by horror writers, and we maintain an official presence at the major fan-based horror and fantasy conventions, such as the World Fantasy Convention and the World Horror Convention.

HWA is also dedicated to recognizing and promoting diversity in the horror genre, and practices a strict anti-harassment policy at all of its events.

As part of our core mission, we sponsor the annual Bram Stoker Awards® for superior achievement in horror literature. Named in honor of the author of the seminal horror novel *Dracula*, the Bram Stoker Awards® are presented for superior writing in twelve categories including traditional fiction of various lengths, poetry, screenwriting, graphic novels, young adult, and non-fiction. In addition, HWA presents an annual Lifetime Achievement Award(s) to a living person(s) who made significant contributions to the writing of Horror and Dark Fantasy over the course of a lifetime.

WHO IS HEX PUBLISHERS?

HEX PUBLISHERS is an independent publishing house in Erie, Colorado, proudly specializing in genre fiction: horror, science fiction, crime, dark fantasy, comics, and any other form that explores the imagination. Founded by writers, Hex values both the author and the reader, with an emphasis on quality, diversity, and voices often overlooked by the mainstream. Hex is owned and operated by Joshua Viola.

Learn more about Hex Publishers at *www.hexpublishers.com.*

A LETTER FROM THE PRESIDENT

LEGEND SAYS THE SANTA ANA WINDS are the Satanis winds—the devil winds—which dry out and cook brush, trees, and grass. Embers turn to fires, and those turn into infernos. The flames have destroyed millions of square feet from California to Colorado in 2020. Containment remains elusive with several fires raging for months. Just as the hungry fires overwhelm everyone unlucky enough to be in their path, so, too, has the novel coronavirus. Just as the fires have spread indiscriminately, this worldwide pandemic has upended nearly every aspect of our world.

Early in 2020, the Horror Writers Association (HWA) neared the start of its first international convention to be held in Scarborough, UK. As infrastructure closed and stay at home orders came down, convention chair Marie O'Regan and I volleyed many emails back and forth. After over two years of planning, pushing the date at the last minute was excruciating on all sides. It's now October 2020, and we are hoping that by the time you're reading this...printed in your hands...that we have finally come out the other side of this global crisis and are enjoying a return to some type of new normal. Enough for us to gather in fellowship, at least, even if it's in cyberspace.

Leading an organization of creators during such a tumultuous time calls for unity. We won't make it through this relatively intact unless we all stand and work together. The fires and scourge have come, and as devastating as they've been, they've also burned down the houses and laid bare some serious issues that need addressing and fixing.

As leaders of thought, each of us imagines a better world. Our works often use the horror we experience as catalysts for commentary. Even if not the work itself, the rise of so many charitable anthologies, groups, fundraisers, and support systems in our community speaks volumes. Our art and how we present it reflects our times, as it always has, and as it is now.

The HWA is not an autocracy. Not with me at the helm. This is an organization run by the most passionate and hardworking volunteers. These amazing people are the HWA. Each is the face of the HWA. Our Board of Trustees. Our Executive Board. Our social media managers. Our Administrator. Those Chapter Chairs who carry the torch and light the way for others. My eternal gratitude to each of you. Special thanks, too, to Larry Berry, who headed an early Denver StokerCon™ committee.

We've grown exponentially this year…more than we ever have. Not only are new chapters being formed in the United States, but we have chapters forming in India, Australia, Canada, Belgravia and Ireland. It's amazing to witness.

Welcome to StokerCon™ 2021!

John Palisano
President, Horror Writers Association

A LETTER FROM THE VICE PRESIDENT

WELCOME TO STOKERCON™ 2021! As I write this, we're still in 2020…yes…that 2020…the one with a contentious U.S. election; multiple social, environmental, and economic crises; and a pandemic. A damn pandemic!

My 2020 self is hoping (praying, begging, crossing fingers, burning sage) that we've turned multiple corners and are enjoying life more thoroughly in 2021. As of now, however, in the waning days of 2020, things are bleak. I blame no one for feeling depressed, anxious, and exhausted.

One of the things that has given me a little bit of joy, a little bit of hope is the horror writing community. Specifically, the people in it. As the HWA's social media coordinator and editor of Quick Bites, I have a front row seat to much of the goings-on. I've seen your vast productivity—so many beautiful books, so many beautiful covers—even in the face of great adversity; I've seen your incredible generosity—donations to HWA funds, as well as to multiple crowdfunding campaigns; and I've seen your humor and your humanity. Is it always rainbows and unicorns and harmony? No…we've certainly had our share of strife. From where I sit, however, we are ultimately more supportive than we are destructive.

The HWA has also had many successful initiatives this past year. Initiatives which are fitting for our times.

Because of the tireless work of our Administrator, Brad Hodson, members of the HWA—and their families and employees—now have access to affordable health insurance. We are ecstatic to be able to offer this important benefit, especially during these difficult times. Make sure to thank Brad when you see him.

In addition to our many other scholarships, we now offer the Diversity Grants. As a member of the subcommittee that developed this, I can say we approached this task with thoughtfulness, intelligence, and care. Representation and diversity have always mattered; they have always been important. The HWA acknowledges this and is committed to doing its part to ensure our organization is welcoming to all.

Although it's been a long time coming, we are now able to offer Horror University Online. Coronavirus made Zoom-users of us all and, thus, provided us with a means to get this StokerCon™ favorite to the public. So far, it has been more popular than we dreamed, and we hope it continues to grow. Stay tuned…

We've had many other successes, as well: virtual (and free!) Librarians' Day, new Chapters in Colorado Springs and India, and all of our many publications, from *Don't Turn Out the Lights* to *Vathek*!

These successes are due to the hard work and enthusiasm of many members of our community. And I would be remiss if I did not call out one of those members: HWA President, John Palisano. Many of you know John as a friendly and fun guy, a great writer, a Bram Stoker Award® winner. And he is all of these things.

But did you know just how dedicated he is to this community? So dedicated, in fact, he conducted interviews for last year's Stokers; put together our virtual Stoker presentation; gave input on all of the above initiatives (and countless others); answered hundreds of emails (at least 50% of which were from me); and a whole bunch of other things he was too busy to mention…all the while personally battling with coronavirus. (Oh yeah, and did his day job and raised his kid, too.)

John loves the HWA, he loves horror, and he loves the people in this community. His passion is palpable, his hard work extraordinary. He's full of gratitude and quick with a kind word. He is a great president, and we're lucky to have him.

Thank you so much for attending StokerCon™ 2021. We appreciate you and your support. And thank you for making an otherwise dreary year one full of progress, positivity, and, of course, the good kind of horror.

Meghan Arcuri
Vice President, Horror Writers Association

CONVENTIONS IN THE AGE OF CORONAVIRUS

T HE COVID-19 PANDEMIC HAS CHANGED EVERYTHING. Around each curve, beyond every corner, something is cancelled or delayed or altered. Throughout 2020 and into 2021, people have missed out on family vacations and holiday gatherings, corporate conferences and professional conventions. Old friends are faces on a Zoom screen. Cloth masks hide our smiles.

Who here feels like Charlie Brown trying to kick that damn football, only to have Lucy yank it away?

As we pen this article, the United States presidential election just ended, the SARS-CoV-2 virus burns throughout parts of the world, and the future remains uncertain. Still, we're roughly six months out from StokerCon™ 2021 and in the thick of planning. Hopefully you're reading this incredible souvenir book snug in your room at The Curtis, swag bag and name badge on the table next to you, with the sounds of footsteps outside your door as your fellow writers—your friends—file in.

Will it happen like this? We don't know, but we know it will happen.

And for that reason, we plan.

As horror writers, we routinely imagine all the things that can go wrong in life, from the mundane to the supernatural, from the personal to the apocalyptic. We send our characters down dark paths, and we craft poems born of nightmares. Yet we hardly expect to face the existential uncertainty that defined 2020 in reality. Of the horror writers we've spoken with over the past year, many have risen above the challenges of a pandemic, political unrest, and prolonged isolation, reached deep, and kept writing. Some have created new ways to keep connected via online events and conventions. And while those adaptations have sweetened a sour year, they're no substitute for being face to face amongst our colleagues and friends, sharing meals and conversation in person, and coming together to celebrate writing and the horror genre.

And for those reasons too, we plan.

Whether we're gathered in Denver on schedule—or on an alternate date or even using those freshly honed online meeting skills to come together virtually—the important thing is that we continue the StokerCon™ tradition of exploring the horror genre, mentoring new writers, and furthering the work of horror authors everywhere.

Regardless of the circumstance under which you are reading this souvenir book, horror writers exist, at their core, as a fellowship. We love to gather, to share, to laugh together and to cry together. The pandemic may knock us down, but it cannot keep us down. Like our characters, we are survivors.

And for all those reasons, we plan.

Welcome to your StokerCon™ 2021.

James Chambers and Brian W. Matthews
Co-Chairs, StokerCon™ 2021

BRAM STOKER AWARDS® EMCEE
JONATHAN MABERRY

JONATHAN MABERRY IS A *New York Times* bestselling author, five-time Bram Stoker Award®-winner, anthology editor, and comic book writer. His vampire apocalypse book series, *V-WARS*, was a Netflix original series. He writes in multiple genres including suspense, thriller, horror, science fiction, fantasy, and action; and he writes for adults, teens and middle grade. His works include the *Joe Ledger* thrillers, *Ink*, *Glimpse*, the *Rot & Ruin* series, the *Dead of Night* series, *The Wolfman*, *X-Files Origins: Devil's Advocate*, *Mars One*, and many others. Several of his works are in development for film and TV. He is the editor of high-profile anthologies including *The X-Files*, *Aliens: Bug Hunt*, *Out of Tune*, *New Scary Stories to Tell in the Dark*, *Baker Street Irregulars*, *Nights of the Living Dead*, and others. His comics include *Black Panther: DoomWar*, *The Punisher: Naked Kills* and *Bad Blood*. His *Rot & Ruin* young adult novel was adapted into the #1 comic on Webtoon, and is being developed for film by Alcon Entertainment. He is a board member of the Horror Writers Association, the president of the International Association of Media Tie-in Writers, and the editor of *Weird Tales Magazine*. He lives in San Diego, California. Find him online at *www.jonathanmaberry.com*.

STOKERCON™ 2021 GUEST OF HONOR
MAURICE BROADDUS

THERE'S ALMOST A SYMBOLIC PORTMANTEAU in the last name of Maurice Broaddus, in that his writing interests are broad and he's invested in strengthening community, always looking for a more inclusive definition of *us*. Born in London, England, Broaddus has been a long-time resident of Indiana, earning a bachelor's degree in biology at Purdue University. He subsequently spent almost twenty years working as an environmental toxicologist. Now a very successful and award-winning writer whose work is being adapted for TV, Broaddus commits himself to education and community organizing, allying with nonprofit organizations such as Kheprw Institute, where he is the resident Afrofuturist.

Writers often tackle social issues, but Broaddus lives his commitment outside of the printed word. As he says on his website: "I do two things: write and work for the improvement of my community." Over the years, he discovered how his passion for storytelling and social change began to complement and empower each other.

"My community work informs my writing and my writing informs my community work," Broaddus says in his interview for this book. His Knights of Breton Court series demonstrates the concept perfectly, a retelling of Arthurian legends told from the perspective of homeless adolescents in Indianapolis. Broaddus has credited volunteer work with Outreach Inc., a local ministry focused on at-risk youth, as inspiring this daring concept, which is often referred to as *"The Wire* meets *Excalibur."*

Broaddus is somewhat unusual among contemporary writers in that he has a true affinity for the novella, those publishing orphans too long to be a short story and too short to be a novel. Selling even one novella can be difficult enough, but Broaddus has pulled off the feat four times, including 2017's steampunk story, *Buffalo Soldier*, a tale of espionage in a reality where the American Revolution played out in quite a different way. But Broaddus' willingness to take a chance with novellas has paid off in a big way with *Sorcerers*, an illustrated story about hip-hop and ancient magic. In 2020, AMC announced they will adapt the story into a TV series.

It should be no surprise someone invested in building his community carries a terrific sense of world-building into his fiction. Of particular note is the keen eye for realistic detail he brings to even the most imaginative concept. For example, when *SF Book Reviews* covered *King's Justice,*

the second novel in the Knights of Breton Court series, Broaddus' gritty realism did not escape notice: "It's simply an incredible work of compelling fiction and the closest most of us will ever get (if we are lucky) to living in a ghetto, pure genius." His knack for world-building has also made Broaddus a natural fit for the gaming community, and he has written for several properties, including *Marvel Super-Heroes*, *Firefly* and *Watch Dogs 2*.

STOKERCON™ 2021 GUEST OF HONOR
JOE R. LANSDALE

![Portrait of Joe R. Lansdale]

FEW AUTHORS WRITE IN AS MANY GENRES as Joe R. Lansdale. The Texas native is just as well known for his horror work as he is for westerns, thrillers, mystery and science fiction—sometimes combining all of them in a single story. To Lansdale, however, genre hardly matters at all. He writes what he wants to write and calls it, as he says in his interview for this book, "the Lansdale genre." His fiction has won the Bram Stoker Award® multiple times, the British Fantasy Award, and the Edgar Award, among many other accolades and prizes.

A prolific writer since the publication of his first novel, *Act of Love* (1981), Lansdale's bibliography includes 45 novels and 30 short story collections. He has written directly for comics and TV and has also seen his work adapted for graphic novels, TV shows, and films.

The diversity of his output is reflected in his influences. Lansdale has claimed James Cain, Ray Bradbury, Robert Bloch and Flannery O'Connor as writers who impact his fiction. Raymond Chandler and Richard Matheson's influence can be detected as well in developing a noir feeling to so many of his stories. And just as O'Connor makes the American South feel like an active character rather than a setting, Lansdale achieves the same effect with the Texas landscapes his characters often wander through in blood-soaked adventures. He is a master of creating a regional voice.

Despite the vast range of topics and interests covered in Lansdale's work, readers know they can expect certain qualities in his stories. Plots featuring outrageous situations and notes of absurdism are prevalent, and electrifying, memorable dialogue spoken by engaging characters are hallmarks of his storytelling. Careful readers will also note how Lansdale almost always avoids ambiguous endings, preferring to bring every story to a definite conclusion. In summary, as Lansdale has often said, his writing strikes "a note of the unusual."

Lansdale is perhaps best known for his Hap and Leonard series, best friend amateur detectives and martial arts experts who get involved with brutal crimes. Their adventures, told over many novels, novellas and short story collections, are even more notable because of the bi-racial makeup of their friendship and Leonard's identity as a gay Black man. The series was adapted into a three-season television show that ran on SundanceTV from 2016-2018.

Regardless of his success as a novelist, Lansdale himself has stated he prefers the short story format, and many critics feel short stories offer the best introduction to his work. A review of *High Cotton: Selected Stories* (2003) in the *Austin Chronicle* calls it "the best introduction to the author you could ask for" and says it shows "an artist at the height of his talents." *The Best of Joe R. Lansdale* (2010) offers another fine representation of his short fiction, compiling some of his most important and famous works.

STOKERCON™ 2021 GUEST OF HONOR
SEANAN MCGUIRE

CALIFORNIA NATIVE AND RESIDENT Seanan McGuire has too much talent for one name, so she also writes under the equally popular pseudonym Mira Grant and, more recently, as A. Deborah Baker. Not only does she hold a record for five Hugo nominations in a single year (2013), she's also been nominated in four different categories—Best Novel, Best Novella, Best Related Work, and Best Fancast.

McGuire's personal interests straddle the literary and the scientific. Her novel *Alien: Echo* is the first young adult novel in the popular *Alien* franchise, and as McGuire notes in her interview for this book, she gave the approaching publishers fair notice about her intentions. "I was asked if I wanted to write a Young Adult *Alien* book; I love the *Alien* franchise; I said yes. I also warned them that I have a biology background and enjoy research, and they said I could create a whole ecosystem to go with my colony world. It was wonderful."

Her biology background certainly plays a key role in her InCryptid series, where Verity Price finds herself practicing her family's long and complicated tradition of cryptozoology. Verity walks a fine line between saving the world from strange creatures while in turn protecting them from sinister agents who want them dead. With cryptids ranging from the size of mice to the length of dragons, the series delights in coming up with unusual creatures plausibly rendered.

Scientific interests aside, McGuire majored in folklore at the University of California, Berkeley, and her research interests and reading provide a key inspiration for so much of her work. This is particularly true of her October Daye urban fantasy series, whose protagonist is half-human, half-faerie who works as a private investigator in San Francisco. Throughout the series (currently approaching 17 titles), McGuire enhances her narratives with layers of allusion. Praising the books, Publishers Weekly marvels at how she "adeptly plunders folklore, nursery rhymes, traditional ballads, and fairy tales for her framework."

StokerCon™ fans may prefer the grittier horror of her alter ego, Mira Grant. *Feed*, the first Grant novel in the Newsflesh trilogy, is a horrific thriller set 20 years after a zombie apocalypse. In other hands, this would be a worn-out scenario, but McGuire breathes fresh life into the subject through skillful world-building, immersing us in the new world's politics

and social media.

McGuire has a caveat for anyone approaching *Feed* for the first time in the aftermath of COVID-19. "If well-researched virological horror is a little close to real life right now," she says, readers are encouraged to try a standalone title called *Into the Drowning Deep*. What's it about? McGuire has a succinct summary: "In which mermaids eat faces." There's also her Parasitology trilogy, which really brings McGuire's interests in biology to the forefront of her storytelling. In a dark tale that Booklist called "firmly anchored in real world science and technology," humanity depends on genetically engineered tapeworms to survive. But what happens when the tapeworms stop wanting to cooperate?

Whether the story is fantasy or horror, part of a series or a standalone, McGuire's readers know they can expect fast-paced storytelling, capable female protagonists, and engaging side characters who never fail to amuse and entertain.

STOKERCON™ 2021 GUEST OF HONOR
SILVIA MORENO-GARCIA

IN AN AGE WHERE CREATIVE WRITING PROGRAMS and workshops flourish, Silvia Moreno-Garcia's work stands out all the more because she has no formal training in the art of fiction writing. In fact, other than a little bit of writing she did as a child, Moreno-Garcia did not seriously approach storytelling as a craft until financial difficulties forced her hand. Unable to find regular employment, with her husband working two jobs, she turned to writing and submitting her work to American publishers.

Her subsequent success has been obvious. Born and raised in Mexico, and currently residing in Canada, Moreno-Garcia now has six novels and two short story collections to her credit. She's also been the editor or co-editor on seven anthologies, including *Historical Lovecraft* (2011) and *Nebula Awards Showcase 2019*. She further champions the weird fiction community as publisher of Innsmouth Free Press.

Critics have noted from the beginning just how well Moreno-Garcia handles voice in her work. Her characters are identifiable and complex. Meche, the adolescent outcast from *Signal to Noise*, demonstrates Moreno-Garcia's abilities to capture feelings of anger, estrangement and wonder as Meche and her misfit friends discover their record collection has magical powers.

Her writing and publishing interests are also keen on making sure other voices get heard. For instance, she edited *Fractured: Tales of the Canadian Post-Apocalypse*, proving end of the world intrigues aren't exclusive to the United States. Her own stories often focus on her native Mexico, particularly Mexico City, and she makes skillful use of Mexican folklore. Her 2019 novel *Gods of Jade and Shadow* finds a young woman in the Jazz Age accidentally releasing the Mayan God of Death and sets her on a quest into the Mayan Underworld. The American Library Association selected *Gods of Jade and Shadow* as its Reading List winner in the fantasy genre. The novel also won the 2020 Sunburst Award for Excellence in Canadian Literature.

Most recently, Moreno-Garcia reviews books for NPR and writes columns for *The Washington Post* in addition to her fiction and publisher responsibilities.

STOKERCON™ 2021 GUEST OF HONOR
LISA MORTON

Novelist, screenwriter and editor Lisa Morton's path to storytelling began in the film industry, though not perhaps in the way one might expect. A cinephile and ardent collector of movie memorabilia, she started her career as a model maker for *Star Trek: The Motion Picture*, helping to create interior shots of V'ger and going on to assist with design work for *Close Encounters of the Third Kind*, *The Abyss*, and *Star Trek: The Next Generation*.

Morton soon found herself growing more and more interested in storytelling. The California native began writing and directing for small theater companies in her home state and contributed to many TV productions. But her greatest success came in the 1990s when her writing interests turned to horror.

As Morton says in her interview for this book, "Horror is my preferred genre (although I've begun exploring mystery more of late), and I love the short form. Novels are hard for me because I have so many ideas I want to explore and characters I want to write about that I'm always anxious to move onto the next thing."

Morton's dexterity with the genre cannot be denied. Between 2006 and 2020, she has won the Bram Stoker Award® multiple times and in several categories, including short fiction, long fiction, novel, graphic novel, and non-fiction. Her bibliography currently stands at seven novels and collections, seven works of academic and popular non-fiction, one graphic novel, numerous novellas and several dozen short stories. She's also edited or co-edited five anthologies, including *Haunted Nights* (2017) with Ellen Datlow.

Those approaching Morton's work for the first time should expect carefully drawn characters and well-developed female protagonists who aren't shy about scratching an itch for adventure. Her stories have a cinematic flair appropriate for her background in film production, maintaining a fast pace without sacrificing creepy atmospherics or Gothic sensibilities.

Aside from her writing and editing activities, Morton has played a conspicuous and critical role in the horror community, serving as President of the Horror Writers Association from 2014-2019. She's also been interviewed for several documentaries, including The History Channel's *The Real Story of Halloween*, and has made guest appearances on popular programs such as *Coast to Coast AM* with George Noory.

STOKERCON™ 2021 GUEST OF HONOR
STEVE RASNIC TEM

Born in Virginia but a long-time Colorado resident, Steve Rasnic Tem remains one of the genre's most prolific and skilled short story writers, whose work often appears in annual *Best Of* anthologies and prominent magazines. Multiple collections of his fiction, such as *The Harvest Child and Other Fantasies*, demonstrate Tem's incredible range of themes and interests. Regardless of subject matter, his writing is marked with cool and controlled language that helps develop understated tensions throughout his narratives.

Tem has not restricted himself to brief fiction. He has published several novels, including the 2015 Bram Stoker Award®-winner *Blood Kin*. As Tem observes, "*Blood Kin* was a book I always wanted to write, and began writing it in high school. The first chapter is pretty much as I wrote it my senior year, tidied up a bit." Set in his native Virginia, the novel offers an intense Southern Gothic experience set in the 1930s, featuring snake handlers and sinister family secrets.

In many ways, Tem's first novel, *Excavation* (1987) introduces several tropes that reoccur in his subsequent work, including the inherent narrative power of family histories and intrigues that lurk just outside of his characters' understanding. Melancholy narrators dealing with personal loss and tragedy are also hallmarks of Tem's work, elevating his storytelling with explorations of grief and other identifiable situations such as marital tensions. As Tem notes in his interview for this book, "I believe that when horror fiction fails to be convincing it generally fails on the level of its realism. By realism I mean its portrayals of the mundane world."

Before her passing in 2015, Tem collaborated on several projects with his wife, Melanie, herself a Bram Stoker Award®-winner for her first novel, *Prodigal* (1991). A series of vignettes they wrote together, published as *The Man on the Ceiling*, won the Bram Stoker Award®, the World Fantasy Award, and the British Fantasy Award. As Tem explains, their first collaboration was the story "Prosthesis," published by *Asimov's Science Fiction Magazine* in 1986. "I had an idea, and I'd written an opening, but I thought it needed a strong female point of view, and I was feeling a bit stuck, so I handed it over to Melanie."

It's fitting this same kind of back-and-forth dialectic is maintained in

Yours to Tell: Dialogues on the Art & Practice of Writing (2017), an essential and engaging book on the craft of storytelling that records Steve and Melanie's conversations with each other on the process of writing.

Tem continues to write at an enviable clip. A new short story collection called *Thanatrauma* is scheduled for release in 2021. His latest novel is *The Mask Shop of Doctor Blaack* (2018). He has also edited two anthologies, including the World Fantasy Award-finalist *High Fantastic: Colorado's Fantasy, Dark Fantasy, and Science Fiction* (1995).

A CONVERSATION WITH MAURICE BROADDUS

by Jeanne C. Stein

L AST SUMMER WAS A VERY EXCITING ONE for Guest of Honor Maurice Broaddus. His book, *Pimp My Airship*, won the 2020 Eugene and Marilyn Glick Indiana Author Award in the Genre category. AMC Networks announced that it will adapt his novella, *Sorcerers*, into a TV series. Plus, HarperCollins recently published the paperback edition of his 2019 young adult novel, *The Usual Suspects*. A trifecta win!

Maurice was born in London, England, but has lived in Indianapolis, Indiana, for most of his life. He holds a Bachelor of Science degree from Purdue University in biology (with an undeclared major in English). A community organizer and teacher, he has over a dozen novels and 100 short stories in print. His gaming work includes writing for *Marvel Super Heroes*, *Leverage*, and *Firefly*.

Jeanne: Your unofficial bio lists exotic dancer, award-winning haberdasher, and credits you with inventing the question mark to name just three among a score of impressive accomplishments. Is your alter ego in a parallel universe perhaps?

Maurice: Possibly. More importantly, it's my continual reminder about the importance of not doing important business things (like creating your author bio) while on a second bottle of Riesling…

Jeanne: You have said that winning the 2020 Eugene and Marilyn Glick Indiana Authors Award was very special to you. Why?

Maurice: I am firmly on the record as saying that I write for me. And that I publish to be read. That's how I've always traveled in my career in order to stay sane since there's so much that is simply out of a writer's control. Like awards.

But I will admit, there's something special about being recognized in your hometown. To have that validation from your community. AND FOR MY MOM TO SEE IT!

Jeanne: Give us the TV Guide description for *Sorcerers*.

Maurice: A young hip hop artist still trying to figure out his place in life discovers that he comes from a long line of magic users. Hijinks ensue.

Jeanne: What is your writing process like? Do you have a daily word count you strive for? Do you adhere to a plot or make it up as you go along? Do you have a favorite place to write?

Maurice: My writing process shifted over the summer. I'd log into Zoom with a couple of writing friends of mine at 10 a.m. and stay logged in until at least 2 p.m. for writing sprints. I turned my front porch into my "coffeeshop" and write from there so that neighbors, family, and friends can "interrupt" me anytime.

I never worry about word counts, but I do say that I'm ALWAYS writing. EVEN WHEN IT LOOKS LIKE I'M JUST STARING INTO SPACE, MOM. I'M WORKING! (In case you couldn't tell, we're also adjusting to my mom having moved in with us.) I am definitely more of a plotting sort of writer. That said, I refer to my outlines as "the lie we've all agreed to." My outlines are roadmaps to get me started, but most times my

characters veer from course such that by the time I get to the halfway point of my novel, I have to sit down and re-outline from there. And again, once I get to the "wrap it up" point of the book.

Jeanne: What's the best thing you've learned from other writers and conversely, what's the best advice you can give to other writers?

Maurice: Writers finish things. This was something told to me by one of my teachers. He said what separates people who want to write/talk about writing from writers is the fact that writers finish what they start. Where this really helps me is in the fight against "the Shiny": I constantly battle ditching what I'm working on to run with the latest shiny idea that pops into my head. Every time I have to remind myself that "writers finish things." If you're going to call yourself a writer, you need to take those ideas you have, get them down on paper, then get to "the end." And it helps battle the imposter syndrome: did you finish what you started? Yes, then you're a writer.

Your angst won't pay the bills. Sometimes we attach a lot of romance to the idea of being a writer. We have to be inspired. We have to wait on our muse. This "advice" was given to me by my wife during one of "my muse has left me" sessions as I stared down a blank page. She reminded me that my "muse" was now named Deadlines. This was a follow up to our "exposure won't pay the bills" conversation. (Her other bit of clutch perspective was "you can go to as many conventions as your writing pays for" which helped me not only guard against the temptation to give away my stories early on, but challenged me to only submit to professional markets).

Do that $#!+. This was told to me by fellow author, Daniel José Older. I was feeling anxious about a project I was working on. It was a novel that was plunging headlong into territories of race, class, and politics. I called up Daniel and that was the advice he gave me. Writers have to be bold and take risks. It can be scary sometimes (which is why it's good to have friends who can nudge you). In the end, taking those risks, accepting those challenges, only makes you a better writer. (The book was *Pimp My Airship*.)

Jeanne: Which book/story/novella was the hardest to write and why?

Maurice: I hate to sound cheesy, but the answer is always going to be "my current one." Every time I get in front of a blank page, it's like I have to convince myself that I actually know how to string words together to form a coherent sentence.

[I suppose I could say my first novel: *Strange Fruit*. It took seven years to write, the bulk of that time figuring out (by doing) how to write a novel. And it never saw the light of day. All the lessons I needed about writing and publishing summed up in one project.]

Jeanne: Being a community organizer and teacher is important to you. How does that translate into action for you and what advice would you give youth (and others) concerning how they can best serve their own communities?

Maurice: For a long time, I struggled with the notion that "I'm only a writer, what can I do?" But what it boils down to is empowering agency: start where you are with what you have. With my neighbors, with my students, whoever I meet, I try to see, learn, and love the person in front of me. Get to know the gifts and talents they bring to the community.

My community work informs my writing and my writing informs my community work. One of the things that I'm doing is mentoring young creatives to be the next generation of dreamers, storytellers, and vision casters. Because that's the work of art informing community work and community work informing the art. The merger of art and social practices, artists and activists. In order to create radical change, we have to be able to envision it. So, we dream the possible future, cast a vision of what a better tomorrow could look like, and then start making steps, charting a

course to get there. Being a resident Afrofuturist of a community organization represents a public statement of the attitude and mindset of the organization and community. It's about creating desired future states in the present by constantly re-imagining the work and the way we move through the world.

Giving back is not just about money. Time, resources, relationships, that's what social capital is all about. I may not have much money, but I can make an introduction to someone who does. When it comes to getting started, the teacher in me wants to respond by asking questions:

Have you met your neighbors? Do you know what organizations are doing work in your community? Which of those organizations have values or do work in an area you are passionate about? How can you join in the work that's already going on (rather than reinvent the wheel)?

Like I said, it's all about starting where you are with what you have. But you have to start.

Jeanne: Tell us a little about your gaming work.

Maurice: I can divide my gaming work into a few categories:

Role-playing games: *Marvel Super Heroes*, *Leverage*, and *Firefly*…which was awesome because 1) I was a fan of each of these already, and 2) anything I wrote for the games became canon!

World-building: Creating worlds/scenarios for the online role-playing games such as *Storium* (since the worlds were historical and realistic, they were used in schools) and *Watch Dogs 2* (which gave me all the street cred I needed with my students). I've done some work for *Dungeons & Dragons* (which I don't know if I can talk about yet).

Tie-in fiction: Stories in *Vampire 20th Anniversary Edition: The Dark Ages*

(Onyx Path), *Pugmire* (Onyx Path), *Powered Up!* (Green Ronin) and *Knaves: A Blackguard* (Outland Entertainment).

Jeanne: What's next?

Maurice: My next middle grade novel, *Unfadeable*, comes out in spring 2021. And book one, *Sweep of Stars*, of my space opera trilogy *All the Stars* comes out in 2022. In between, look for a dozen new short stories. So far.

More information about Maurice Broaddus is available on his website at *www.mauricebroaddus.com*.

A CONVERSATION WITH
JOE R. LANSDALE
by Dean Wyant

JOE R. LANSDALE IS A MASTER STORYTELLER known in the horror community for his multiple Bram Stoker Award®-winning works, but horror isn't the only genre he writes. Thrillers, comic books, mysteries, and westerns help define Lansdale's robust portfolio. With a résumé like that, it's no surprise Hollywood came calling. From *Batman: The Animated Series* to the well-received *Hap and Leonard* on Sundance TV, Lansdale is a force to be reckoned with. Among his various accolades, he has been honored with the Bram Stoker Award® for Lifetime Achievement, as well as British Fantasy, American Horror, and Edgar awards.

Dean: Your impressive body of work has been keeping us up all night for many years now. Did you ever expect you'd have the reputation you do now when you first put pen to paper?

Joe: I did not. I only wanted to be able to sell, and hopefully make some kind of living at it. It went far better than I ever expected.

Dean: It's known that you don't plot your manuscripts because you like to be as surprised as your readers. After authoring so many stories, does your writing process still surprise you?

Joe: It does surprise me. I like being surprised. I didn't start out working that way, but over time I found out that's what works for me. I like to work a little bit each day, three hours on average, in the morning when I get up. That works best for me. I can be a hero every day. I also don't do multiple drafts. I do one and correct as I go, follow with a touch up. Now and again there's a little more, but that's it. Editors may then have suggestions that if I like I do, and if I don't, I don't. I love the proofreaders. They find spelling and gaffs of that nature.

Dean: You're a successful multi-genre author. Which is your favorite to write?

Joe: The Lansdale genre. I like them all and am part of all of them, but on the whole I'm Lansdale. I write stories.

Dean: Who is your biggest literary inspiration?

Joe: Nostalgically, Edgar Rice Burroughs. And comics, primarily Gardner Fox. Later on, so many. Flannery O'Connor. F. Scott Fitzgerald, Mark Twain, Jack London, Raymond Chandler, Harper Lee, Hemingway, James Cain, Philip José Farmer, Bradbury, Matheson, Beaumont. Bill Nolan. There are many. Gerald Kersh. The list would go on for a long way. Certain writers influenced me more at certain times, others usurped some.

Dean: You often utilize violence, sex, and abuse in your books. Have you experienced any pushback in recent years over those themes?

Joe: Not really.

Dean: Are there any subjects or themes you refuse to explore?

Joe: Probably. But I'll know it when it comes up. I think some things

I might explore, but not in an exploitive way. It depends on the subject and the method of attack.

Dean: Your father couldn't read or write, and your mother didn't attend school for long. How did your love of the written word come about under such circumstances?

Joe: My mother, no doubt. She was a big reader and encouraged me early on. She loved writers and passed that on to me.

Dean: What can we look forward to reading (or watching) from you next?

Joe: I have *More Better Deals* out right now, and behind it will come a collection of novellas, *Fishing for Dinosaurs*, to be followed by *Moon Lake* next year from Little, Brown & Co/Mulholland Books.

More information about Joe R. Lansdale is available on his website at *www.joerlansdale.com*.

A CONVERSATION WITH SEANAN MCGUIRE

by Bret Smith

IN 2010, AUTHOR SEANAN MCGUIRE was awarded Best New Writer at the Aussiecon Four Worldcon and that award was just a prelude to her remarkable career. Since then, she has earned a Nebula Award, Hugo Award and Locus Award for her *Every Heart a Doorway* novella. In 2013, she was on the Hugo Award ballot a record five times. Last year, she became the first three-time winner of the Young Adults Alex Award with her novel *Middlegame*, which also won the Locus Award for Best Fantasy and was nominated for a Best Novel Hugo.

Seanan loves to write strong female characters and is attracted to stories and films that apply real science. I first fell in love with her horror Newsflesh series (*Feed, Deadline, Blackout, Feedback*), which she wrote under the pen name Mira Grant. This series thrilled me with its post-apocalyptic world and realistic portrayal of zombies, politics and medical science. For even more science fiction horror, there's her Parasitology trilogy (*Parasite, Symbiont* and *Chimera*), which explores the tragic tale of genetically-engineered tapeworms that spell bad news for humanity.

I was honored to get the chance to interview Seanan by email.

Bret: You write under your name, Seanan McGuire, as well as Mira Grant in the horror and science fiction genres. More recently, you've written as A. Deborah Baker, with *Over the Woodward Wall*, a book-within-a-book that began in your Hugo-nominated science fiction novel *Middlegame*. Why so many pseudonyms? Any insight into how you picked these names?

Seanan: Well, Seanan McGuire is my name, so that wasn't hard. Mira Grant is a complicated horror movie joke that I have refused to explain for over a decade now, and the "dot com" was available. A. Deborah Baker is a fictional character from the book *Middlegame*, where she is the author of the Up-and-Under series, so I couldn't steal "her" book. As to why I write under different names, it's all about saturation and marketing.

Bret: For horror readers and StokerCon™ attendees who are new to the name Mira Grant, where do you recommend that they start with your books?

Seanan: Either with *Feed*, or, if well-researched virological horror is a little too close to real life right now, *Into the Drowning Deep*, in which mermaids eat faces.

Bret: You are an award-winning writer of horror, science fiction and fantasy in all formats (short stories, novellas and novels). Do you have a preferred format? A favorite genre? How do you choose with so many options available to you?

Seanan: I write the story I want to tell in the way it needs to be told. That dictates almost everything else.

Bret: You have written tie-in stories for the *Predator* and *Star Wars* franchises. Can you tell us the story behind writing the first-ever Young Adult *Alien* novel, *Alien: Echo*? And what was your inspiration for creating the fascinating planet Zagreus and the relationship between the characters Olivia and Kora?

Seanan: I was asked if I wanted to write a Young Adult *Alien* book; I love

the *Alien* franchise; I said yes. I also warned them that I have a biology back-ground and enjoy research, and they said I could create a whole ecosystem to go with my colony world. It was wonderful. It had been suggested when I was brought on that I might want to center a queer romance, so they were always written with that in mind.

Bret: Many readers may not know your background in science fiction folk music or "filking," and that you have won the filking Pegasus Award six times. You started writing poetry, lyrics and music well before publishing fiction. Do you play an instrument? Did you perform in high school plays?

Seanan: I do not play an instrument—I'm purely a vocalist—and yes, I performed in my high school drama department. My earliest documented poetry was age six. So it started a long time ago.

Bret: I first met you at Denver's AnomalyCon and since then you've signed books for me at three San Diego Comic-Cons and two Worldcons. With the pandemic cancelling events in 2020, what do you miss most about conventions?

Seanan: I miss airports the most, I think. I love to travel. I'm real tired of the same four walls.

Bret: You are a big fan of Marvel comics and have written for the *Spider-Gwen*, *Ghost-Spider*, *Nightcrawler* and *King In Black* series as well as being a cartoonist of your own webcomic. Are you a collector and what led to you writing comics?

Seanan: They called me. Seriously, it's not a very interesting story. They called, I screamed a lot, and then I answered. I am a collector; I love comics.

Bret: *The Walking Dead* television series created a resurgence of interest in the zombie apocalypse, and you released your Newsflesh series of horror books at the same time. How do you feel about these books now, considering the 2020 pandemic? And why does the CDC know your name?

Seanan: I feel like I had a much more optimistic and even idealistic idea of what this would all play out like than reality has proven to reflect. That breaks my heart a little. As to why the CDC knows my name, I researched my zombie virus (a Coronavirus, no less) with their help.

Bret: Considering the huge revival the horror genre is experiencing in films and television, which of your works would you like to see Hollywood adapt?

Seanan: Right now, *Into the Drowning Deep* is in development, but I'd honestly love to see someone tackle *Feed*.

Bret: Given the opportunity, is there any author, living or dead, you would jump at the chance to co-author a story with?

Seanan: Stephen King. He's been my favorite author since I was nine.

Bret: Being an owner of five cats myself, I love that you, too, are a "cat-person". What's the fascination for you?

Seanan: They're my cats. I love them. They tolerate me. I don't need anything else from them.

Bret: You are continuing to expand your urban fantasy *October Daye*, *InCryptid*, and *Wayward Children* series and have written in most genres. So, what's next? What would you like to do that you haven't done?

Seanan: I'd really like to revise and republish my superhero fiction now that I'm a little better known.

More information about Seanan McGuire is available on her websites at *www.seananmcguire.com* and *www.miragrant.com*.

A CONVERSATION WITH
SILVIA MORENO-GARCIA
by Mario Acevedo

I FIRST HEARD OF SILVIA FROM buzz about her debut novel, *Signal to Noise*. However, it was several years before we met in person, in Denver at a party of a mutual friend and fellow writer, Rudy G. It was an exciting experience for me to finally meet someone that I've known from a distance and whose work I admired. I think we traded books. Since then, I've kept tabs on her impressive career that continues to push the edges of genre fiction, inverting tropes, and creating stories that are intensely atmospheric.

Signal to Noise won a Copper Cylinder Award, and Silvia's second novel, *Certain Dark Things*, was picked by NPR as one their best books of 2016. *Gods of Jade and Shadow* was the 2020 American Library Association Reading List winner in the Fantasy category and won the 2020 Sunburst Award for Excellence in Canadian Literature of the Fantastic. *Mexican Gothic* is a *New York Times* bestseller, a LibraryReads Best Pick, an Indie Next Best Pick, and is currently under development as a Hulu original series.

Mario: Let's start with the easy question. What brought you to writing horror?

Silvia: Some of the earliest stuff I remember reading was horror. Poe, Quiroga, Lovecraft. My mother had a lot of horror books around, both in English and Spanish. Works by Stephen King and other folks. And I liked watching old horror movies and read horror comic books as a kid.

Mario: Your books bring an insight of Mexican society and culture largely overlooked by the American audience, which tends to view Mexico through a lens of cliché. In your stories, the characters are distinctly modern, or appropriate to the time of the narrative, and yet the Mexican setting is crucial to the setting and the plot. What guides you in the writing of the story?

Silvia: I think the problem is that writers of color are normally allowed to tell a small range of stories. If you're Mexican, it's expected you'll write either magic realism (which is frankly so old fashioned, we went through the whole McOndo movement to get away from that about two decades ago!) or a story about suffering immigrants. I refuse to perform whatever Frida Kahlo-meets-the-migra fantasies people have of me so what you get is what I feel is my Mexico, and that means a multifaceted Mexico. That's the pop music-soaked Mexico of the 1980s like in *Signal to Noise*, the Jazz Age fantasy of *Gods of Jade and Shadow*, and the postcolonial legacies high up in the mountains of Hidalgo in *Mexican Gothic*. It's different things because we are not a monochromatic, single story.

Mario: A compelling attraction to your writing is the power of your prose. What other writers or works have influenced you? Are there rules that you adhere to that guide your writing style?

Silvia: The only rule I can remember right now, and it's not really a rule but a preference, is that I don't like to write novels in first person. I've done stories in first person, but nothing longer. I've always been fascinated by writers who do multiple POVs that offer contrasting, unreliable narratives—I'm thinking of *The Beguiled* here—and I am always interested in writers who have 'unlikeable' protagonists, which is why I'm so taken with noir and hardboiled writers and people like Jim Thompson.

Mario: Writing horror and gothic can be a challenge to avoid getting campy or too familiar. How then do you conceptualize your stories?

Silvia: I really think people are too afraid of tropes. They think just because they can recognize a trope, it's bad. But if you look at something like *The Only Good Indians*, that's trading on tropes. Both the 'Indian curse' idea and the 'sins of the past.' It evokes both *It* and *Ghost Story*, but it builds something completely different with those ideas. I read a quote somewhere that the big secret is that a book is made of other books. That's obviously true.

Mario: What are you looking forward to as a Guest of Honor for StokerCon™?

Silvia: I don't normally attend cons in any capacity so I honestly have no idea what is supposed to happen.

Mario: What is your writing process? Do you outline?

Silvia: I outline and then I revise quite a bit, which I've discovered is not a very good idea nowadays. When I shopped manuscripts around initially, I assumed that editors help you 'shape' a book but turns out they want it all ready-made. I had rejection letters that were like 'this is good, but it might need some revisions' and I was left standing there thinking 'uh... but I can make those revisions if you give me an offer. What do you want?' It was kind of naïve of me to think that talent was 'nurtured' but I managed to survive the Darwinian process that is publishing so I guess I'm pretty decent as far as writing goes.

Mario: Your books jump from time period to time period, which adds a fresh perspective to anyone reading about Mexico. Is this an ongoing process on your part of exploring and analyzing Mexico?

Silvia: It was never a coherent plan. I did want to write three noir novels set in Mexico in three different years, but totally not connected. It's what I dubbed in my head as my 'noir cycle' that began with *Untamed Shore* set in 1979 in Baja California and now I have *Velvet Was the Night* set in 1971 in Mexico City, but then I changed my mind and if I do a third noir it will probably be set in Vancouver. Then again, I feel I should try a totally different genre, like Western. So, who knows?

Mario: Congratulations on the adaptation of *Mexican Gothic* into a drama series. What was that experience like? What changes has this brought to your life as a writer?

Silvia: No changes on a day-to-day basis, really. TV shows and movies take a long time to make so there's no telling when or if this will air. At a general level, the success of *Mexican Gothic* means there is interest in me that didn't exist before and it's not the hardscrabble situation I used to have where I couldn't get anyone to look at my manuscript or stuff like that.

Mario: What are you reading and what do you recommend?

Silvia: I write a column with Lavie Tidhar for *The Washington Post*, so please check that out since we talk about different books each month. I'm reading Usman Malik's *Midnight Doorways* which is a collection of speculative short stories. They have a very rich, sensory language.

Mario: What's next for you?

Silvia: I have a lot of books out in 2021. My vampire novel *Certain Dark Things* and my romantic novel of manners *The Beautiful Ones* will both be reprinted by Tor. *Velvet Was the Night*, a noir set in Mexico in the 1970s, will also be out in the summer. And I have a novella called *The Return*

of the Sorceress.

More information about Silvia Moreno-Garcia is available on her website at *www.silviamoreno-garcia.com.*

A CONVERSATION WITH LISA MORTON

by Carina Bissett

MANY PEOPLE KNOW LISA MORTON as the face of the Horror Writers Association. After all, she was the president of the organization for five years. I first met Morton when I joined the HWA in 2016, after being awarded the HWA Scholarship. I quickly learned that she was much more than a name. Not only is Morton an incredible writer, she is also an advocate for diversity and inclusion in the genre, something this international organization continues to build upon.

Morton has been writing for more than two decades now, and her incredible list of accomplishments runs the gamut: she is a prolific writer of screenplays, short fiction, poetry, creative non-fiction, novellas, and novels; she has edited several anthologies; she's worked on set as an actor and as a producer; and she's well-known as an expert in everything Halloween. Over the years, Morton has won six Bram Stoker Awards® in the categories of Short Fiction, Long Fiction, First Novel, Non-Fiction, and Graphic Novel. She also has been awarded the Black Quill Award for Best Dark Genre Anthology and the Halloween Book Festival Grand Prize.

It was an honor for me to interview Morton for the StokerCon™ Souvenir Book. She continues to be an inspiration for writers worldwide, especially for women like myself who are working in the genres of dark fiction and horror.

Carina: Many people know you in your role as the past president of HWA. What is it like returning as a Guest of Honor for StokerCon™ 2021?

Lisa: It really is a tremendous honor. When I was overseeing these gatherings as HWA's President, one of my goals was to recognize the accomplishments of the Guests and treat them with great respect, so that's why it's really very gratifying to be on the other end of the StokerCon™ experience.

Carina: You have written in a wide range of genres and formats. If you had to pick your favorite, what would it be?

Lisa: I think it has to be the horror short story. Horror is my preferred genre (although I've begun exploring mystery more of late), and I love the short form. Novels are hard for me because I have so many ideas I want to explore and characters I want to write about that I'm always anxious to move onto the next thing.

Carina: Out of your numerous accolades and awards, is there any one in particular that stands out for you?

Lisa: The best praise I ever got was the day my dad—who was not a reader AT ALL—called me at work to tell me how much he loved my novel *Netherworld*. He knew many of my inspirations for that book, and we talked about it in a conversation I just never expected to have with him. No award or rave review could ever match how special that phone call was.

Carina: You have always been prolific, and this year is no exception. How do you stay motivated? Are you able to juggle multiple projects or do you work on one at a time?

Lisa: Well, accepting too many invitations and over-committing yourself is a darned fine way to stay motivated! I wish I could say I'm a multi-

tasking maven and can work on more than one project at a time, but I just can't; I get so intensely focused on whatever I'm working on that I can't see anything else but that. Fortunately, I write quickly.

Carina: The pandemic and restrictions due to COVID-19 have put a halt to the output of many creatives. Do you have any tips for people struggling to produce during these difficult times?

Lisa: Like many other writers, it's been difficult for me to keep writing during the pandemic. I read an article that called it the condition of acedia, which is when you have such a hard time seeing a future that you lose interest in getting anything done. I've spent the last year going in circles on what I should do for a next big project: I've got two non-fiction book projects that I've pitched to publishers and both proposals were enthusiastically accepted (yes, I simultaneously pitched two major projects that would require months of research, at a time when I can't even get into most libraries), and yet I keep thinking maybe I should decline both of those and try another novel instead. That sense of a failing future that just sits all the time in the back of your head like a raven blurting out "Nevermore" makes you question every possible new project.

Carina: What does a typical writing session/day look like? Do you have any special habits or rituals that help you get started?

Lisa: I don't, and I also don't have a typical writing session. Much of my writing time goes to non-writing work—interviews, presentations, contracts, maintaining my website and social media presences, all the business stuff that goes along with the creative stuff—so the writing tends to get squeezed in whenever. If I had my druthers, I'd be up every morning at 8 a.m. and sitting in my backyard office with a cup of tea, writing, but more often I'm sitting at my indoor desk squinting at contract terms or trying to keep my deadlines and interview times straight.

Carina: More and more women are writing in the genres of horror and dark fiction. Have you seen a shift in the horror community as a result? Do you have any advice for women who feel as though they are struggling to fit in with what has been historically a male-dominated field?

Lisa: I am so thrilled with the veritable tsunami of insanely gifted women who have entered the genre over the last ten years or so. When I was getting started in the early 90s, you could count the number of published female horror writers on your fingers and toes; all too often anthologies would include one or even no women. If I were to name my ten favorite new horror writers from the last ten years, I think all but maybe two would be women. As far as new female writers entering the field, I'd say don't be afraid to seek out some of us who have been around for a while. Social media makes it easy to connect with other writers, and it can be a tremendous relief to know that there are other writers working through the same things you are. I'd also encourage newer writers to join HWA's Mentorship Program, where you can even ask to be paired with a female writer.

Carina: What projects are you currently working on, and what can we expect to see coming out in the future?

Lisa: I wish I knew the answer to that right now! I can say that I'm thrilled to have my first "greatest hits" collection (*Night Terrors and Other Tales*) debuting at StokerCon™ (and I'm very happy to have the book coming out from Kate Jonez's company Omnium Gatherum). There are a few film things lurking, like my first novel *The Castle of Los Angeles*, and others I can't talk about right now. As usual, there'll be lots of new short stories in a variety of anthologies and magazines, and…well, who knows what else at this point?

More information about Lisa Morton is available on her website at *www.lisamorton.com*.

A CONVERSATION WITH STEVE RASNIC TEM

by Jeanni Smith

I CAME RATHER LATE IN LIFE to the horror genre, and a high point of my new-found appreciation for being creeped out is a collaboration with my husband, Bret, and Joshua Viola of Hex Publishers on *It Came from the Multiplex*, an anthology of stories with an 80s movie theme. Steve Rasnic Tem contributed one of the eeriest stories in the book and that is how I became such a fan of his work.

He has written eight novels, including the Bram Stoker Award®-winning *Blood Kin*, *Deadfall Hotel* and *Ubo*. Beautiful yet unsettling, *The Man on the Ceiling*, a novella written with his late wife Melanie and later expanded into a novel, received World Fantasy, Bram Stoker and International Horror Guild Awards. He has also published almost 480 short stories, many of which are brought together in such collections as *Figures Unseen: Selected Stories* and *The Night Doctor and Other Tales*. His latest novel, *The Mask Shop of Dr. Blaack* is written for a Young Adult audience. A dive into his bibliography shows he is also a poet, has written stories for comic books, edited anthologies and collaborated with Melanie on the nonfiction book *Yours to Tell: Dialogues on the Art and Practice of Writing*. He is very involved with the issue of climate change, working to broaden awareness about how each of us can take responsibility for lowering our carbon footprints, and the ramifications if global warming goes unchecked.

I'm grateful I was given the opportunity to ask him a few questions (I have so many!), and I hope you enjoy this interview as much as I did. Read on to find out more about his fascinating life and work.

JEANNI: My first introduction to your work was "Late Sleepers," a very subtle short story you wrote for our anthology, *It Came from the Multiplex: 80s Midnight Chillers.* When I read that story and then later *Blood Kin, The Night Doctor,* and other works, I was reminded of molasses. Your stories begin so quietly, smoothly, and often sweetly, but as I read further, that gentleness becomes something sticky and uncomfortable that I can't extricate myself from, but I can't look away either. This is accomplished with very little violence or graphic depiction, yet I feel my terror or anxiety growing with each word. What is it that makes you see frightening things in the mundane or commonplace?

STEVE: I think sometimes horror writers make the mistake of focusing all their effort on the fantastic (or graphic) portions of the narrative. But I believe that when horror fiction fails to be convincing it generally fails on the level of its realism. By realism I mean its portrayals of the mundane world. The characters are unbelievable or undermotivated, the dialogue is unrealistic, the descriptions of real things are flat and unoriginal, the suspense isn't quite realized (because suspense begins in the commonplace world, bridging you into the fantastic), and in general they fail to adequately inhabit the protagonist and/or narrator. That last point is crucial—fail to do that and everything is ill-fitting and seems forced.

How do we experience horror in real life? We don't encounter werewolves slobbering all over our faces. We're not fending Dracula off with a cross and a string of garlic. We don't find a bunch of severed heads in our bed when we wake up in the morning (at least not usually).

In real life, most of us experience horror as manifestations of anxiety. If we're lucky, those anxieties are the everyday fears about money, health, relationships, etc. But depending on age, ethnicity, nationality, and other factors, our commonplace world may include bullets and explosions or the

fear our children won't return one night because of the color of their skin. Or that we're in heightened danger from some disease or pandemic. Or that we're going to die alone.

These anxieties prey on our imagination. We imagine dangers in the shadows, in the dark house, in the dusty basement, in the idling car on the corner, and we feel it in those little silhouetted details, those faces we can only see parts of, those ordinary commonplace things which somehow resemble other terrible sometimes supernatural things.

So that's where you start. You start with the real world and the anxiety that real things evoke (or you establish it as a subfloor to a more fantastic imagined reality) and you move on from there into the unreal and imagined. Then you will have earned your slobbering werewolves and your sinister Draculas and your severed heads. If you can maintain the connection between the two realms in your story—the real and the unreal— you're more likely to create something powerful and emotional.

JEANNI: How did growing up in a tiny, heavily religious town in the Appalachian Mountains of Virginia inform your storytelling? Were your parents or grandparents an influence on your style or subject choices?

STEVE: You never completely escape your upbringing, at least that's what I believe. Whether you're allowing it to develop you or you're working against its influence, you're still being molded by the experience. One of the things I remember most about my childhood in southwest Virginia is watching Walter Cronkite on the evening news as he reported on the 60s, and thinking it was like a broadcast from another world because it had absolutely nothing to do with us. We were pretty isolated, and the roads at that time were such that it took a while to get to anywhere that wasn't isolated. I knew people who had never been more than 35 miles from home their entire lives. There were kind, good people there for sure, and it was a beautiful place to grow up. In fact, I still think of it as one of the most beautiful places I've ever been. At the same time, that kind of isolation can lead to some isolated viewpoints, and at times some strange, unmonitored behavior on the part of individuals who lack a broad social context. So, I heard stories, and my parents and relatives told me stories, and I began to think that within that safe, beautiful world, weird and mysterious things had happened. My novel *Blood Kin*, alternating between southwest Virginia in the 30s and some sort of now, is about some of those things.

Blood Kin was a book I always wanted to write, and I began writing it in high school. The first chapter is pretty much as I wrote it my senior year, tidied up a bit. I scribbled impressions and ideas for the novel over the years in various notebooks, even arranging for a college friend to take me to a couple of snake handling church services for the experience.

JEANNI: Your late wife Melanie was also a successful author. When did you first collaborate with her and what was it like to write together? Do any of your children or grandchildren write?

STEVE: Our first collaboration was a science fiction story, "Prosthesis," which was published in *Asimov's Science Fiction Magazine* in 1986. I had an idea, and I'd written an opening, but I thought it needed a strong female point of view, and I was feeling a bit stuck, so I handed it over to Melanie. She immediately had a strong feeling for the story and wrote a few pages. She handed it back to me, and we proceeded that way, passing the story back and forth until it was done. We were communicating through fiction, which added additional texture to a story which was in part about communicating with the other.

After that, we frequently collaborated by simply handing each other the beginning of a story. Sometimes from the inception of an idea we knew it would benefit from collaboration. Sometimes it was during a time in which I was getting a lot of invitations to contribute to anthologies and I couldn't handle them all, so we decided to collaborate on a few of those invitations. In other cases, we just wanted to play with the male and female points of view.

It was easy collaborating with Melanie because although we were inter-ested in different themes, we had similar aesthetics, similar ideas about what was good and bad writing. And we had no personal ego invested in those collaborations—we just wanted to create good fiction. The most satis-fying aspect was when our collaborations created a new third voice which was different from what we would have written as individuals.

I have one grandchild in her twenties who is interested in writing and who is a voracious reader. Melanie used to give her coaching sessions. Whether she becomes a writer or not, I'm extremely proud of her.

JEANNI: In *The Man on the Ceiling*, you say you have to position yourself to be available for stories. What was the most unlikely place you ever encoun-tered a story idea and has that story been written and published?

STEVE: For the most part we were talking about positioning ourselves emotionally and psychologically. You have to be open to stories, to new ideas and approaches. Genre writers sometimes narrow their imaginations too early in the process. For example, horror writers can get to the point where they're only seeing horror ideas, and sometimes only a particular kind of horror idea. That's an obstacle to both growth and good writing.

But being open to story can mean being open in different settings. "2 PM: The Real Estate Agent Arrives" came to me while I was driving early in the morning and passed a couple of real estate signs. The story is very short, a little over 50 words, and poetically structured. I wrote it in my head while driving, jotted it down when I got to the office at my day job, then spent two weeks off and on revising it. It appeared in the British magazine *Crimewave #10* and has been reprinted several times.

"Ancient Grass" came to me when I ran out of gas near a large stretch of tall, unmown grass. I had to walk a mile to a gas station to get some help, with nothing to look at but all that grass. As one of the mechanics was driving me back to my car, I had the idea and wrote it that weekend. It appeared in the small magazine *After Hours*.

The idea for "A House by the Ocean" came when Melanie and I were staying in a nice B&B facing the ocean in Hastings, England. I'd never spent much time by the ocean, and one day I was so impressed with how the gray waves were coming up and splashing over the road in front of us. The ocean's horizon line was level with our second story bay window, and even though I knew better, for a moment I couldn't imagine what was holding all that water back. I started the story in that room, setting it in North Carolina, and worked on it for about a year. It appeared in my 2014 ghost story collection *Here with the Shadows* (Swan River Press, Ireland).

So I suppose ideas can happen anywhere.

JEANNI: What do you do with all the ideas that come to you and how do you choose which ones to give life to?

STEVE: Most of my ideas go into a notebook on my desk (I used to have several; now I've boiled them down to one). If an idea seems to fit one of the submission guidelines or invitations stacked on my desk, I may write the idea down on that particular printout and start thinking about it. And sometimes I get ideas which are so compelling to me I drop everything else and start writing to make sure I get the inspiration and tone down as quickly as possible (even though I'll be working on another story or two at the same time). The ideas that take priority are frankly the ones that are for markets that pay the most.

JEANNI: What have you written that has pushed you furthest out of your comfort zone?

STEVE: Technically, the most challenging work was *The Man on The Ceiling*. It's meta-fiction, and we were throwing out the usual rules of fiction and trying to create our own, feeling our way through and deciding what did and did not work. There were also some obvious emotional challenges

because we were writing about grief and the death of our son.

But the work which challenged me psychologically, emotionally, and technically was *Ubo*, a novel addressing violence and its origins. It took decades before I thought I knew enough to write that book. It was my "bucket list" novel—I first had the idea in college. The human propensity for violence is what frightens me the most and I rarely include graphic violence in my fiction. I wanted to write a novel which explored our violent tendencies while at the same time making it readable. I didn't know how to write such a book, but I believed one day I would have the necessary skill. I built a massive reference library on the subject and when I finally decided to commit to finishing it (around 2014), I created stacks of these reference materials on a long table, organized by historical figure and type of violence. I thinned the piles, narrowing the events and rearranging the stacks according to the sequence of the book. These stacks became my physical outline, which I converted into a traditional paper outline.

JEANNI: What was your most frightening encounter with a human or an animal?

STEVE: I'll give you an answer for both. The most frightening human being I ever knew was my father. He terrified me nearly every day from the time of my first memories until around the age of 14 when I was big enough not to be physically intimidated by him. He was an angry, haunted man, fraught with demons, and his alcoholism made him worse until the time came when the drinking rendered him helpless. And yet I also loved him, because little kids tend to love their parents no matter what.

As a father myself, I find it strange to think about. Being a father has been extremely important to who I am. I've always seen part of my role as being a source of psychological nourishment for my children. That's been my mission. If my children saw me the same way I saw my father, I would feel like a complete failure as a human being.

As far as animals go, it was those trips to the snake handling church as part of my research for *Blood Kin*. Some of the most physically intense moments of my life were watching those snakes, waiting for them to strike. My youngest son once wanted to have a snake for a pet. I felt bad about it, but I had to exercise my veto. I offered to let him keep a giant Madagascar hissing cockroach instead.

JEANNI: Has it been hard for you to write since the unsettling events of 2020 have changed our world so drastically?

STEVE: Initially it was. I thought a lot about what would be the "normal" for any fiction I wrote when the current normal was so thoroughly compromised and uncertain. If you were to write a number of stories in which people are in masks and social distancing, those tales might be considered quaint relics in a few years. On the other hand, if you fail to include that background and our habits change forever, the fiction might seem equally outdated. So, for a few months I didn't write at all. I read, and I accumulated ideas.

When I started writing again, I began exploring the themes of isolation, loneliness, and the distance between people. We really aren't well-suited to this kind of hermetic lifestyle. Writers have to write. As I often say, it is our task to give testimony, to say what we saw and what we felt and what we imagined during our relatively brief time on the planet.

JEANNI: For StokerCon™ attendees who may not be familiar with your work, where would you suggest they start? One of your novels or a short story anthology?

STEVE: For people new to my work, I recommend my *Figures Unseen: Selected Stories*, published by Valancourt in hardcover, paperback, e-book, and audio formats. For that collection I chose 2-4 stories from each of my collections as representative. The result is a good sampler. When anyone

asks me what I do I simply point to that book.

JEANNI: When you read or watch TV or a movie, what do you enjoy the most? What other ways do you decompress?

STEVE: Reading, of course. I read every day, and I try to read one short story every day. But movies have always been my primary means of decompression. Before the pandemic, I was going to see movies in the theaters at least twice, sometimes three times a week. That's felt like one of my biggest losses since all this began. At least now, with all the streaming services and cinema premieres at home, I can still have a movie night on my big TV, but it's not quite the same. Currently I watch 4+ movies a week on TV.

I also enjoy watching reality competition TV shows in which you see people who are really good at something. *Masterchef, Project Runway, So You Think You Can Dance, The Great Pottery Throwdown, Blown Away* (that one was glass blowing), etc. I find those shows inspire me creatively. There are also the "architectural" shows like *Grand Designs* and Apple TV's *Home*. I can't get enough of those.

But the one thing I really have to have in order to maintain balance is comedy. Especially standup. I have to laugh at least a couple of times a day or I don't feel fully human. When you're writing horror, that counter-influence is important.

JEANNI: Which of your stories or novels would you most like to see filmed?

STEVE: I've always thought my novel *Deadfall Hotel* would make a great TV series. It's about a massive, highly atmospheric hotel, which I'd describe with tongue firmly in cheek, as a place where supernatural creatures go for vacations. It's also a commentary on the horror genre itself. The main characters are the caretaker, the new hotel manager, and his daughter. The chapters follow the seasons, and feature such guests as a werewolf, a vampire, a cult, a thing-without-a-name, etc. It could be done as an anthology movie, but in a series, you could go on for several seasons, focusing on a different supernatural figure each episode.

Another interesting film project would be my and Melanie's novelette "Bees from the Hive" in our collection *In Concert*. It's a suspenseful story about three childhood friends and their oddly sadomasochistic relationship.

JEANNI: Answer a question that you wish I would have asked you, something you would like fans at StokerCon™ to know about you.

STEVE: I suppose it would be that I have tried other art forms. I draw and paint. I took classes at both the Denver Art Students' League and the Rocky Mountain College of Art and Design in drawing, painting, cartooning, digital art, etc. I make no claims of being great at it, but I've always found that it centers and fulfills me, and sometimes working out the imagery for a story through drawing is quite helpful. You can find examples in the Gallery portion of my website at *www.stevetem.com*.

Some of that work has been for public consumption. I did the illustrations for my "The World Recalled" chapbook for Wormhole Books. I did a painted experimental graphics story, "Shadowhouse," for issues 2-4 of *Blurred Vision: New Narrative Art*. I also wrote and illustrated a couple of comics stories for a magazine called *Slambang*. I've also made a couple of animated short films, one of which, "The Swimmer," based on one of my poems, appeared in film festivals in Seattle and Vancouver.

I've also written a few comics stories over the years for companies like Kitchen Sink, Caliber, and Shockwave. I love comics, so it's something I'd like to do more of in the future.

More information about Steve Rasnic Tem is available on his website at *www.stevetem.com*.

THE HWA POETRY SHOWCASE THRIVES!

by John Palisano

THE HWA's SEVENTH VOLUME OF POETRY showcasing the best of our members' poetry launched in late 2020. Expertly edited by Stephanie M. Wytovich and again with a beautiful cover from notable artist Robert Payne Cabeen, the team was rounded out by judges Gwendolyn Kiste and Carina Bissett. Dark poetry is an important art to the HWA. Poetry dates back to the earliest civilizations. Even then darker, more supernatural elements were present. From *The Epic of Gilgamesh*, *The Odyssey* and *The Iliad*, through *The Tell-Tale Heart*, horror poetry continues to be important and popular, represented in current times with works from such practitioners as can be found throughout our annual poetry showcase volumes.

Putting these showcases together takes a phenomenal amount of work, so let's celebrate the editing team, the production team, as well as the massive list of very talented dark poets.

This year's volume includes works from: Colleen Anderson, Michael Arnzen, Michael Bailey, Garrett Boatman, Robert Payne Cabeen, G. O. Clark, Frank Coffman, David E. Cowen, Ashley Dioses, Stephanie Ellis, Alexander P. Garza, Teel James Glenn, Owl Goingback, Janna Grace, Kerri-Leigh Grady, Miriam H. Harrison, R. J. Joseph, Naching T. Kassa, Pamela K. Kinney, Kendall Krantz, K. P. Kulski, Gerri Leen, Donna Lynch, Lisa Morton, Donna J. W. Munro, Lee Murray, Annie Neugebauer,

Corey Niles, Joanna Parypinski, Cynthia Pelayo, Saba Syed Razvi, Sarah Read, Terrie Leigh Relf, Loren Rhoads, Kelly Robinson, Sumiko Saulson, Ann K. Schwader, Jordan Shiveley, Marge Simon, Angela Yuriko Smith, John Claude Smith, Christina Sng, Jessica Stevens, Roni Rae Stinger, Chad Stroup, Sara Tantlinger, Ingrid L. Taylor, Steve Rasnic Tem, Kyla Lee Ward and Mercedes M. Yardley.

ANN RADCLIFFE ACADEMIC CONFERENCE SHOWCASES HORROR STUDIES' SCHOLARSHIP FOR FOURTH YEAR

by Michele Brittany and Nicholas Diak

HORROR HAS LONG ENTERTAINED AUDIENCES over the centuries, but horror studies is a relatively new academic course of study that has its genesis with our namesake, Ann Radcliffe, a British writer of fiction who also sought to critically understand the horror genre. In the two centuries since Radcliffe's brief treatise, "On the Supernatural in Poetry," the study of horror has been making strides to bring deeper understanding to horror offerings in popular culture and our need to consume and feed on the endorphins of fear. While this path of enlightenment has most often been paved by academics, there is a growing trend of fiction writers critically assessing horror as well. We see this as a return to Radcliffe's roots of writing and understanding horror as a reflection of social issues and concerns.

In 2016, when we proposed the Ann Radcliffe Academic Conference, we were seeking to create a conference that would appeal to horror scholars and provide them the opportunity to showcase their research in a presentation format. We sought to nurture a conference that encouraged inclusion of scholarship represented by diverse participants. In addition, we felt it was very important to foster a safe and supportive environment. We believe we have been successful based on the overwhelming positive feedback we have received, but also by the number of participants who have returned to present year after year.

Arising from the success of the conferences thus far, the Ann Radcliffe Academic Conference now has a book *Horror Literature from Gothic to Post-Modern: Critical Essays* (McFarland & Company). This is the HWA's first academic title and it is comprised of fourteen essays that cover a breadth of horror scholarship. For example, given this unprecedented time of COVID-19, Rahel Sixta Schmitz's "Mapping Digital Dis-Ease: Representations of Movement and Technology in Jim Sonzero's *Pulse* and Stephen King's *Cell*" is eerily timely and relevant in its discussion of viruses, while J. Rocky Colavito's "ScatterGories: Class Upheaval, Social Chaos and the Horrors of Category Crisis in *World War Z*" reminds us just how quickly our world can change. Naomi Simone Borwein introduced conference attendees and readers to new academic theories regarding Australian horror in "Synchronic Horror and the Dreaming: A Theory of Aboriginal Australian Horror and Monstrosity" and Emily Anctil demonstrates the importance of horror at a young age with her "'Not a Bedtime Story': Investigating Textual Interactions between the Horror Genre and Children's Picture Books." This book gave presenters an opportunity to solidify their contribution to academic scholarship.

Back for a fourth year, the conference continues to attract non-fiction and fiction writers, HWA members and non-members as well as many returning presenters! As always, the conference programming is free for StokerCon™ attendees. Panel sessions are grouped by common overarching topics, so convention-goers can come for one, some or all of the panels, receiving a variety of perspectives on numerous horror topics. Do stop by, listen to our panelists, and engage in lively Q&A sessions at the conclusion of each panel session!

FINAL FRAME
HORROR SHORT FILM COMPETITION

by Jonathan Lees

I<small>F BEING SHUT IN A DIMLY LIT ROOM</small> with hundreds of softly breathing strangers sounds like the impetus for a modern horror story, it is hard to believe that it used to be a cherished ritual.

One of the harder parts of dealing with the pandemic is the separation from family and for us, Final Frame is family, consisting of film-makers, judges, and of course, our audience. Each StokerCon™ event turns strangers into familiars and friends: the people you can't wait to see every year. In 2020, we lost the ability to celebrate in-person, yet that didn't stop an amazing array of judges from choosing their favorite films eventually deeming Natalie Erika James' haunting *Drum Wave* the Grand Prize Winner before she went on to global acclaim for her debut feature, *Relic*.

Rob Savage first screened at Final Frame with his humorous yet heartfelt, *Dawn of the Deaf*, then followed up with the deliciously demonic, *Salt*. Despite the struggles of the current climate, he recently took the film world by surprise when he released the much heralded and pandemic-produced, Zoom room shocker, *Host*. Carlen May-Mann and Beck Kitsis, the dynamic women who swapped roles as producer for each other's films, *The Rat* and *The Three Men You Meet At Night*, are off prepping their first features. We have been lucky to witness filmmakers with an intense amount of passion and promise (Anthony Cousins, Izzy Lee, Kayla Stuhr, Chris McInroy,

Alvaro Rodriguez Areny, and Ethan Evans) return with a vengeance.

Final Frame is also a competition based on opinion. We like to think our guest judges, Josh Malerman, Mick Garris, Lisa Morton, Mike Flanagan, and Rebekah McKendry, to name a few, have pretty damn good opinions but nothing is more engaging than hearing what captivates our audience. At the end of the evening when everyone shuffles off to the next event or party with little dark scenes replaying in their heads, they share their thoughts effusively despite the differences, and listen to each other. If only our world could match this energy.

We revel in our shared fears, our communal terrors. If that sounds like what the nightly news and our social feeds have become, like a possessed typewriter that no one can stop, you aren't wrong but we can imagine better than that. I refuse to relinquish the hope that this year will see us return to celebrate in a safe space, cheer each other on, and we all can dream in the dark once again.

LIBRARIANS' DAY

by Becky Spratford

STOKERCON™ 2021 WILL MARK THE 5th Annual Librarians' Day. It is hard to believe we have made it five years, but both the HWA's work with the library community and Librarians' Day itself have grown into a nationwide initiative that now offers branded and recognizable horror-themed programming and assistance for libraries all year long. As a result, the HWA has become a go-to resource for library workers as they add more horror to their collections and seek out horror programming options for their communities.

Because 2020 was an extraordinary year and many of you may be new to Librarians' Day, I want to give a recap of the programming the Librarians' Day team delivered to the world last year. It was year two of the Summer Scares program where a committee of library workers and a writer spokesperson selected three horror titles in each of the adult, YA, and middle grade reading levels. With Stephen Graham Jones leading the way, the committee added a free guide for libraries that included summaries of the titles, read-aloud options, book discussion questions, and programming ideas, allowing the Summer Scares program to be fully implemented without extra work on the library's part. When the pandemic hit, the Summer Scares team and the selected authors took the program online, recording videos with the authors to post on the HWA's YouTube page, and encouraging libraries to discuss the titles. Many of our authors made virtual appearances for those book discussions, too. The feedback has been overwhelmingly positive as libraries went out of their way to thank the HWA for making the program accessible and for helping them get more horror onto their shelves.

Due to the pandemic, Librarians' Day was moved to YouTube and presented in November of 2020, with our sponsors, NoveList, Library-Reads, and Flame Tree Press assisting. Here is the series of panels that were filmed for the event:

The Scary Truth About Horror Reviews
(Sponsored by Cemetery Dance) Featuring *New York Times* Book Review Horror Columnist Danielle Trussoni, Booklist and Library Journal Horror Reviewer Becky Spratford, and Cemetery Dance reviewer and owner of Night Worms Sadie Hartmann. Moderated by Ashley Rayner from the Chicago Public Library.

Horror and Libraries: A Not So Scary Partnership
Featuring Gillian Cargile-King from Northern Illinois University, Konrad Stump from Springfield-Greene [MO] County Library, Cathleen Keyser from NoveList and Gregg Winsor from Library-Reads. Moderated by Lila Denning from the St. Petersburg [FL] Public Library.

Summer Scares 2020: How to Feature Horror for All Ages at Your Library
Featuring members of the Summer Scares Committee and the announcement of the 2021 Summer Scares Spokesperson.

The State of Horror Today: A Conversation
Featuring authors Daniel Kraus, Stephen Graham Jones, and Cina Pelayo. Moderated by Becky Spratford.

Meet Flame Tree Press
Featuring editor Don D'Auria and Flame Tree Press authors John

Everson, J. G. Faherty, J. H. Moncrieff, Melissa Prusi and Steven Hopstaken. Moderated by Emily Vinci of the Schaumburg Public Library.

Breathing New Life into Horror Classics

A lively conversation with the co-editors of Poisoned Pen Press's Haunted Library of Horror Classics series Les Klinger and Eric Guignard, former HWA President Lisa Morton and Los Angeles Public Library librarian Daryl Maxwell about the behind-the-scenes creation of the series and the use of horror titles in library book clubs and programming. Thank you to Sourcebooks for organizing and sponsoring this panel!

All of the panels featured HWA members from bestselling authors to up-and-comers and were free to view on the HWA's YouTube page. During the month of November, the Librarians' Day team and all panelists were available for Q&As which were collected on the Adult Reading Round Table's website [arrtreads.org]. Despite COVID-19, Librarians' Day in 2020 was the biggest and most successful one yet. While an in-person event would have been limited to 100 library workers, when we went live on November 1, there were over 400 people registered and over 1,000 subscribers to the HWA's YouTube channel. Our reach grew exponentially, and more attention to horror in the library world means more sales and more readers for all horror writers.

This year, Librarians' Day is back at StokerCon™, where we will be offering another full day of continuing education for library workers. Joining Librarians' Day coordinator Becky Spratford to run this year's event is Summer Scares committee member Konrad Stump. A variety of programs will be offered including roundtable discussions with authors and publishers, presentations about horror programming, and a panel about the 2021 Summer Scares line-up featuring Silvia Moreno-Garcia. All attendees will also receive free swag from the authors and publishers who are participating. Anyone who purchased a full StokerCon™ ticket, is welcome to attend Librarians' Day.

The best thing about the Librarians' Day and Summer Scares programming is that while they serve as an outreach to libraries by encouraging them to purchase horror titles and offer more horror-themed programming, it has also allowed many horror authors to make connections with their local libraries. While you are attending StokerCon™, consider adding Librarians' Day to your schedule. With five years under our belts and a successful virtual event in 2020, library workers and horror writers are working together to bring the scares to library patrons all over the country. Join us as we celebrate the scariest genre with a full day of learning, networking, and tons of creepy fun.

Becky Spratford
HWA Librarians' Day Coordinator
Summer Scares Co-Organizer

2020 SILVER HAMMER AWARD

THE HWA PERIODICALLY GIVES THE SILVER HAMMER AWARD to an HWA volunteer who has done a truly massive amount of work for the organization, often unsung and behind the scenes. It was instituted in 1996, and is decided by a vote of HWA's Board of Trustees.

The award is so named because it represents the careful, steady, continuous work of building HWA's "house"—the many institutional systems that keep the organization functioning on a day-to-day basis. The award itself is a hammer with an engraved plaque on the handle. The hammer is also a satisfying allusion to The Beatles song, "Maxwell's Silver Hammer," a miniature horror story in itself.

The HWA is a worldwide organization promoting dark literature and its creators. It has over 1,700 members who write, edit and publish professionally in fiction, nonfiction, video games, films, comics, and other media.

This year, the Board has elected to award two exceptional members for their outstanding work:

CARINA BISSETT and BRIAN W. MATTHEWS

Carina has worked extensively in Colorado to bring to life a new Colorado Springs chapter and has been a tireless supporter of our members.

In addition, she's taken on the responsibility of heading up our HWA Membership Committee and has done an outstanding job.

"I stumbled across the HWA during one of the darkest times in my life. I was on the precipice of succumbing to absolute despair when I received notification that I'd won the HWA scholarship. That phone call connected on a Wednesday, a long summer night in 2016. I'll never forget that moment, but it's what came afterwards that was the real surprise. Not only did the HWA offer me hope, but it also gave me purpose. In my attempt to return a small measure of goodwill, I started volunteering as a jury member, first for the scholarships and then for the Stokers. Later, I added other responsibilities. I took a position on the HWA Membership Committee and another as co-chair of the local chapter in Colorado Springs. I reviewed poetry submissions, supported women writers, and moderated conference panels. And I loved it all. Every single minute I've spent volunteering for the HWA has been a minute well spent. It is rewarding work, and I find great joy in contributing to an organization dedicated to providing a safe and supportive space for members. I'm grateful to be a part of this creative and compassionate community. There isn't a day that goes by when I'm not involved in one volunteer task or another. This is a blessing. It is a light that continues to shine in my life, and I don't need anything more than that."

—Carina Bissett

Brian W. Matthews has risen to the occasion not once, not twice, but three times as a co-chair of our StokerCons™. First, in Grand Rapids and now for both the virtual and in-person conventions celebrating Denver. He has served on the Lifetime Achievement Award Committee, currently serves as a jurist for the Bram Stoker Awards®, and for the past several years has organized and run the pitch sessions for StokerCon™. In addition to his role as convention co-chair, he also serves as the Bram Stoker Awards® Show Coordinator. We would not have been anywhere near as successful without him.

"A friend once told me the HWA is like a family; she called it a fellowship. We pull together to help one another, committing our time and our hearts to making the organization a better place for everyone. That's the spirit of volunteering. To be recognized with the Silver Hammer Award for outstanding volunteerism is an honor I will cherish forever."

— Brian W. Matthews

2020 RICHARD LAYMON PRESIDENT'S AWARD

THE RICHARD LAYMON PRESIDENT'S AWARD FOR SERVICE was instituted in 2001, and is named in honor of Richard Laymon, who died in 2001 while serving as HWA's President. As its name implies, it is given by HWA's sitting President.

The award is presented to a volunteer who has served HWA in an especially exemplary manner and has shown extraordinary dedication to the organization. We are proud to announce this year's winner:

BECKY SPRATFORD

"I am very honored to be awarded the Richard Laymon President's Award. Ironically, in my work on Summer Scares for the HWA, I am usually the one giving others this type of recognition and honestly, I am not sure how to react. Now that the roles are reversed, the work I have done to grow the HWA's outreach to Libraries, including recruiting library workers to join the organization, growing the reach and scope of Librarians' Day, and coordinating the Summer Scares Reading Program have given me some of the greatest professional satisfaction of my life. I have also had a lot of fun amidst all the work and made some lifelong friends along the way. Connecting libraries with horror books and authors is fulfilling but seeing how well both the library workers and authors have taken to each other has been inspiring. I am proud to serve the HWA in this way and very humbled to be recognized for it."

— Becky Spratford

2020 SPECIALTY PRESS AWARD

THE HWA SPECIALTY PRESS AWARD is presented periodically to a specialty publisher whose work has substantially contributed to the horror genre, whose publications display general excellence, and whose dealings with writers have been fair and exemplary.

The award was instituted in 1997, largely due to the efforts of long-time HWA member and specialty press aficionado Peter Crowther.

ABOUT THE AWARD

WHO MAY RECEIVE THE AWARD? To be eligible for this award, a publisher must specialize in horror, dark fantasy, and occult literature. This needn't be the publisher's only specialty, but it must be a substantial one. In addition, works of horror, dark fantasy, or occult literature must have been published by the press during the year prior to the award's presentation.

HOW ARE RECIPIENTS CHOSEN? The HWA Specialty Press Award is a "Trustees' Award." The winner is decided by a majority vote of HWA's Board of Trustees.

HOW OFTEN IS THE AWARD GIVEN? The award is given only during years when the Trustees feel an exemplary candidate is clearly visible and deserves recognition for its contributions.

And this year's winner is:

CRYSTAL LAKE PUBLISHING

Since its founding in August 2012, Crystal Lake Publishing has quickly become one of the world's leading publishers of Dark Fiction and Horror books in print, eBook, and audio formats. With several Bram Stoker Award® wins and many other wins and nominations, Crystal Lake Publishing puts integrity, honor, and respect at the forefront of their publishing operations. As of this date, they've published over 100 titles across the genre and have many satellite programs that help both new and established authors.

"Thank you to the HWA for awarding Crystal Lake Publishing with this amazing award. Being noticed and celebrated for our efforts emphasizes that we're on the right path, and we commit to taking you with us on the Crystal Lake journey as we go from strength to strength."

–Joe Myhardt, Founder, Owner, Editor, Publisher

2020 HWA LIFETIME ACHIEVEMENT AWARD RECIPIENTS

THE HWA IS PROUD TO ANNOUNCE the recipients for the Lifetime Achievement Award for 2020.

The Lifetime Achievement Award is the most prestigious of all awards presented by HWA. It does not merely honor the superior achievement embodied in a single work. Instead, it is an acknowledgment of superior achievement in an entire career. While this award is often presented to a writer, it may also be given for influential accomplishments in other creative fields. The Lifetime Achievement Award is the only award that is not decided by a vote of the entire Active membership, instead it is selected by a committee of diverse writers and HWA members appointed by the President of the HWA.

The committee this year consisted of:

Kevin Wetmore (Chair, non-voting)
Linda Addison
Gwendolyn Kiste
Rena Mason
Lee Murray
Paul Tremblay

The recipients of the HWA Lifetime Achievement Award for 2020, by unanimous decision of the committee, are:

CAROL J. CLOVER

JEWELLE GOMEZ

and MARGE SIMON

2020 HWA LIFETIME ACHIEVEMENT AWARD RECIPIENT
CAROL J. CLOVER

CAROL J. CLOVER IS A PROFESSOR EMERITA of Medieval Studies (Early Northern Europe) and American Film at the University of California, Berkeley. While much of her scholarship has concerned medieval Icelandic culture, her 1992 book *Men, Women and Chain Saws: Gender in the Modern Horror Film* was a seminal work in the serious study of contemporary horror cinema and especially "slasher" films. Clover argued against film critics who saw the films as victimizing women, instead focusing on the victim/hero—the young woman who defeats the killer. Clover coined the term "final girl," and articulated a structural and gendered approach to understanding films such as *Friday the 13th*, *Halloween*, and similar horror cinema that has exhibited a profound effect not only on how scholars understand the genre, but also has entered the popular vocabulary and understanding of how to read these films. The volume was reissued as a "Princeton Classic" in 2015 and her influence in the genre can be seen in such recent horror narratives as *Final Girl*, *The Final Girls*, *Scream Queens*, and every rebooted slasher film of the last twenty years.

2020 HWA LIFETIME ACHIEVEMENT AWARD RECIPIENT
JEWELLE GOMEZ

JEWELLE GOMEZ IS A WRITER, novelist, playwright, activist, critic, poet, and television writer, among many other identities and activities. She is the author of seven books including the double Lambda Literary Award-winning vampire novel, *The Gilda Stories*, currently celebrating its 30th year in print. She also authored the stage adaptation of that novel under the title *Bones and Ash: A Gilda Story*, which began touring in 1996 and was performed in thirteen American cities by the Urban Bush Women company. Her work centers on women's stories, in particular women of color, and LGBTQ+ rights and culture. Gomez calls herself "the possible foremother of Afrofuturism." Her poems and short stories appear in over one hundred anthologies. She has also worked as a critic for *The Village Voice*. Her work bringing horror and speculative fiction from a lesbian, feminist perspective is found not only in her own writing, but in her activism, her teaching, her lectures, and her mentoring. Her impact on the field is substantial, and her work has expanded the margins of horror in an inclusive and genre-reshaping fashion.

2020 HWA LIFETIME ACHIEVEMENT AWARD RECIPIENT
MARGE SIMON

MARGE SIMON'S POEMS, SHORT FICTION, AND ILLUSTRATIONS have appeared in hundreds of publications, including *Amazing Stories*, *ChiZine*, *Daily Science Fiction*, *Dreams & Nightmares*, *Niteblade*, *The Pedestal Magazine*, *Strange Horizons*, *Vestal Review*, and many, many more. She has published over a dozen books of poetry and short fiction and won three Bram Stoker Awards® for Best Poetry Collection for *Vectors: A Week in the Death of a Planet* (2007, co-written with Charlee Jacob), *Vampires, Zombies & Wanton Souls* (2012, illustrated by Sandy DeLuca) and *Four Elements* (2013, co-written with Rain Graves, Charlee Jacob and Linda Addison). Simon's service to the profession is incalculable, including mentoring numerous poets and writers, serving as the president of both the Small Press Writers and Artists Organization and the Science Fiction and Fantasy Poetry Association, as well as serving as Chair for the HWA Board of Trustees. She has also illustrated five Bram Stoker Award®-winning collections and has worked collaboratively with a number of different authors. Simon is the second woman to be acknowledged by the SF&F Poetry Association with a Grand Master Award.

2020 BRAM STOKER AWARDS®
FINAL BALLOT

THE HWA IS PLEASED TO ANNOUNCE THE Final Ballot for the 2020 Bram Stoker Awards®. The HWA is the premier writers organization in the horror and dark fiction genre, with more than 1,700 members. We have presented the Bram Stoker Awards® in various categories since 1987 (see *www.thebramstokerawards.com*).

The HWA Board and the Bram Stoker Awards® Committee congratulate all those appearing on the Final Ballot.

SUPERIOR ACHIEVEMENT IN A NOVEL

Jones, Stephen Graham – *The Only Good Indians* (Gallery/Saga Press)

Katsu, Alma – *The Deep* (G.P. Putnam's Sons)

Keisling, Todd – *Devil's Creek* (Silver Shamrock Publishing)

Malerman, Josh – *Malorie* (Del Rey)

Moreno-Garcia, Silvia – *Mexican Gothic* (Del Rey; Jo Fletcher Books)

SUPERIOR ACHIEVEMENT IN A FIRST NOVEL

Hall, Polly – *The Taxidermist's Lover* (CamCat Publishing, LLC)

Harrison, Rachel – *The Return* (Berkley)

Jeffery, Ross – *Tome* (The Writing Collective)

Knight, EV – *The Fourth Whore* (Raw Dog Screaming Press)

Reed Petty, Kate – *True Story* (Viking; riverrun)

SUPERIOR ACHIEVEMENT IN A GRAPHIC NOVEL

Archer, Steven (author/artist) – *The Masque of the Red Death* (Raw Dog Screaming Press)

Brody, Jennifer (author) **and Rivera, Jules** (artist) – *Spectre Deep 6* (Turner)

Douek, Rich (author) **and Cormack, Alex** (artist) – *Road of Bones* (IDW Publishing)

Holder, Nancy (author), **Di Francia, Chiara** (artist), **and Woo, Amelia** (artist) – *Mary Shelley Presents* (Kymera Press)

Manzetti, Alessandro (author) **and Cardoselli, Stefano** (artist/author) – *Her Life Matters: (Or Brooklyn Frankenstein)* (Independent Legions Publishing)

Niles, Steve (author), **Simeone, Salvatore** (author), **and Kudranski, Szymon** (artist) – *Lonesome Days, Savage Nights* (TKO Studios)

SUPERIOR ACHIEVEMENT IN A YOUNG ADULT NOVEL

Cesare, Adam – *Clown in a Cornfield* (HarperTeen)

Kraus, Daniel – *Bent Heavens* (Henry Holt and Company/Macmillan)

Snyman, Monique – *The Bone Carver* (Vesuvian Books)

Thomas, Aiden – *Cemetery Boys* (Swoon Reads/Macmillan)

Waters, Erica – *Ghost Wood Song* (HarperTeen)

SUPERIOR ACHIEVEMENT IN LONG FICTION

Iglesias, Gabino – *Beyond the Reef (Lullabies for Suffering: Tales of Addiction Horror)* (Wicked Run Press)

Jones, Stephen Graham – *Night of the Mannequins* (Tor.com)

Kiste, Gwendolyn – *The Invention of Ghosts* (Nightscape Press)

Landry, Jess – *I Will Find You, Even in the Dark (Dim Shores Presents Volume 1)* (Dim Shores)

Pinsker, Sarah – *Two Truths and a Lie* (Tor.com)

SUPERIOR ACHIEVEMENT IN SHORT FICTION

Arcuri, Meghan – "Am I Missing the Sunlight?" (*Borderlands 7*) (Borderlands Press)

Fawver, Kurt – "Introduction to the Horror Story, Day 1" (Nightmare Magazine Nov. 2020 (Issue 98))

Malerman, Josh – "One Last Transformation" (*Miscreations: Gods, Mon-*

strosities & Other Horrors) (Written Backwards)

O'Quinn, Cindy – "The Thing I Found Along a Dirt Patch Road" (*Shotgun Honey Presents Volume 4: Recoil*) (Down and Out Books)

Ward, Kyla Lee – "Should Fire Remember the Fuel?" (*Oz is Burning*) (B Cubed Press)

SUPERIOR ACHIEVEMENT IN A FICTION COLLECTION

Koja, Kathe – *Velocities: Stories* (Meerkat Press)

Langan, John – *Children of the Fang and Other Genealogies* (Word Horde)

Lillie, Patricia – *The Cuckoo Girls* (Trepidatio Publishing)

Murray, Lee – *Grotesque: Monster Stories* (Things in the Well)

Taborska, Anna – *Bloody Britain* (Shadow Publishing)

SUPERIOR ACHIEVEMENT IN A SCREENPLAY

Amaris, Scarlett and Stanley, Richard – *Color Out of Space* (SpectreVision)

Green, Misha – *Lovecraft Country, Season 1, Episode 1: "Sundown"* (Affeme, Monkeypaw Productions, Bad Robot Productions, Warner Bros. Television Studios)

Green, Misha and Ofordire, Ihuoma – *Lovecraft Country, Season 1, Episode 8: "Jig-a-Bobo"* (Affeme, Monkeypaw Productions, Bad Robot Productions, Warner Bros. Television Studios)

LaManna, Angela – *The Haunting of Bly Manor, Season 1, Episode 5: "The Altar of the Dead"* (Intrepid Pictures, Amblin Television, Paramount Television Studios)

Whannell, Leigh – *The Invisible Man* (Universal Pictures, Blumhouse Productions, Goalpost Pictures, Nervous Tick Productions)

SUPERIOR ACHIEVEMENT IN A POETRY COLLECTION

Manzetti, Alessandro – *Whitechapel Rhapsody: Dark Poems* (Independent Legions Publishing)

McHugh, Jessica – *A Complex Accident of Life* (Apokrupha)

Pelayo, Cynthia – *Into the Forest and All the Way Through* (Burial Day Books)

Sng, Christina – *A Collection of Dreamscapes* (Raw Dog Screaming Press)

Tantlinger, Sara – *Cradleland of Parasites* (Rooster Republic Press)

SUPERIOR ACHIEVEMENT IN AN ANTHOLOGY

Bailey, Michael and Murano, Doug – *Miscreations: Gods, Monstrosities & Other Horrors* (Written Backwards)

Murray, Lee and Flynn, Geneve – *Black Cranes: Tales of Unquiet Women* (Omnium Gatherum Media)

Kolesnik, Samantha – *Worst Laid Plans: An Anthology of Vacation Horror* (Grindhouse Press)

Tantlinger, Sara – *Not All Monsters: A Strangehouse Anthology by Women of Horror* (Rooster Republic Press)

Yardley, Mercedes M. – *Arterial Bloom* (Crystal Lake Publishing)

SUPERIOR ACHIEVEMENT IN NON-FICTION

Florence, Kelly and Hafdahl, Meg – *The Science of Women in Horror: The Special Effects, Stunts, and True Stories Behind Your Favorite Fright Films* (Skyhorse)

Heller-Nicholas, Alexandra – *1000 Women in Horror* (BearManor Media)

Keene, Brian – *End of the Road* (Cemetery Dance Publications)

Peirse, Alison – *Women Make Horror: Filmmaking, Feminism, Genre* (Rutgers University Press)

Waggoner, Tim – Writing in the Dark (Guide Dog Books/Raw Dog Screaming Press)

Wetmore, Jr. Kevin J. – *The Streaming of Hill House: Essays on the Haunting Netflix Adaption* (McFarland)

SUPERIOR ACHIEVEMENT IN SHORT NON-FICTION

Joseph, Rhonda Jackson – "The Beloved Haunting of Hill House: An Examination of Monstrous Motherhood" (*The Streaming of Hill House: Essays on the Haunting Netflix Adaption*) (McFarland)

Pelayo, Cynthia – "I Need to Believe" (Southwest Review Volume 105.3)

Robinson, Kelly – "Lost, Found, and Finally Unbound: The Strange History of the 1910 Edison Frankenstein" (Rue Morgue Magazine, June 2020)

Sng, Christina – "Final Girl: A Life in Horror" (Interstellar Flight Magazine, October 2020)

Waggoner, Tim – "Speaking of Horror" (The Writer)

STOKERCON™ 2022 ANNOUNCEMENT

REMEMBER WHEN WE SAID Colorado just loves you to death? Well, that's very true. It's also true that death isn't quite so final a thing when it comes to the horror genre. In fact, sometimes it's just the beginning. As we noted in the introduction, Denver was supposed to host StokerCon™ 2021, and we developed this souvenir book to highlight some of the best talent and great features Colorado has to offer for the horror community. We're now proud to say the pieces that follow can also serve to whet your whistle for StokerCon™ 2022. Because when it comes to hosting horror conventions, and when it comes to celebrating this important genre, Denver will not be denied. You thought you escaped our clutches when 2021 went virtual, but the reality is you only pushed your fate forward a year. So read the following pieces in anticipation of what we have in store for you here in the Mile High City.

May 12–15, 2022.
StokerCon™.
Denver.
The Resurrection.

THE HEX ARTWORK GALLERY

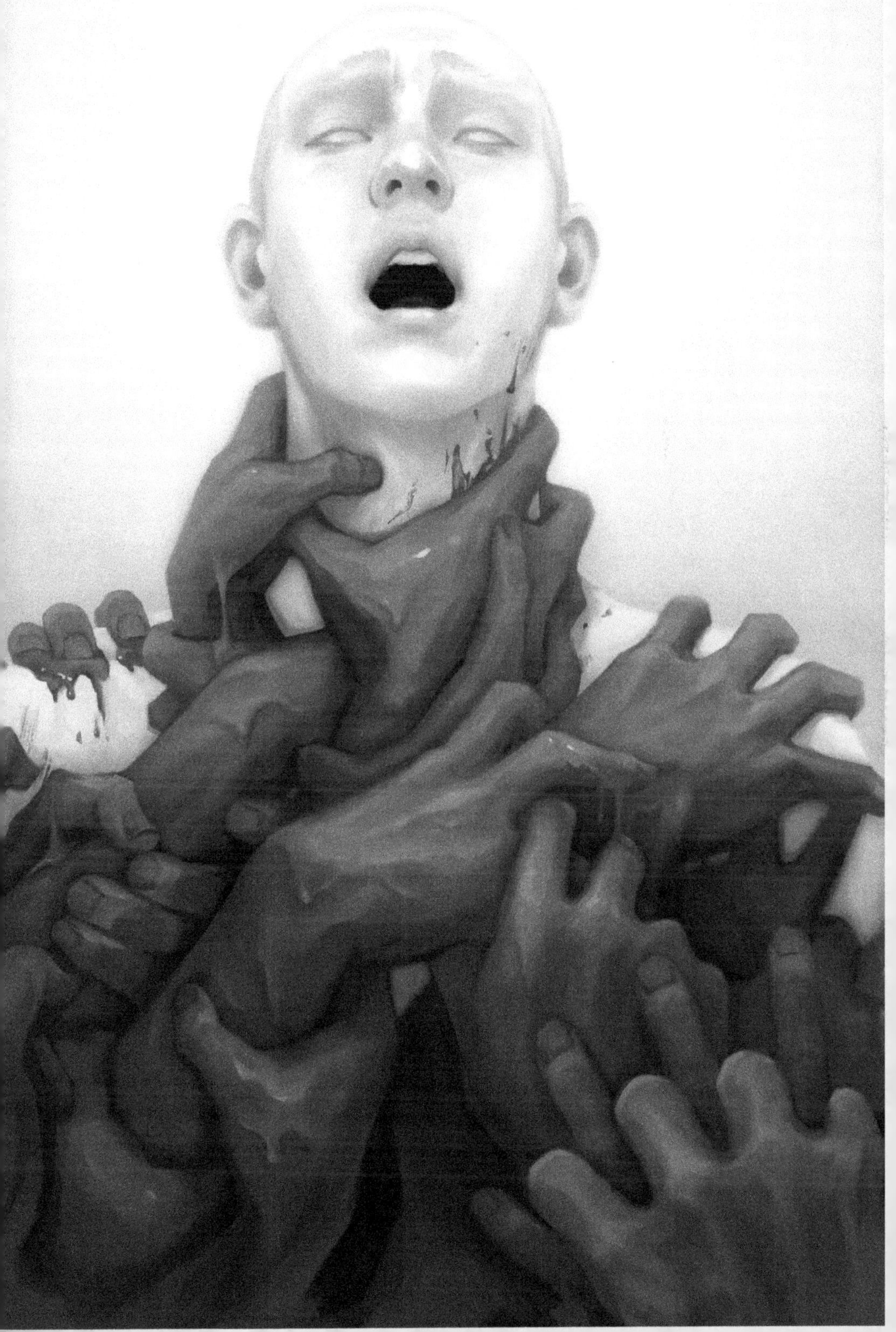

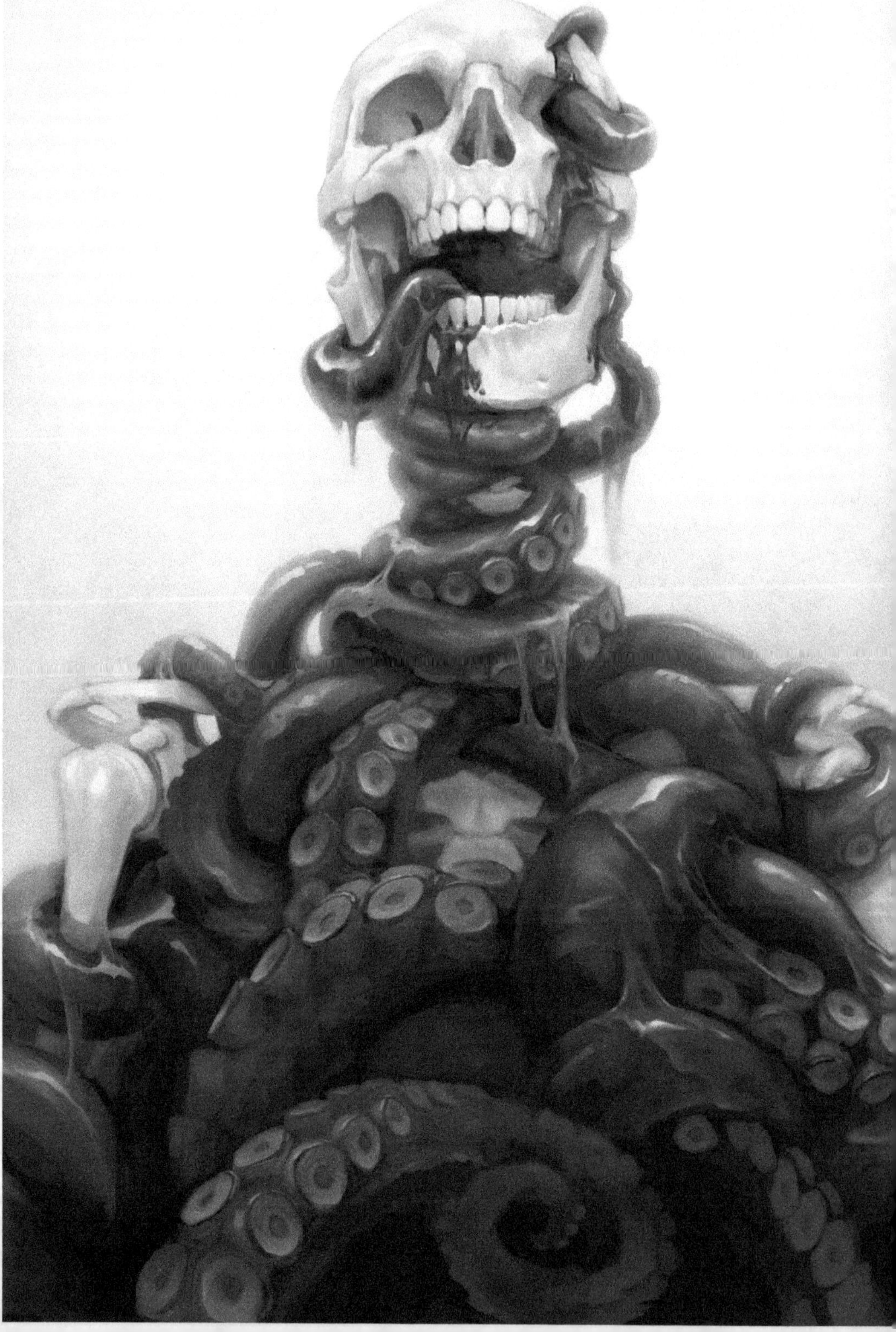

THE STATE OF HORROR

by Sean Eads

WE ALL KNOW HOW THE STORY GOES: a writer with an intense interest in the supernatural stays at a famed and supposedly haunted building in Colorado. It inspires him to write a book based on the experience, which then gets adapted into one of the most memorable haunted house movies of all times.

Yes, we've all seen *The Changeling* starring George C. Scott, based on Russell Hunter's paranormal experiences at the Henry Treat Rogers mansion in Denver's Cheesman Park neighborhood back in the 60s.

I know, I know. You were expecting me to be referencing Stephen King's *The Shining*. But I subverted your expectations. All the cool *artistes* do it these days.

I bring up the example of *The Changeling* to remind you that Colorado has a broader relationship with horror fiction than the uninitiated might expect—though in fairness, the state's prominence in both *The Shining* and *The Stand* are more than enough to put Colorado on any horror enthusiast's map. But ghosts, goblins, demonic possession, zombies and werewolves aren't typical things Colorado conjures up in the mind. Dusty plains, sawtooth mountains, gold and silver mines, Butch Cassidy, cattle rustlers, and Colfax Avenue saloon brawls make us better suited for Louis L'Amour than Lovecraft. We seldom manage more than a few Sasquatch sightings a year, and our climate just gets too darn unpredictable for chupacabras between Labor Day and June.

So, what does Colorado have to offer for those with a taste for dread? Quite a bit, actually.

For one, we have our own cannibal. Our beloved gourmand Alferd Packer easily stands up to Wisconsin's Ed Gein or New York's Albert Fish, dining on five men when the wilderness trip he was leading in 1874 got caught in a blizzard. You do what you do to survive, capiche? Alferd's exploits are so famous, his life story was even adapted into *Cannibal! The Musical!* Just think of him sitting by a roaring fire, burping in contentment with a fully belly. That's what we call cozy Colorado horror.

You'll also be interested to know that Colorado claims at least one vampire, which isn't too shabby considering the state's relative youth (not even 150 years old) and general absence of the sort of creepy Gothic architecture that seems to attract bloodsuckers. You can visit the grave of Fodor Glava in Lafayette (and read about it in Josh Viola and Carter Wilson's short horror story, "Grave Mistake", in *Terror at 5280'*). Mr. Glava was from Transylvania, which means he must have been an old-school vampire for sure. Supposedly, the vampire lent his name to the well-known travel book publishing company, but this is likely a malicious rumor started by Frommer's.

Heck, in Colorado it's even possible for flower beds to be haunted. Paranormal investigator Richard Estep insists Denver Botanic Gardens has its share of malcontent spirits because it was built over a large city cemetery. Apparently, this happened *Poltergeist*-style, with the removal of hundreds of headstones to clear the area, without disinterring the corpses. No wonder the soil is so fertile there. If you're curious to learn more, check out *The Dead Below* to read more of Estep's account of the strange happenings at Denver's most famous garden.

Not all horror needs to be supernatural, of course. In the 50s and 60s, Denver was home to the most powerful mafia family west of the Mississippi. Clyde, Eugene and Clarence Smaldone held a tight grip on organized crime in Colorado, starting off as bootleggers before branching out into gambling and loan sharking. More than a few people who got on the bad side of these three brothers came to violent ends. Personally, I'd rather

have to deal with a few Romero-style zombies than a couple of mafia hitmen looking to settle a score.

Speaking of murder, we're squarely in the middle of the fifty states, statistically speaking, when it comes to serial killings. We have infamous ties to Ted Bundy, who twice escaped Colorado jails in a bold fashion that would put Andy Dufresne to shame. Even more chilling, you'll find Colorado has reported 155 victims of serial killers, which means on average 2.65 per 100,000 people in the state will fall prey to someone's sinister trap. Terrifying!

Colorado isn't a stranger to horrific illnesses either. After all, squirrels and prairie dogs routinely test positive for bubonic plague in our great state. If a zombie virus were ever to be spread by fleas, Colorado would surely be ground zero for the outbreak.

Now some will accuse me of bad taste and scraping the bottom of the barrel by citing a mafia family and serial killers as examples of Colorado's horror roots. They'll ask why I instead don't talk about the hundreds of haunted buildings so neatly analyzed by Phil Goodstein in his book, *The Ghosts of Denver: Capitol Hill*. Fair enough. I *could* go into depth about the innumerable accounts of paranormal encounters reported by people across the state. Together, we could delve into the strange and often sinister conspiracy theories surrounding Denver International Airport, from its importance in the Illuminati's New World Order, to its controversial murals, to the notorious 32-foot fiberglass statue of a demonic blue horse with glowing red eyes, referred to by locals as *Blucifer*. The statue's unsettling appearance comes with an equally unsettling history, as the statue's architect was killed during its construction when a portion of the sculpture fell on him.

I'll forgo all this to focus on Colorado's most important contribution to horror, which rests on the shoulders of the great authors who've called this state home or been influenced by time spent here. Stephen King is, of course, the obvious example. He moved his family to Colorado following his mother's death in 1974, and lived in Boulder for less than a year. But how influential those months proved to be! A stay at the Stanley Hotel in Estes Park became the well-known inspiration for *The Shining*, and his memories of Boulder must have been pleasant, because he chose it as the gathering point for the good survivors in *The Stand* (as opposed to the bad survivors, who naturally gravitate toward Las Vegas).

A lesser-known fact is how his time in Boulder inspired *It*. As King relates—

In 1978 my family was living in Boulder, Colorado. One day on our way back from lunch at a pizza emporium, our brand-new AMC Matador dropped its transmission—literally. The damn thing fell out on Pearl Street. True embarrassment is standing in the middle of a busy downtown street, grinning idiotically while people examine your marooned car and the large greasy black thing lying under it. Two days later the dealership called at about five in the afternoon. Everything was jake—I could pick up the car any time. The dealership was three miles away. I thought about calling a cab but decided that the walk would be good for me. The AMC dealership was in an industrial park set off by itself on a patch of otherwise deserted land a mile from the strip of fast-food joints and gas stations that mark the eastern edge of Boulder. A narrow unlit road led to this outpost. By the time I got to the road it was twilight—in the mountains the end of day comes in a hurry—and I was aware of how alone I was. About a quarter of a mile along this road was a wooden bridge, humped and oddly quaint, spanning a stream. I walked across it. I was wearing cowboy boots with rundown heels, and I was very aware of the sound they made on the boards; they sounded like a hollow clock. I thought of the fairy tale called "The Three Billy-Goats Gruff" and wondered what I would do if a troll called out from beneath me, "Who is trip-trapping upon my bridge?" All of a sudden I wanted to write a novel about a real troll under a real bridge. ...Sometime in the summer of 1981 I realized that I had to write about the troll under the bridge or leave him—IT—forever.

I always enjoy authors revealing their sources of inspiration. Though I've lived in Colorado since 1999, I'm from Kentucky, and I was living there when I read both the novel and King's account (from *Bare Bones*, a collection of King interviews published in 1988, though what I've excerpted here comes from stephenking.com). I'd never been to Colorado, so the description that stood out to me the most was, "In the mountains the end of the day comes in a hurry." I still experience a little thrill over the evocativeness of those words. It just feels the way horror should—isolation, a sense of helplessness, building dread, and a disorientation of the senses. I suppose to some degree all horror stories, even those that take place in the day, represent a yearning for lost sunlight.

If King's relatively brief flirtation with Colorado could influence him to write three terrific novels, imagine how impactful it must be for those authors who reside here on a more permanent basis. Let's take a look at some of horror's finest practitioners who call Colorado home.

First, the late, great Edward Bryant, who won back-to-back Nebula Awards in the late 70s, but whose fiction always had abiding elements of dark fantasy and horror. Born in New York and raised in Wyoming, he moved to Colorado in 1972. I had the honor of knowing Ed fairly well over the last ten years of his life, and though we often talked about the mechanics of storytelling, I never thought to ask him how Colorado itself may have influenced his writing. Still, I think it obviously did. Just consider the opening to his story "Jody After the War," found in his first collection, *Among the Dead and Other Events Leading up to the Apocalypse*:

Light lay bloody on the mountainside. From our promontory jutting over the scrub pine, we looked out over the city. Denver spread from horizon to horizon.

There it is again, that interplay of mountains and sunlight, establishing the scene, anchoring the mood. Perfectly Ed, perfectly Colorado. In addition to his collaborations with Harlan Ellison, his participation in George R. R. Martin's *Wild Cards* series, and the movie adaptation of his suspense story, *While She Was Out*, Ed would go on to contribute to some significant horror anthologies, including Kirby McCauley's *Dark Forces* and John Skipp and Craig Spector's signature anthology of zombie fiction, *Book of the Dead*.

It is likewise impossible to discuss Colorado's influence on horror fiction without bringing up Steve Rasnic Tem and Dan Simmons. Tem has won the World Fantasy Award and the British Fantasy Award, and his novel *Blood Kin* was recognized with a 2014 Bram Stoker Award®. But his true mastery rests in short fiction, as evidenced by the few hundred stories he's published over the course of his career. Dan Simmons meanwhile is a prime example of the *sui generis* author, excelling in every genre and capable of blending multiple genres in a single work. Winner of the Locus Award, World Fantasy Award, and the Hugo Award, among many others, Simmons' work is often enmeshed in literary and historical references, and several of his novels have been optioned by Hollywood studios. You may be most familiar with *The Terror*, adapted into a 10-episode miniseries by AMC in 2018.

And no one could write about contemporary Colorado horror without bringing up Stephen Graham Jones. Not that he requires much in the way of an introduction to most readers (he is, after all, a Bram Stoker Award® winner, too), but not everyone may know that he came to Colorado as a Texas transplant and that he's a Blackfeet Native American novelist and short story writer who specializes in the dark and weird. He's also a creative writing teacher at the University of Colorado-Boulder. But above all, this is a man who *writes*. Stephen King's legendary prolificacy has nothing on Stephen Graham Jones. Still a couple of years shy of 50, he's published twenty-two books. Publishers Weekly says his latest novel, *The Only Good Indians* "renders both supernatural and psychological horror with powerful cultural specificity" and concludes, "This is a must-read for horror fans."

But you probably already knew that.

It's definitely not fair to limit my sample size of Colorado horror authors

to four people. Connie Willis, Carrie Vaughn, Paolo Bacigalupi, R. Alan Brooks, Betsy Dornbusch, Mario Acevedo and Warren Hammond are all terrific, award-winning authors, too, with an international audience. The simple fact is I'd need a few thousand more words just to list all the names of talented Colorado authors who've at least dabbled in horror or dark fiction with striking results, even if such efforts aren't necessarily representative of their body of work.

Colorado's impact on and support for the horror community has never been more invigorated. MileHiCon is in its 52nd year; 2021 hopes to see the inauguration of the Colorado Festival of Horror as a yearly event; the new Colorado Springs Chapter of the Horror Writers Association is growing; and recently a group of enthusiasts launched the Denver Horror Collective. There's plenty to read, plenty to watch, and plenty to hear in Colorado to tingle the spine. But don't forget to go for a hike or two during your free time.

And don't forget your flashlight.

I hear that in the mountains, the end of the day comes up in a hurry.

TO FLAME UNHOLY LIGHT

by Alvaro Zinos-Amaro

L UIS JIMÉNEZ'S THIRTY-TWO-FOOT, nine-thousand-pound, electric blue sculpture of a rearing horse in the median of Peña Boulevard, the main road of Denver International Airport, is a bold, confrontational work. Since its unveiling in early 2008, it has endured a stream of steady praise as well as derision, even suffering graffiti vandalism in 2019. One thing it hasn't been is ignored. Its fiberglass composition and bright red eyes, intended by Jiménez as a tribute to his father's neon sign-making shop, where he worked at an early age, make *Blue Mustang* indisputably contemporary, but the color choices themselves, and the steed's pose, also evoke a mythological sensibility.

Consider those red eyes, which casual observers have described with that very non-casual term, "demonic." Glowing red eyes have held audiences captive in their imaginative thrall since at least the days of *Beowulf*, a thousand years ago. To quote from J.R.R. Tolkien's translation of the epic poem: "In angry mood he [Grendel] went, and from his eyes stood forth / most like to flame unholy light."

Blue horses are older still, and are often associated with dark deeds. Cerulean horses of a dark hue appear in two works by Ovid (43 BC – 17/18 AD), the epistolary *Heroides* (*The Heroines*) and the calendar-structured poem *Fasti* (*The Book of Days*). In the former, the horses are ridden by the sea god Triton: "Soon the winds will fall, and o'er the smooth-spread waves will Triton course with cerulean steeds" (Letter VII, lines 49-50). The fictional letter containing these lines is essentially Queen Dido's suicidal pleading with Aeneas not to leave for Italy. Not exactly cheery fare. In *Fasti* the horses feature in the couplet that deals with the rape by Pluto of Proserpina (the Latin version of Persephone, the Greek goddess of the underworld): "Her uncle sees her and having seen her carries her swiftly away; bears her on his dusky horses to his kingdom" (Book 4, lines 445-6). The adjective "dusky" is based on the Latin "caeruleis," or cerulean. Blue horses appear again in the 1st century tragedy *Hercules Furens* (*The Mad Hercules*) by Seneca (4 BC – AD 65): "Now, carried aloft by cerulean steeds, the Titan looks out from the heights of Oeta" (132-133). In some translations the word "azure" is used instead of "cerulean." Different words, same tragedies.

The horse's pose in Jiménez's sculpture reminds me of various depictions of one of ancient history's most famously wild horses; it took none other than Alexander the Great to tame Bucephalus (who, incidentally, was supposed to have a blue eye). If you look at Scottish sculptor Sir John Robert Steell's bronze depiction of the horse in "Alexander Taming Bucephalus" (1883), and ignore Alexander, you'll glimpse some of the same defiant energy as in the Jiménez piece. *Blue Mustang* is often referred to as Blucifer, which happens to have a nice alliterative overlap with Bucephalus. In a regrettable poverty of affection, *Blue Mustang* is also sometimes called the Devil Horse and, even more friskily, Satan's Stallion.

Given such roots, it's unsurprising that the evocative power of blue horses has proved an undying inspiration for artists. The German Expressionist painter Franz Marc, for instance, created in 1913 the spellbinding oil painting "The Tower of Blue Horses," sadly lost after World War II. More recently, Joy Harjo, a writer of the Muscogee (Creek) Nation, and in 2019 named the 23rd Poet Laureate of the United States, published an arresting poem titled "Promise of Blue Horses," which may be found in her collection *How We Became Human: New and Selected Poems 1975-2001* (2004). It begins with the following striking lines: "A blue horse turns into a streak of lightning, / then the sun-"

Blue Mustang's compositional audacity exists in a context of real-life

tragedy. In 2006, while Jiménez was working on the massive sculpture at his studio in Hondo, New Mexico, the horse turned not into a streak of lightning but rather an instrument of death: part of it fell on its creator, fatally severing his femoral artery. Jiménez's death shocked his family and friends, was mourned across the art world, and shook the local community. The governor of New Mexico had flags lowered to half-staff. Upon learning of this tragic event, the more paranoid of Blucifer's spectators have taken to calling the statue "haunted" or "murderous."

Jiménez was a prolific artist, and *Blue Mustang*, though titanic, shouldn't overshadow a career that featured over seventy-five distinctive solo exhibitions. Early pieces like *American Dream* commented on the alienation of "others" from mainstream U.S. culture; work from the late sixties engaged with the Vietnam War; *Border Crossing (Cruzando el Rio Bravo)* is a poignant reflection on immigrant anguish; later works, like *Vaquero, Steelworker, Fiesta Jarabe (Fiesta Dancers)*, or *Sodbuster, San Isidro*, probe everyday life on the border between the U.S. and Mexico through the depiction of working-class folks like laborers and farmers.

Besides the enduring quality of the work itself, Jiménez's legacy may be felt in the way he inspired and mentored others. Jesús Bautista Moroles, a sculptor of note who received the 2008 National Medal of Arts, served an important apprenticeship under Jiménez. Moroles chose to work in granite rather than fiberglass, and his pieces tend to be more abstract than those by Jiménez, but "the work of both artists reflects their Mexican heritage" (*Latino Visions*, James D. Cockcroft & Jane Canning, 2000).

Though examples of blue horses in classical literature and art precede and perhaps inform *Blue Mustang*, the bright blue Jiménez chose for his sculpture may have been an homage to Mexican muralism, which Jiménez had studied at Mexico University.

The specific breed of Jiménez's horse is also significant. The mustang is a powerful symbol of the Old West frontier spirit; it speaks to us about the forging of new paths, in this instance maybe even metaphysical ones. The origins of the stallion in the U.S. relate back to one of the themes that Jiménez explored throughout his career, namely that of cultural displacement. Spanish conquistadors brought horses, including the mustang, to the U.S. some five hundred years ago. Indeed, "in 1492, no horses had been seen in North America for thirteen thousand years" (*A Little History of the United States*, James West Davidson). Transporting them across the Atlantic proved difficult, but it was done nevertheless. The tropics also saw their passage, and in fact became known as the "horse latitudes" because "calm seas were even more dangerous [than the Atlantic]—the fierce heat could kill the poor animals in their dark, stuffy quarters" (*A Little History of the United States*). Once in the so-called New World, the descendants of horses that were deliberately freed or managed to escape moved across grasslands in huge herds. The word for such animals was the Spanish term for stray, or *mestengo*. The Mexican version of this term is *mesteño*, which is also the title of the 1997 eight-foot piece by Jiménez, on display at the University of Oklahoma, that served as the model for *Blue Mustang*.

Former museum director Brooke Barrie described Jiménez's oeuvre as operating "at the boundary between popular culture, ethnic identity, daily life, and aesthetic process" (*Contemporary Outdoor Sculpture*, 1999). These elements are all evident in *Blue Mustang*. But, with the addition of a dark affect, that summation also offers a remarkable view into another, very different form of creative expression that is currently experiencing a renaissance of sorts: horror.

Think about any of the best-regarded horror books or films of the last few years and you'll find elements of pop culture, ethnic identity, daily life, and yes, oftentimes comments on the aesthetic process itself by means of structural experimentation or meta-narrative games. It's not surprising, when we appraise Jiménez's collective work in this light, and see it so vividly exemplified by Blucifer, that many observers would find the piece creepy or disquieting. 1969's *Man on Fire*, for example, startlingly conflates Cuauhtémoc, an Aztec ruler whom Spanish conquistadors tortured by fire,

with Thich Quang Duc, the Buddhist monk who committed self-immolation to protest the Vietnam War. Like *Blue Mustang*, it's not hard to imagine this sparking gloomy flights of literary fancy.

In a 1985 interview with Peter Bermingham, Jiménez said the following about his process: "I'm working on an intuitive basis. And I guess I've been blessed with a good subconscious. I can't take any credit for it, because most of the time I don't know what's really going on. I just know that I'm putting it down, and then as I begin to develop it, I become more aware of why that idea is important to me."

Blue Mustang projects a primal power that seems very much at home with this intuitive means of conception. Its cunning and confident execution offers a brilliant balance of the mythical with the modern, the aesthetic with the artisanal, the grand with the intimate. It challenges us, juxtaposing questions about our place in worlds both real (remember the various strands of history, from the conquistadors and their horses to frontier life) and imagined (try not to succumb to the mesmerism of that "unholy light" in the mustang's eyes), to which there are no easy answers.

It is also an invitation.

Rear up, it seems to be saying, and run wild.

THEY PASS BY THE HORSE

by Jonathan Maberry

The thousands come and go.
> Come and go.
> In laughing groups of visitors.
> In weary family bunches.
> In pairs and clusters.
> Or alone.

He watches them all.
> He loves the loners, though.
> The ones who aren't smiling the right way.
> The ones who look here, and there, and there.
> And don't like to be looked at.
> Except by Blucifer.

The ones he likes are the ones who stop.
> Who turn.
> Who look up at him.
> The ones who see him.
> See.
> Him.

The ones who look into those red eyes.
> Who can read the power.

Of the eyes.

Of his massive body.

The ones who see his potential.

And feel it match their own.

These people smile a lot.

Because they don't want to be seen not smiling.

They know the words and phrases.

They blend in because that's how it works.

Becoming what is expected.

Becoming normal.

They are exactly as normal,

As he is a horse.

The scale is the same.

The implication is the same.

The inferences are as wildly wrong.

Which is correct.

They pause to regard him.

To see him.

To feel him.

To know him.

A fellow traveler.

A kindred soulless.

The younger ones, the ones just starting this work

Say, "I will behave here."

"I will not cause trouble in your town."

They believe that until they see those eyes.

And realize their mistake.

Then they linger longer and listen more clearly.

They hear the whispers from his screaming mouth.

Not a warning. Not a caution.

They realize what it is.

An invitation.

Come and play in my fields.

The young ones grow older in wisdom.

Right there.

Right then.
With joy.
Released.
Unfettered.
The big horse pretending to be only that.
Watches the young ones grow.
He watches the older ones open up.
He haunts them, and goes with them in spirit.
As they run in red fields.
As they scream with red mouths.
As red as his eyes.

COLLATERAL DAMAGE

by Angie Hodapp

M ARCY HATES HER NEW BOSS. His name is Blake, and he's as douchey as his name. For one thing, he's wearing loafers with a sapphire-blue suit and carrying a shiny blue motorcycle helmet to match. Who rides a motorcycle dressed like that? And another thing: Didn't Van Dykes go out in the nineties?

So far, Blake has told Marcy how to alert airport security if she sees any suspicious behavior. How to ring up customers. Which key unlocks the kiosk's drawers and which unlocks the cash box. That failing to restock at the end of every shift—especially the refrigerator magnets and shot glasses because they're his bestsellers—is a fireable offense. How to spin the red plastic clock hands on the cardboard Be Back Soon sign when she has to use the restroom. That restroom breaks longer than five minutes are also a fireable offense.

"And don't steal," he tells her.

"Also a fireable offense," she says with a crisp nod.

He narrows his eyes like he can't decide if she's mocking him. She is, but *don't steal* was a direct hit, a reminder that she's lucky to have this job, lucky to have a probation officer who knows people who know people. It's not easy to score an honest paycheck when you have a record.

Marcy smiles, and Blake's gaze falls to her chest. "It's basically a job any moron could do," he tells her breasts. "I own eight kiosks in this airport, so I'm usually around, but if you have questions, ask Trey." He jerks his head at the next kiosk over, which is called Colorado Dew and sells locally made skin-care products.

Trey is enthusiastically pumping lotion from a bottle marked "sample" into the open palms of three gray-haired women in beige orthopedic shoes and elastic-waisted jeans. They ooh and ahh as they smell their hands and rub the lotion into their wrinkled skin.

"That dude could sell meth to a Mormon." Blake hands her the keys, which are on a red plastic coil she's supposed to wear around her wrist.

Selling meth to Mormons isn't any harder than selling hand lotion in Colorado. Stupid analogy. Stupid Blake. What'll be harder is selling this shit: Colorado- and Denver-themed keychains and travel mugs, bottle openers and coasters, beer koozies and cheap teddy bears wearing Broncos, Nuggets, and Avalanche tees. All mass produced in China and marked up probably like eight-hundred percent.

When Blake leaves, Marcy perches on her stool and looks over at Trey, who is now upselling the old ladies on little pots of lip balm. He's so into it. Casual laughter, leaning in, intense eye contact. It's all an act, Marcy knows. Everyone is always acting. Some people are just better at it than others.

Another woman stops at Colorado Dew. She has a kid with her, a boy who's maybe six. Both have white-blond curls and freckled noses. The woman picks up a bottle of something, which she sniffs before turning over to read the label.

Marcy glances at the kid.

The kid is staring at her.

She blinks. She's never liked kids. They smell weird, they're loud, and they chew with their mouths open. They have other bad manners, too. Like staring.

Then she realizes maybe he isn't staring at her. Maybe he's staring at all the shiny things hanging on her kiosk. The mom is occupied (Trey is showing her how to dab something under her eyes) so Marcy grabs a keychain off a peg. It's a blue-enameled horse rearing up on its hind legs, glittery red crystals for eyes—a miniature version of Blucifer, the massive

statue just outside the airport.

She dangles the keychain in front of the kid. "Check this out. Want to buy it?"

The kid flips her off.

She returns the gesture, which earns her a sharp, disapproving look from a business man hurrying by.

The kid gives her a gap-toothed grin and steps closer. "I'm going on an airplane to Omaha."

Marcy dangles the keychain again. "Two bucks. You want it or not?" She has no idea how much Blake charges for the Blucifer keychains, but it seems reasonable that a six-year-old might have a couple ones in his pocket. Why not try to get what she can?

"I don't have that much money."

"How much money do you have?"

He pulls three quarters from his pocket, holds them out on a fat little hand.

"Sold," she says.

He hands her the coins, and she hands him the Blucifer.

"Timothy!" The woman rushes over. She grabs his arm and glares at Marcy. "What's going on here?"

"He bought a keychain."

"With my own money," he says.

"You don't have any money," the woman snaps. To Marcy, she says, "Give it back."

This woman is rude. Marcy seethes. She hates rude people.

She shrugs and hands the kid two quarters. He doesn't notice he's been shorted because he's busy working up a squall. He grips the Blucifer in his fist, anger-panting at his mother, his face going red. His mother stares at him in horror, calculating whether the magnitude of the tantrum he's about to throw will fall within the scope of her current ability to manage.

Marcy smiles at the woman. "You know what? He can just have it."

The kid's panting slows. The woman's shoulders sag. "Are you sure?"

"I'm sure. Hey, Timmy, enjoy your Blucifer. Have fun in Omaha."

The woman drags the kid toward their gate. The little shit doesn't even turn around to say thank you.

Trey saunters over to Marcy. "I had that lady on the hook for the Colorado Dew Eye-Brightening Serum. Twenty-four bucks per two-ounce bottle."

His teeth are straight and white. He's wearing a mint-green button-down embroidered with the Colorado Dew logo and khaki slacks. His high-and-tight is pomaded to perfection.

She flips him the quarter. "I'll have to owe you the rest."

"You lifted this off that kid, didn't you? You bitch!"

Marcy's hackles rise. She doesn't like the b-word, never has, but when Trey laughs, she realizes he was saying it in a conspiring way, like they're buddies. Like they're both in on the joke.

"Get it where you can," she says.

"Girl, absolutely. People are a goddamn mess who deserve what happens to them."

Marcy's pulse hops. That's right, what Trey said. That's exactly right. "Hey, what's up with Blake?"

"Blake's a tool."

Her pulse hops faster. This guy gets it.

"He has a hard time keeping employees," Trey continues. "Everyone he hires quits after a couple months. Not because he's a tool, but because… this'll sound crazy, but you might as well know. It's because they get scared of him. Like, *scared* scared."

Marcy rolls her eyes and twists a dyed-black piece of hair around her finger. She can't imagine being scared of Blake. She's lived on the street. She's had her ass beat plenty, but she's delivered more beat-downs than she got. Hell, she knows strung-out grannies walking East Colfax who could kick Blake's ass.

"Rumor is he's some sort of Satan worshipper."

"Ooh. Scary."

"I'm serious. The girl you replaced said Blake is a demon and the stuff he sells is possessed. Someone else said he's into, like, talisman magick or some shit. And they weren't the only ones to say stuff like that."

"Maybe Blake shouldn't hire junkies."

Trey leans back and makes a show of looking her up and down.

Marcy snorts. "I'm not a junkie. I'm a dealer."

That earns a raised eyebrow. "Got anything good?"

"What are you into?"

Trey laughs. "Girl, you're my new BFF."

Blake comes back at four. He's still wearing his douchey blue suit, still carrying his sparkly blue helmet. His eyes scan his merchandise like he'll be able to tell if she swiped something.

"Busy day?" he asks her breasts.

"Sold a couple magnets."

"Did you restock? Magnets are hot. I told you this morning."

She didn't but says she did.

"Good. See you tomorrow."

Marcy hands him the keys and bolts. She doesn't like the way her stomach feels when he's around—like she just downed a jug of sour milk.

She's almost to the employee lounge when Trey comes speed-walking toward her.

"Oh-em-gee, Girl, did you see?" He spins her around, links his arm through hers, and marches her back into the terminal.

"What's going on?"

"The most terrible thing." He steers her to the nearest gate, where a crowd stares in shock at the TV on the wall. The sound is off, but the images and captions scrolling across the screen tell the story: Flight 1467 from Denver to Omaha crashed. All 232 passengers and crew are dead.

Marcy gasps. Timmy and his mom were on that flight. She's sure of it. Rude Timmy and his rude mom. They're dead.

She knows she should feel horror and grief over this tragic loss of life. And she does. She does feel those things. But she has to dig for it. A giddy sense of exhilaration pushes itself open inside her, hard and fast like the time-lapse video she saw one time of a black rose blooming.

"Look at that." Trey shakes his head. "Look at them crying like they knew any of those dead people, like they're not going to go on living exactly the same as before." His voice goes high. "Ooh, watch me be sad! Watch me cry! Marvel at my empathy! What a joke."

Trey is right. Jesus, he really gets it.

"Look at that," Marcy says.

That night, Marcy barely sleeps. She lies on the threadbare carpet of her rundown apartment and watches the ceiling fan spin slowly in the dark. She thinks about Timmy.

People are a goddamn mess who deserve what happens to them.

Trey tossed that out there like he was ordering a cappuccino, like it was no big deal, because that's what truth should be: no big deal.

She closes her eyes and conjures the image of Timmy's mother dragging him away, the Blucifer keychain clutched in his rude, selfish little fist.

The Blucifer keychain. She sits up.

A pinpoint of light zips through her brain. Zip, zip, zip. She watches it career off the spongy folds inside her skull. The light is the part of her mind that makes connections, and right now it is very, very busy. She grabs her laptop off the coffee table, opens it, Googles talisman magick.

Hours later, she has a theory and an idea. She can't wait to tell Trey.

"Interesting," Trey says. "Let's try it."

They watch the people moving past, dragging their baggage this way and that, all in various states of hurry. Soon, an older couple walks by, the woman loudly berating her husband for taking too long to buy a newspaper. If they miss the hotel shuttle, dammit, they'll have to wait thirty whole minutes for the next one. The old man's cowed, poor thing. That hag's probably been belittling him for decades.

"Do it," Trey whispers.

Marcy unties her shoe, then follows them. The man stops at a water fountain, and the woman lets out another high-pitched tirade. Marcy kneels beside the woman's suitcase and eyes the luggage tag. Lucille Stearns. Quickly, she stuffs a Blucifer keychain into a side pocket that's not quite zipped.

Lucille looks down at her. "What do you think you're doing?"

Marcy smiles, not entirely certain she hasn't been found out. "Tying my shoe, Ma'am."

Lucille's face puckers with suspicion. She swats her husband's elbow and drags her suitcase toward the sign for ground transportation.

Back at the kiosk, Marcy writes Lucille Stearns in the notebook she bought this morning at Hudson News.

"Now what?" asks Trey.

"Now we wait."

Wednesday, a man who's just landed in Denver stops at Marcy's kiosk and buys a pink teddy bear in a Colorado-flag tee.

"For your granddaughter?"

"My girlfriend's daughter."

The man looks sixty, and he's wearing a wedding ring. Marcy raises an eyebrow.

The man chuckles. "You know how it is."

Marcy knows exactly how it is. She rings up the sale, noting the name on his MasterCard, and slips a Blucifer keychain into the bag along with the bear.

When he leaves, Marcy tells Trey what she did and writes Kenneth Jesperson in her notebook.

Thursday, Marcy sees an uppity type applying bronzer in the ladies' room. The girl is already wearing more makeup than a Kardashian, and as Marcy washes her hands, the girl poses for a mirror selfie, pushing her lips out like a duck and holding two fingers in a peace sign beside her heavily contoured cheek. As she posts it to Instagram, Marcy reaches behind her to snag a paper towel and peek at the phone. On her way out, she drops a Blucifer into the girl's slouchy boho-chic shoulder bag.

At the kiosk, Marcy searches @MileHiBabe0313 on Instagram. "Tiffany Fellows," she tells Trey. She writes the name in her book.

Friday, Blake stops by.

"I did inventory last night," he says. "We're missing some Blue Mustang keychains."

You're missing all of them, Marcy thinks. There are two left, and they're both in her purse. "That's weird," she says.

"You know what's even weirder? There were a couple in the drawer last week, and they're missing too."

She tries to look thoughtful, despite the sour-milk feeling in her gut. "I restocked those on Wednesday. Or maybe yesterday."

His eyes bore into hers.

Marcy lets her lip tremble a bit. "I swear, Blake, if I knew anything, I'd tell you."

He doesn't want to believe her. "What did I say about stealing?"

"Fireable offense."

"That's right. Keep your nose clean. I'm watching you."

That night, she Googles her boss, finds his address. Beside his garage is a sapphire-blue Yamaha crotch rocket. She pops open the seat compart-

ment and drops in a Blucifer.

Saturday morning, the terminal is busy. Trey's on fire. He grins and fawns and samples and laughs and calls everyone Girl, even the men, and compliments their hair, their earrings, their shoes. No one walks away from Colorado Dew without a bag and a receipt.

Marcy sells the occasional piece-of-shit souvenir and waits. At last, Trey gets a break. She rushes over to his kiosk. Her insides boomerang against her ribs.

"It worked." Her voice shakes. "We did it." She opens the notebook, to which she has added careful notes. "Timmy and his mom died Monday. Plane crash. Duh. Lucille Stearns and her husband died Tuesday at the Grand Hyatt downtown. Actually, seven dead and four hospitalized because there was a carbon-monoxide leak on the fourth floor. Kenneth Jesperson was killed in a house fire Wednesday night. So were his girlfriend, her daughter, and three of her daughter's friends. Sleepover. Thursday, Tiffany Fellows crashed head-on into an SUV carrying a family of five. No survivors." Marcy lets out a maniacal giggle that sounds more like a hiccup. "Tiffany was thrown free but not clear, if you know what I mean. There was a half-typed text on her phone, which she was holding in what was left of her hand."

Trey pales. "Are you bullshitting me?"

She slides him the notebook. "Google them yourself."

He pulls out his phone. Marcy waits.

After a couple minutes, Trey's skin goes from merely pale to chalk white. "Jesus. This is...I mean...you killed..." He starts counting on his fingers, then gives up and flaps his hands in the air. "You killed like three hundred people."

"Don't exaggerate. It was two hundred and fifty-one, and there was always going to be collateral damage. But you said it yourself: People are a goddamn mess who deserve what happens to them. The point is, we did it together."

"Did what?"

"Took out the trash. Made the world a better place."

"You did this! I didn't have anything to do with it!" He presses his fingertips into his temples like he's fighting off a headache. "How many of those keychains are left?"

"Two. They're in my purse."

"If you're carrying them around with you, why aren't you dead?"

"It has to be a gift. If you buy or steal a charmed object, it doesn't work." She spent hours studying talisman magick online, and she found an old blog post that went on and on about how the spirit of giving can be just as important as the practitioner's intent.

"Hold on. That kid Timmy—technically, he paid you a quarter. That means his Blucifer can't be what caused that plane crash."

"Technically, I stole that quarter, and then I gave it to you right after, so I didn't profit from the exchange. Pretty sure that means the magick was still good." She furrows her brow. "No, wait. There's only one keychain left. I put the other one in Blake's bike last night. Talk about trash, am I right? Anyway, I'm going to use the last one to learn how to make more. This blog I found says—"

Trey stumbles back a few steps, his mouth hanging open. Marcy thinks he's about to freak out on her, but then she realizes he's looking at something behind her.

Slowly, she turns.

Blake stands at her kiosk. He holds up a hand, lets something shiny and blue dangle from his finger. Marcy doesn't have to look at it to know what it is.

"You want to tell me how this ended up in my bike last night?" He takes a step closer.

Marcy sees her purse clutched in his other hand. Her mouth goes dry.

"Give me that."

"You're a thief and a liar. You know what else you are? You're a murderer."

Part of her wants to bolt. That sour-milk feeling she gets when Blake's around makes her stomach clench, but she feels something else now, too. She feels his power. It crackles in the air, reaching for her. She's never wanted anything more.

"Why aren't you dead?" she asks.

Blake stretches thin lips over clenched teeth. His eyes go glittery and red, like cut rubies. "I invented this game, little girl. Don't play with other people's toys."

Marcy glances at Trey. To his credit, he hasn't run, but he isn't helping her either. He's just standing there, slack-jawed and stupid. She sighs.

Lightning fast, she lunges for her purse. "Help! Security! Purse-snatcher!"

Marcy and Blake play a violent tug-of-war for what seems like an age. Marcy screams Purse-snatcher! Security! Help! over and over. A crowd gathers. Two men move in to assist her, but when they see Blake's red eyes—or maybe when they feel the crackle of his power, Marcy isn't sure which—they shrink back.

Blake is strong, but she can tell he's holding back. He's playing with her. Why?

She'll worry about that later. Get the purse. Get the Blucifer. Run. That's the plan. Zip, zip, zip.

From the corner of her eye, she sees two security guards closing in, the crowd parting to let them through

"Drop the purse!" one of them yells. "Get down!"

Blake lets go. Marcy stumbles back and nearly falls, but she has it now.

She has the last Blucifer. She's won. Then she looks at Blake. When she sees a grin spread wide across his face, she realizes her mistake.

"Consider it a gift," he says, stroking his Van Dyke.

No, no, no! She shoves her hand into her purse, digs around for the Blucifer, digs through keys, pens, tampons, Kleenex, loose change. Where is it? Where the hell is it?

"She has a gun!" Blake's voice is a cannon booming off the shiny walls and marble floors of the terminal. In its wake, everything falls silent.

Then.

People scream. People run. People duck behind trash cans. People fall flat on the floor and cover their heads.

To Marcy, it all seems so impossibly slow and terribly absurd. The world around her moves like a syrupy dream. She has to find the Blucifer. She has to throw it far, far away. As far away from herself as she can.

The security guards skid to a stop a few yards away. They stand with weapons drawn, like superheroes on a movie poster. "Drop it! Hands in the air!"

Her fingers close around the sharp little horsey shape of the last Blucifer. Its magick crackles in her hand. It's already alive. It already knows where it came from and what it's here to do.

Throw it. Throw it! She pulls it from her purse.

The bullets crack-crack-crack around her. She wants to clap her hands over her ears, but she's still holding the Blucifer, and now she's falling. She's fallen and so has Trey, and there's blood, so much blood, and she and Trey are face to face. His eyes are open but empty.

"There's always collateral damage," she tells him as her throat fills with blood.

The last thing Marcy sees is Blake's face. The last thing she hears is his voice. "People are a goddamn mess who deserve what happens to them."

The last thing Marcy feels is Blake peeling the Blucifer from her cold, dead fingers.

BLUCIFER'S PROPHET

by Mario Acevedo

There is no education like adversity.
BENJAMIN DISRAELI

I REPEAT THE QUOTE IN MY HEAD. For me, for us, it's another day in this camp, another day of dealing with prisoners, another day of stress that I don't need. The quote gives context to what I'm doing, refreshing me, like a breeze through a stale room.

I stuff the book, *Thoughtful Musings: Quotes to Live By*, into my cargo pocket. The book is a souvenir I picked up from the remains of a bombed-out house months back. I pass through the concertina wire and enter the detention area. Today's mission is to deliver prisoners to Blucifer's Prophet.

Corporal Jameson unlocks the door of a confinement cell and swings it open.

Afternoon sunlight pours past me. I swat at flies. The prisoners inside stir, blinking at the glare, raising hands to shield their eyes. The enclosure smells like a stable that needs mucking. Using my tablet, I call up the Plan of the Day and recite the prisoner roster. "Zarrella. Isaacs. Horvath."

I only bother with the family names. Prisoners seldom stay long enough to make it worth learning their first names.

The prisoners I called help each other to their feet and shamble out the door. My squad groups them by family into three files, arranged from youngest to mom, the dad is last. Guards stand by, ready to pounce with electric cattle prods.

The prisoners are ordered to their knees. From where I stand behind them, I can see the bottoms of their dirty, bare feet; grimy, tattered clothes creased over the sharp edges of their bony frames; matted, greasy hair teeming with lice.

They represent the hold outs. The wrong thinkers. One bad apple spoils the entire bunch and all that. Normally we'd leave their bodies to rot in the streets or hanging from cherry pickers. But the Prophet has other plans.

The Isaacs mom turns her head. "Where are we going?"

I read from my tablet. "The re-education camp at the old Rocky Mountain Arsenal."

Whispers of optimism ripple from prisoner to prisoner. The camp means they've been given a reprieve. Clean clothes. Food. Rewards for good behavior and right thinking.

I keep my gaze on the Zarrella dad. Yesterday he went psycho. After subduing him, we bound him by threading coat hanger wire through the palms of his hands. I remember how his fingers twitched like the legs of a tortured crab when Jameson used the cordless drill.

Presently, he's hunched over his knees, hands behind his back, the wire looped around his hands. Blood soaks the lower back of his shirt, still wet from what seeps from his wounds.

Doing that kind of work is hard on the troops, and the lieutenant rewarded Jameson with a coupon for a free drink from the coffee truck. Small acts of empathy like that do wonders for morale. I remember the quote I read to Jameson afterwards.

Great things never come from comfort zones.
BEN FRANCIA

Jameson walks down the files and beeps her tracker reader against each prisoner's plastic collar. A blip flashes beside their names on my tablet.

Eleven blips. Matches the head count.

Specialist Kendall brings the crate with chains and padlocks. He and a couple of other guards measure a length of chain, one per family. They loop the chain around each prisoner's neck and secure it with a padlock.

Lieutenant Collins appears from the direction of the mess tent. She halts by the prisoners. Takes a whiff. Winces. "Sergeant Gonzales, make sure your squad takes precautions. I don't want anyone infected."

"All under control, LT." I give her jazz hands to show that I'm wearing gloves, then point to my face mask, my safety glasses. Several of the guards do the same. Sometimes, you have to highlight the obvious to our officers.

As Collins nods in approval, we lead the prisoners toward the shit buckets where they drop trou or raise skirts, depending, to do their business. Mrs. Zarrella performs her wifey duties by working her husband's pants and wiping his ass.

Afterwards, we let them wash up with soapy water and clean rags. Not for their sake, but for ours. We don't need an outbreak of cholera or other nastiness.

Kendall brings a bucket filled with hunks of rock-hard bread and apples soggy with rot. Each family gets a big plastic cup they dip into a rain barrel and pass around. The bread is too hard to chew so they soften the pieces with water. The Zarrella wife lovingly feeds her husband. The families sit in circles, bound by their neck chains, eating silently.

The scene brings to mind the first line of my favorite quote:

Give us this day our daily bread…
MATTHEW 6:11

Three vehicles rumble close and stop, civilian types commandeered for the war: an SUV, a panel truck, and a four-door pickup.

The rental company logo on the panel truck shows through faded slap-dash camouflage. Jameson and I unlock the rear door and scroll it open, releasing the smell of piss and vomit. Worse, on hot days, bloated bodies tumble out, the result of heat stroke or asphyxiation. Wasn't supposed to happen but with the hurry up and wait of military SNAFUs, you tend to forget about the prisoners.

I shout, "Load up, everyone."

The prisoners rise to their feet, tame as cattle. We march them to the truck, each family tethered neck-to-neck. With food in their bellies, they're more compliant and less likely to get carsick during the ride, which is good for us since we'd have to mop the mess.

Collins climbs into the SUV, Jameson drives the panel truck, Kendall's at the wheel of the pickup, me riding shotgun. The rest of the squad is scattered among the vehicles.

We proceed past the barracks, the motor pool, the teeing area for the officer's golf course, and out the main gate. We drive north from Aurora, through the waste lands of what was Chamber Heights and Fitzsimmons. People watch from the distant rubble, resembling curious prairie dogs.

After driving up a wide, weedy incline we reach Interstate 70. We rumble across the divided highway, by habit circling the grass and weeds sprouting from the cracked concrete and asphalt, favorite places where the enemy used to hide IEDs.

A Wi-Fi tower marks the location of the sentry house, part of the wall of junk that demarcates the southern perimeter of the old airport property. Scuffed and stained orange traffic cones and bullet-pocked Jersey barriers channel us to the sentry bunker where our little column pulls short.

Two guards exit the bunker, rifles at the ready, wearing special Blucifer arm bands—blue with twin red dots. The guard sergeant approaches the SUV, salutes, and exchanges words with the LT.

While waiting for the go-ahead, I take in the view. It's a panoramic vista of what remains of the Denver metroplex. The sun lingers above the distant, jagged skyline, standing in relief against the foothills. The afternoon light turns yellow, curdling the haze over the city into a syrupy

amber, where helicopters buzz about like moths.

Kendall clears his throat. He's the oldest in my squad, older than me, but never rising above the rank of corporal and was recently busted back to technician. Again. For the usual. Drunk on duty. In any other unit, he would've been bounced loose but we need bodies.

His glance swivels toward me and to the back of the pickup. It's just him and me in the cab, the rest of the crew is in the bed. Gazing forward, he says, "Brianna," his voice low.

"What?"

He juts his chin toward the panel truck. "The Horvath girl."

Ahh. He's talking about the teenage daughter. "What about her?"

"Give her a couple days of hot rations. A bath. Something to wear other than rags, she'd be looking really good."

He adjusts his posture. "Too bad you missed the early days of the Purge. Back then, the women, particularly the young women," he raises his eyebrows at the truck, to Brianna inside, "were sent to work as 'therapy pillows.' Good times."

I've heard the stories. But with so many women now in the upper ranks of the Tri-Force Alliance, the comfort camps were disbanded.

"Now female prisoners get the same treatment as the men." Kendall draws a finger across his throat. "Equality."

We finally proceed up the well-worn path that meanders over the undulating ground. Reaching Peña Boulevard, we follow it north, the stretch of broken pavement twisting like a fractured spine. Ahead of us, the tops of the old airport terminal are stained orange by the setting sun. The remains of airliners lay scattered like emaciated carcasses.

The airport was the first in the area hit by the pandemic. The government immediately quarantined the airport and surrounding property. The pandemic spread, the economy cratered, and then the rebellion started, which morphed into civil war. For some reason, when people thought of civil war, they pictured two sides shooting at each other from neat rows, flags waving. It was actually a dirty mess fought in the shadows: car bombs and suicide bombers, homes attacked with Molotov cocktails and burned to the ground, kidnappings and assassinations, kneecappings, snitches found tortured and dead. The victor was not the most righteous, or the best equipped, but the most vicious. Our side won. Then came the Purge and now we're in the Cleansing.

Kendall says, "What's the word, sarge?"

"About what?"

"From that book of yours."

I share something from memory. "Forgive your enemies—"

Kendall cuts me off, chuckling. "And then hang them. I already know that one. How about something else. More topical?"

"Topical?" I reply. "That's a big word for you."

"Gimme a break, sarge. I read."

"Topical to what?" I ask. "Like happiness?"

Kendall adjusted his grip on the wheel. "Yeah, I could do with a dose of happiness."

I dig the book from my pocket, flip to a dog-eared page, and read:

To increase your happiness, randomly wish for someone else to be happy.
CHADE-MENG TAN

Kendall smiles. "Yeah, I like that one."

We drive a bit, then he asks, "You gonna ask me who I want to be happy?"

"Wasn't planning on it. I figured these wishes are like wishes when you blow out candles on your birthday cake. You keep them secret or they won't come true."

Kendall grunts in approval.

Twilight creeps upon us. The sky darkens, revealing a spill of stars. We flip on our headlights and carve garish swaths in the murk.

I keep my attention forward, waiting for the crimson eyes of Blucifer to

appear. I can't count how many times I've made this trip and every time, it's a bit hard to let go of what I see. Anxiety clots in my throat and I clench my teeth to keep down the bile.

One of the local guards appears beside the road. She waves, signaling that we douse our headlights, and we're swallowed by the darkness.

A pair of tiny crimson lights appear low over the ground. As we continue, the red lights grow brighter and rise above the horizon. Then a dark outline materializes around the lights, the silhouette of a huge rampart horse, eyes blazing.

We pass several pits filled with freshly turned dirt. One pit remains empty, about six meters square and two meters deep. A tractor sits on the edge of this pit, its excavator arm raised like the neck of a robotic dinosaur scanning the horizon for a meal.

The smell of burning fuel wafts from the direction of a crew tending a portable gasoline stove. Blue flames shimmer beneath pots set on the burners. Steam lifts from around their lids.

Other guards direct us where to park. We all dismount and form a circle around the back of the panel truck. Kendall and I crack open the rear door and heave it upwards. Within the gloomy enclosure, prisoners gaze at us, blinking and uncertain, like chickens on the way to the butcher.

"We're here!" I shout. "Get out!"

They clamber to the ground, chained together, treading carefully on the rough dirt because of their bare feet. It takes them a moment to get their bearings. They realize the enormous black shape is the horse towering above us. A collective gasp erupts, "Blucifer."

They tremble in panic, not knowing which way to run.

Collins grouses, "Goddamn it, Gonzales, I thought you'd have this under control."

"They're not going anywhere." The LT was naïve if she thought the prisoners would react any other way. People know about Blucifer and the Prophet.

I raise my voice but keep it calm. "Relax," I tell the prisoners. "This is just the transfer point. In a few minutes you'll be over there." I point to the airport terminal. "On warm bunks. Getting fed. Tomorrow your re-education starts." A lie but they buy it.

Collins says to me, "Sergeant, your balaclavas."

Meaning this event will be broadcast, and so we guards must hide our identities.

A team of videographers appear, already wearing balaclavas, to aim phones and record the proceedings. We all look like dark phantoms with human eyes grafted onto our blob-like heads, made even more bizarre because of our safety glasses.

My guards snap at the chains to force the prisoners to their knees. I hand out zip ties and my guards go down the files, securing the prisoners' wrists behind their backs, even the Zarrella dad. Can't take chances.

Then we wait, the night's chill creeping upon us.

There's a *whoosh!* On the ground beneath the horse's front hooves, a pair of torches burst into flame. The flare of light rips through the darkness. The illumination shrinks to the torches, each a blossom of fire.

Blucifer glows in terrible spectacle, the statue animated by the reflected light dancing and glistening on its fiberglass form. Our eyes are drawn to its immense snout, lips drawn back, teeth bared, an expression of murderous vengeance.

From between the rear legs, a figure clad in a white robe emerges to stand between the torches. A hood obscures the face but there is no doubt who this is: Blucifer's Prophet, the avatar and symbolic leader of the Tri-Force Alliance.

Sleeved arms reach upward and fold back the hood. Man or woman or something else, I don't know and even now I can't tell.

A shock of green hair spills around a translucent mask that both reflects the shimmering light and reveals the flesh underneath. Eyes glisten from oval cutouts.

The Prophet's voice booms from speakers hidden inside Blucifer. "Our

struggle is near its end. In the previous phase, the recalcitrants were by necessity quickly dispatched. But we've learned that such swift justice was not enough to prevent contamination. Now, during this Cleansing, we must perform the difficult steps required to maintain the peace and return ourselves to a civil society."

The videographers sidestep to better positions.

I know what's coming. The taste in my mouth becomes metallic and I adjust my weight to maintain equilibrium on ground that seems to have shifted. Groping into my cargo pocket, I touch the edges of my book. I need a quote to strengthen my resolve, to steel me for the unpleasantness that will unfold.

> *God widens the back to carry the load.*
> IRISH PROVERB

Collins says, "Sergeant Gonzales."

Now it begins. I bark commands. We gag the prisoners with sticks tied across their mouths. The night is going to be stressful enough without them screaming and hollering. Even so, the boys and girls squeal like piglets. Their mothers and fathers bellow in terror.

The Prophet continues, "You have refused to see the truth even when it was obvious before you. If you wish to be blind, then blind you shall be."

Jameson has already put on insulated gloves. She crouches in front of the Isaacs kid, a boy about ten. Jameson straddles his little frame and grips his head, working her gloved fingers to skin his eyelids back. The boy squirms and his eyes bulge, glistening with horror and helplessness.

His mother and father spit froth from around their gags. My guards plant a boot in the small of their backs and yank on the neck chains, choking, controlling them the way you would feral dogs. I seize the boy by his neck and hold firm.

A pair of guards bring a stock pot. Steam puffs from the hot water. They set the pot in front of the Isaacs boy. Jameson draws a ladle from the pot and cautions me. "Watch your hands."

Videographers lean close.

The eyeballs glisten, straining. Lips distend around shiny pink gums and small white teeth.

Jameson empties the ladle. The scalding hot water cascades into the left eye, then the right. Though small, the boy thrashes with animal fury. Vapor plumes upward. Steam curls from the sockets of his ruined eyeballs. The air is filled with the odor of boiling meat. Water dribbles around his nose and into his mouth. An inhuman cry escapes from around the gag, a keening sound that tears into my ears.

Though we have been briefed and are ready, the scene is one of organized pandemonium. Prisoners strain at their restraints. I didn't expect this much blood, spurting from under the zip ties or frothing from screaming mouths. We jerk hard on the chains to keep them under control.

Jameson remarks, "It's like a baptism."

The ordeal lasts twenty minutes. The prisoners sob as they squirm on the wet ground, the air clouded by vapor. The worst of the night is over for us, and I breathe easier. I remember why we're doing this: for the greater good, to make a better world.

Do something today that your future self will thank you for.
SEAN PATRICK FLANERY

The Prophet watches. "You were blind to the truth. Now you are blind to everything. But take heart. You will serve as an example to others. Your misery was not in vain. Now, from the earth you emerged, so to the earth you shall return."

The tractor growls to life. Its lamps blare on, the illumination turning the area into a collage of fleeting lights and shadows.

We hoist the prisoners to their feet and push them toward the open pit.

They stumble zombie-like, whimpering, their scalded faces shining bright red, what's left of their eyes wrinkled like stewed prunes. At the edge of the pit, we halt the prisoners. Jameson beeps her reader against their collars. Have to keep our records current. Then guards snip the collars off and remove the chains and padlocks. These cost money. The guards kick the prisoners, one by one, into the pit where they flop on top of each other like fish in a bucket.

The Horvath mother slips out of her zip ties and pulls the gag from her mouth. She squirms from under the pile of prisoners to grope along the bottom of the pit, wailing, "I'm blind! Why? Why are you doing this?"

Collins nudges me. I nudge Kendall. He grabs a shovel and scrambles into the pit, where he conks the Horvath mom on the skull. She convulses, then lies still.

Kendall climbs out, muttering, "Man, she was really bugging me."

The tractor growls again. Its front dozer blade lowers, slicing into the mound of dirt and advances, pushing a roll of dirt into the pit. The broken earth heaps and scatters across the prisoners.

A videographer pivots toward Blucifer. The flames on the torches shrink, taking the illumination with them, until the fires fade into glowing stubs. The Prophet has vanished. Blucifer gazes down upon us like a god weighing the merit of this sacrifice.

The leader of the videographers yells that they are done recording and with that, we all remove our balaclavas. Fresh coffee and donuts are passed around while we wait for the pit to be filled in.

Collins slaps me on the back. "Gonzales, good job tonight. What does your book say about this?"

I pull out the book and turn to a random page. I lean toward a light from the tractor and read:

Sometimes we look back and 10 years from now we think 'Boy, those were great old days.' Well, you know, we're living in the good old days.
JOEL OSTEEN

THE CURSE OF THE DREAMCATCHER

by Sam Knight

"LOOK, DADDY!" A little girl on the other side of the bus shouted. "There it is!" She couldn't have been more than five or six, and her icepick-sharp voice pierced the road noise, stabbing into Thomas's ears.

He hated shuttle busses.

Scowling, Thomas looked up to see her pointing at the giant blue horse statue rearing up between the highways to the airport. He looked back to his phone.

"Look at its eyes!"

A boy, barely beyond toddler, crawled over the girl to get to the window. He stood on the seat, pressed his face to the glass, and shouted with glee. "They glow!"

Next to them, holding a squalling baby in a travel seat, their father's glazed eyes gave no indication of noticing his children.

Two women, across from Thomas, continued talking like they were the only two people in the world.

"It is like a dreamcatcher!" the girl said. "I can't think of any of my troubles now!"

The boy laughed, jumping up and down on stubby legs. "Me either!"

"It's like magic!"

"Like magic!" the boy echoed. He lost balance, teetering on the seat.

The girl caught his arm.

The father didn't react.

Thomas, already irritated because he was at the start of three business trips, gave up trying to read emails. He put his phone away and closed his eyes, pondering the idea of Blucifer being a dreamcatcher.

Who the hell would have told a kid something like that?

Still, helping people forget their troubles as they journeyed out into the world would at least put some value on the creepy blue statue. Why something like that was lording over the entrance to Denver International Airport was beyond him.

The girl cried out again. "He can see *everything!* He talks with his eyes!"

Thomas opened his own eyes just in time to see the giant horse's glowing red eyes glare through the window.

Murderer...

A sepulchral voice shuddered through Thomas like tires skidding on asphalt, then it was gone.

He looked around the bus. The father was looking around too. Their gazes met, and the other man looked away, roughly pulling the boy back into a seat.

Had the father heard that voice too? Somehow, Thomas knew the voice meant that man.

What he didn't know was if the voice had been real.

Keeping his eyes on the road ahead, Thomas felt the man's heavy gaze upon him the rest of the trip.

It had been a long few days. Thomas was exhausted and ready to get home. Old sodium lights made the passenger pickup level of the parking garage a sickly orange, leaving white cars jaundiced and dark cars lost to shadows. They made him feel much the same way. The putrid, fog-like exhaust covering the airport didn't help either, but Thomas was glad for the cool, quiet of the night.

The crisp autumn chill, despite the smell, was cleansing the fatigue of the flight home.

He glanced at the time. He'd already waited twenty minutes for the shuttle that was supposed to come every fifteen. At least, judging by the empty curb around him, there wouldn't be any shrieking kids this time.

Or their creepy father.

Thomas had been too busy the last several days to think about the other morning. Now, so close to where it happened, the memory of that voice made the night chill turn cold.

He shivered. Maybe it hadn't been real.

When the shuttle pulled up, he was still staring at his feet, thinking how that voice had made him feel like a piece of chalk being dragged across a sidewalk.

Maybe it had been a seizure.

He nodded to the driver, a middle-aged woman with short blonde hair, as he boarded. She nodded back tiredly, taking his parking receipt.

The bus was empty. Thomas dropped his carry-on into the first row and sat sideways next to it, keeping his knees away from the metal handrail in front of him. His angle left him facing the driver, who fussed with paperwork while waiting to see if anyone else showed up.

Pulling up local news on his phone, Thomas found himself staring into the eyes of the father from the other morning. A mugshot with a headline. The man had murdered his wife. Stabbed her over fifty times.

And then he'd gotten on a bus with his kids, sat across from Thomas, and gone to the airport.

The hair on Thomas's neck prickled. He put the phone away. Maybe he'd heard a voice that morning, maybe he hadn't, but the idea that the man was a murderer had definitely been in Thomas's head—and it had been right.

The bus, silent but for the mumbling motor and hissing heater vents, became stale and hot. Thomas pulled at his collar and looked out the window. Night had swallowed the world beyond the sodium lights of the open-sided building, leaving only pinpricks of streetlights in the distance.

"What do you think of Blucifer?" he asked the driver, trying to break the feeling they were alone in the world.

"I try not to." She didn't look up. Her sandpaper voice made Thomas want to clear his throat. "Thing gives me the heebie-jeebies."

Thomas looked back out the window, wondering where the statue was from here.

"It's that way," the driver pointed, correcting his gaze. "I see that goddamned thing sixteen times a day."

Thomas looked, expecting to see red eyes, but she was pointing to a concrete wall.

A young couple, huffing, came into the bus smiling. "Thanks for waiting!" the man said, pulling two suitcases behind him. The woman echoed the sentiment as she handed the driver their parking receipt.

The driver shut the doors, and the bus pulled away from the curb.

When Thomas finally saw the Blue Mustang, he was surprised how visible it was at night, how prominently it had been placed. Spotlights made it impossible to miss even if the eyes hadn't glowed demonic red.

It was terrifying.

The eyes flashed at him as the bus rounded the bend, turning away from the statue.

Adulteress...

Thomas jumped. The voice came from everywhere, from nowhere, and he was sure it was real. He glanced at the couple.

Snuggled up in the last row, they caught him looking, smiles fading from their faces. Had they heard it too? Had the voice grated over their souls, demanding attention, as it had his?

Maybe, maybe not, but the returning smirk on the woman's face said she knew that he knew this wasn't her husband, and she didn't care.

Thomas shifted to face the front of the bus, jamming his knees into the bar so he wouldn't be tempted to look at them again.

"Morning," the young bus driver grunted, sunken eyes making him look as tired as Thomas felt. He held out a piece of paper marking where Thomas had parked.

"Morning." Thomas took the receipt and shuffled in, trying not to bump anyone. He sat next to a woman in a business suit, making eye contact and smiling only long enough to not be rude.

He'd dreaded this bus ride all weekend and did not want to go past the demonic horse again. He did not want to see its eyes, and he did not want to hear that voice.

That voice, along with the voices of the children from last week, had stolen his sleep. He could hear the girl innocently calling Blucifer a dream-catcher, see the boy bobbing up and down excitedly on stubby legs. And he could hear the voice of Blucifer—a missed warning of impending doom, whispered to only him. It weighed upon his soul.

"I can't think of any of my troubles at all now!"

"Me either!"

"It's like magic!"

There had been more news about them. And their baby brother. None had survived their father. Neither had their grandparents in San Antonio. The man had killed them all after they landed.

Thomas found no solace in knowing Blucifer had been a dreamcatcher for the children, that it had taken away their troubles and worries for a few moments. It hadn't mattered in the long run. It hadn't prevented the death of an entire family.

And the monstrous beast had been the opposite of a dreamcatcher for him. It had given him a horrific burden to bear, an unrelenting knot in his stomach that ached incessantly.

If only he had said something, anything, perhaps those children and their grandparents would be alive. Something simple could have triggered a reaction, maybe set him off enough to get police involved, and then maybe those kids would still be alive.

Or maybe they wouldn't.

But at least Thomas would know he'd tried.

Eyes on the road, Thomas watched for the Blue Mustang, wondering if he should have said something to the cheating couple the other night. Was there a reason the voice told him about them? Was there something he could have prevented?

Or was it just an overflow, a leakage, of too many dark thoughts caught by the dreamcatcher? Where did bad thoughts go when a dreamcatcher took them?

If there is power in them, Blucifer must be horrifically powerful by now. How long had it been there? Ten years? Fifteen? How many had it collected?

Thomas looked to the cars on the highway and wondered how many went by every day. A thousand? Ten thousand? How many people was that? How many evil notions?

The road made a subtle S curve, rose over a hill, and then Thomas spotted it. It had to be a mile away, but he knew he was looking at Blucifer— and he felt it looking back.

Was it taking darkness from people right now? From all those cars on the road ahead?

It didn't feel like it. It felt like he had been singled out, like it was trying to give horrible thoughts to him instead.

Thomas looked away, eyes scanning the other passengers. What would Blucifer take from them? Would a macabre voice whisper into his soul again?

As the bus passed the towering equine figure, the red eyes were dim, a strange gray, washed out in the direct morning sunlight. Almost like it was sleeping.

Thomas twisted in his seat to watch the beast go by. They were almost out of sight of the monstrosity when the voice came.

Addict...

Heavy snow blew sideways, slapping people across the face even under the cover of the cement structure. The shuttle was already full of faces in the windows when it pulled up to the returning passenger waiting area. The driver inside opened the door and called out that the next bus was only five minutes away, quickly shutting the door on the groans of those waiting, moving on before anyone could argue.

Thomas turned his back to the wind. Weather delays had taken a toll, and it felt like years since he'd been home.

He found himself staring at the wall the bus driver had pointed to, so long ago, when she'd indicated the direction Blucifer awaited. He could almost see the glow of red eyes through the concrete.

The memory of the last thing the voice had said bothered him.

There had been too many people on the bus. He hadn't been able to figure out who the addict was. Or even if there was one.

Not that he could have done anything anyway. What do you do when you see an addict? Stand up and point at them? It would have been as futile as calling out an adulteress.

He berated himself for the knot in his gut that wouldn't go away. He felt terrible about the dead family, but none of these things were his problem. It was not his responsibility to stand up and point out people because a voice whispered in his head.

He stomped his cold feet and grimaced.

Was he going insane? Or had Blucifer really whispered terrible things to him? He didn't know which truth would be worse, but whatever it was, he'd had enough. He would cancel the last business trip. Quit his job if he had to.

Once he got home, he decided, he wasn't ever going past that goddamned blue demon again.

The bus pulled up, splashing dirty slush onto the curb, and people crowded forward, pressing to get on. Thomas filed in with them until he saw the driver. It was the kid with the sunken eyes, but now those eyes were wide and wild, and his movements were quick and jerky as he took parking receipts.

He's high, Thomas realized. The driver was the addict.

Thomas pushed his way back, off the bus, and got out of line.

His heart pounded as he watched the others move ahead, giving him curious looks. He should say something. But what? Who would listen?

The last passenger entered, and the driver waved to Thomas. "There's still standing room!"

Thomas shook his head and stepped back. The kid shrugged and shut the door.

Shivering, unsure what to do, Thomas stared after the bus as it pulled away.

The next shuttle didn't come for nearly an hour. Enough people were lined up behind Thomas to fill three or four buses. He shuffled in first, unable to feel his toes and grateful for the warmth. He recognized the driver as he handed over his parking receipt.

"Sorry about the delay," she said in her raspy voice. Her eyes were red and puffy. "There was a bad accident."

"Seventeen people died," a woman behind Thomas said, holding up her phone. "At last count. Fifteen-car pileup involving a bus."

The driver shook her head and didn't meet anyone else's eyes as she gathered their receipts.

Thomas felt ill, a growing dread twisting inside him as he took a seat. He swallowed, throat dry, as he listened to passengers discuss the accident, getting updates from their phones.

When the bus drove past the Blue Mustang, Thomas began to tremble. He tried not to look, but he could feel its eyes upon him, calling. Beckoning. Compelling him to look at it.

Unable to resist, he turned and met the weight of its gaze through the window. The red eyes stabbed into his soul.

Coward...

WILDFLOWER

by Warren Hammond

I LOOK OUT THE WINDOW OF THE Westin conference room at the asphalt cloverleaf carrying a never-ending stream of parking shuttles and rental car buses. A jetliner comes in for a landing. The 737 is Southwest blue just like the one that carried me to Denver this morning. The lawyer has kept me busy ever since but we're currently on a well-earned break from another stack of paperwork. This one is full of questionnaires that dig deep into every uncomfortable corner of my life.

I aim to keep telling the truth. Mostly.

The door opens and the lawyer steps in. My lip curls in a failed attempt at a smile. I know it comes off as more of a snarl, but it's the best I can do.

After several more questionnaires, he rolls through the liability waivers and non-disclosures. You may be deprived of food and water: Initial here. You may be forcibly dunked underwater: Initial here. Efforts will be made to do no permanent damage, but loss of teeth and broken bones do sometimes occur: Signature and date here.

I sign everything with the pen I keep in my purse. It was a gift from my father when I was deployed to Iraq. There's really nothing so special about it, but I like its heft, how it feels heavy in my hand.

In the distance, I see a statue at the airport's entrance. A well-muscled mustang reared on two legs. It's an unnaturally bright blue with feral red eyes that glow as if it has been possessed. If I still had any heart to smile, I'd smile now because it reminds me of Wildflower, the horse my rancher father couldn't tame. I'd never forget the day he came home to find his thirteen-year-old daughter sitting calmly on its bare back. That might've been the most memorable moment of my forgettable life.

The lawyer places a small duffel on the table. "You'll need to put this on," he says.

I unzip the bag and look inside. "Why?"

"Mr. Brock insists."

"Does everybody have to do this?"

He sorts papers into piles then stacks them all up in the precise order he wants. "Yes," he says. "Everybody."

I can't begin to count the number of double takes I draw as I follow the lawyer out of the Westin and into the main terminal. I'm in a panda onesie with black buttons running up my white belly. The hood adds a black-and-white face above my own. I'm sweating despite wearing nothing but my underwear underneath the thick, fuzzy fabric.

"This is humiliating," I say to the lawyer.

He acknowledges with a shallow nod that seems to say this is exactly the point. We take an elevator down, and once inside the parking garage, he calls for a van that pulls up a minute later. The driver loads my suitcase in the back and opens the sliding door so I can join a giraffe and a fox. They introduce themselves, but I instantly forget their names. I didn't come all the way from Nevada to make friends.

The van takes us west on I-70 past the city and up into the mountains before turning south. Giraffe and Fox talk quite a bit for the first hour or two. Giraffe works in banking. Wife and three kids. He says he's making the pilgrimage to Mr. Brock's because coaching Little League just doesn't do it for him. He needs something more. Something different. Since he happened upon Mr. Brock's website six months ago, he hasn't been able to think of anything else.

Fox is a surfer but also does some rock climbing. He once volunteered

to crew a sailboat that went to all seven continents and Bali too. He's always looking for the next big thing.

They don't say much to me. They can sense I'm not interested.

"Did you watch the promotional video?" asks Giraffe.

"About fifty times," says Fox.

"You know the part when Mr. Brock says he knows what we need? I don't normally go for anything mystical like fortune tellers or psychics, but when he looks right into the camera, I feel like he's talking directly to me. Like the video was made for me and only me. The guy's probably full of shit, but I figured there's only one way to find out."

Conversation dwindles along with the daylight as each turn the driver takes leads us into more and more remote territory. Exactly where we're going is a mystery. Somewhere near the New Mexico border is all it says on Mr. Brock's website.

The road twists and turns. Out the window I only see an occasional light as we head farther from the last signs of civilization. We turn onto a dirt road, and the van's jostling wakes both Giraffe and Fox. The van stops, and I check the clock on the dash before it goes dark. 11:27 PM.

The driver opens the door, and I embrace the nighttime chill that seems to blow right through my panda suit. I step down to the ground, and with nothing to protect the soles of my feet other than a thin layer of rubberized padding, I wince at the poke of rough gravel. I hear the roar of running water—probably a stream nearby.

"Head on in," says the driver.

I take my bag and wheel it a few steps before the bumpy terrain convinces me I'm better off carrying it. Fox makes it to the entrance first and opens a steel door. I follow him into a sizeable room with cots lined up against the back wall.

A voice comes over an intercom. I instantly recognize the same smooth confidence from the videos on his website, and I hope he really does know what I need.

"Welcome to BrockLand," he says. "You'll find a bathroom to your left. To your right is a closet. Get your bathroom supplies out and put everything else in the closet. The door has a push-button lock, and only I have the key. You have two rules. No cell phone and you are absolutely prohibited from entering the blue building next to the river. Your twenty-four-hour observation period starts now. See you tomorrow at midnight."

Cameras are everywhere. Six of them in this room alone. Another two in the bathroom. Outside, cameras are mounted on ski poles every twenty feet or so. I barely sleep. Based on the lack of snores from my roommates, it's the same for Giraffe and Fox.

By morning, I'm freezing. My blanket is intended for a child so I can't completely cover myself no matter how tight a ball I form. I go into the bathroom for a hot shower. I climb into the tub and pull the curtain to hide myself from the camera lenses before I remove my panda suit. The water is lukewarm at best so I make it quick and get back into my onesie.

A knock on the door alerts us to the fact that breakfast has arrived—a variety pack of sugary cereals and a half gallon of milk. The day passes slowly. I take several walks to the river and around the fenced property making sure to never go near the blue building. It's a simple rectangle of corrugated steel. Reminds me of an oversized storage unit.

Giraffe and Fox talk a lot. They have little in common beyond them both paying six-thousand dollars for the privilege of coming here to Brock-Land. Our dinner is a loaf of white bread served with half-consumed jars of peanut butter and jelly. Though it's chilly outside we eat at the picnic table. When we go back in, we find wrist and ankle cuffs on our cots. Also, we each find a strange contraption of metal and leather.

"A gag," says Fox. "One of my exes worked for a dentist. They use it to hold your mouth open." He tips his onesie hood back and shows us how it works. It has clips to peel your lips back and a rubberized bit to keep your

teeth from closing. When he has it in place, his lips are stretched so far out I can see the shape of the lower part of his skull.

"Jesus," says Giraffe.

His tone is drenched in dread. Like it just got real. What did he think he was signing up for? BrockLand is extreme survival horror. It's not a haunted house.

Fox says, "You can do this, bro. You came to push yourself, right? To see how far you can go."

The next few hours go on like that as each tries to pump the other's confidence.

Me? I stay quiet. I know it's going to be bad.

It's midnight. As instructed, we file up the rocky path to the blue building. Giraffe slips the gag over my head, and I let the bit into my mouth as he fastens the straps behind my head. The icy breeze makes my exposed teeth hurt. I return the favor then help Fox tighten his straps, before we all assist each other into our wrist and ankle cuffs. We're all ready.

The door opens. It's Mr. Brock. He wears a gray jumpsuit, heavy boots, and has a pair of night vision goggles propped on his head. "You each have a safe word," he says. "Panda, fox, and giraffe, okay?"

We nod.

He looks at me. "Say it."

I do my best with the gag in my mouth. Sounds more like handa than panda. The others take their turns saying ox and girass.

We hop toward the door and Mr. Brock guides us through before shutting us in with the clang of a latch. The space is pitch black. I blink my eyes but can't tell the difference between closed and open.

I'm pushed, and the breath is knocked out of me when I strike the floor. I'm yanked by my hair before being lifted and dumped into a tub of ice-cold water. I'm dunked and dunked again. I'm shivering so forcefully I can't control my arms or legs. I'm repeatedly slapped then dragged back out to the floor. Something hard and weighty strikes my skull and everything goes dark.

I'm awake. I'm still shivering but not as bad as before. I keep my eyes closed in hopes that Mr. Brock won't notice I'm back in the present.

Loud sobs sound to my right. I hear the word ox over and over but then I hear splashing and assume Fox is getting the ice-bath treatment. I'm struck in the back, and the groan that escapes my mouth alerts him to the fact that I'm lucid. Something is shoved in my mouth. It tastes like dirt, and I jerk my head back so hard it bounces off the floor. Dazed, I can feel that whatever is in my mouth is moving. I blow air out of my lungs and shake my throbbing head to get the bugs out.

I see sparks and think my head trauma is making me see stars, but then I feel the clamp of a jumper cable biting into my thumb.

"Handa! Handa!"

I edge closer to the fireplace so my panda suit can dry. I don't know where this cabin is—never saw it when I walked the property earlier in the day, but here I am after being transported upon a wagon attached to the back of an ATV.

Mr. Brock sits in an armchair. His jumpsuit has bloodstains on the knees. My blood? Fox's or Giraffe's?

"I know what you need," he says. "Now let's see if you know, or will it take another round in the blue building?"

I struggle for words. I can't believe this is actually happening, but I know it is. I can't believe he knows anything about me, but I look at his face, and I know he does.

"Want to start with an easier question?" he asks. "Why are you here?"

"I wanted to know what it felt like."

"To be tortured. Yes, that's why people come here. Except for Giraffe. He seemed to be under the impression that none of this was real. It happens sometimes. People think it's all ketchup and special effects."

"It says it's all real on your website."

He shrugs. "I don't know how much clearer I can make it."

"Is he okay?"

"He'll be ending his stay early, but no refunds. Now tell me why you wanted to know what being tortured feels like."

I hesitate. Though I think he already knows, it's something I never talk about. To anybody. Ever.

But it's what I think about. All the time. Even when I'm not thinking about it, it sticks to me like tar. It sucks away every drop of happiness and drowns every ounce of joy. It has crushed everything I once was or ever hoped to be.

It drove me away from my husband. My two precious girls who I'm sure I'd no longer recognize after so many years.

"Where did it happen?" he asks. "Where did you lose who you were? Where did your former life die to be replaced by this empty shell?"

I say it. "Abu Ghraib."

Every muscle in my body seizes as the voltage passes through me. "HANDA!"

I'm back in the blue building. Have been for what seems like hours but has probably only been thirty minutes. I don't understand why I'm here again. I told Mr. Brock that I learned what it felt like to be on the other side. I learned just how wrong what I did was—orders or no orders.

The cosmic scales of justice are even-steven, I told him. I received the same punishment I doled out to so many others, so thank you, Mr. Brock for showing me the way. Now, we're all done here.

Yet the torture continues. When I can think straight, I listen for Fox, but I don't hear any cries of ox.

I'm lifted into a chair. The gag is removed from my mouth and dropped to the floor. A flashlight shines directly into my eyes. "Tell me about the first time," he says.

"I ordered the prisoner to strip naked," I say. "I went to the latrine to fill a bucket and—"

"No go back farther. Before Iraq. Take me to the ranch. To the first time."

I don't understand how he can know about that. His research team is obviously top notch, so I can't be surprised he found out I was stationed at Abu Ghraib, but how can he know about Wildflower? I was alone on the ranch that day. My mother was visiting Gran, and my father had gone to town.

Mr. Brock clamps on the jumper cables, and I'm sparked into talking.

"The horse was wild," I shout.

A danger. My father warned me not to go anywhere near her. But I went to the stable anyway and climbed up to sit on the wall over her. She was a beautiful horse. Young with powerful muscles rippling under her black coat. Her spirit was just as savage and dangerous and unbroken as that statue by the Denver airport, and she eyed me suspiciously before bucking her head in defiance.

I zapped her with the cattle prod.

It took several hours, but I zapped her over and over and over. I gave her the juice until her coat was shiny with sweat and her eyes were filled with fear. Wielding the weighty prod, each jolt I dispensed heightened my intoxicated senses. I kept at her until all I had to do was lift a hand to make her twitch.

Then I led her to the corral and waited until I saw the cloud of dust in the distance that signaled my father's return before climbing the fence and transferring myself onto the horse's back.

A slight thirteen-year-old girl in complete control over a five-hundred-

pound beast. I'd never felt so proud. So in control. So powerful.

"Oh my god," I said.

"You just realized something," said Mr. Brock. "Tell me."

"All this time, I've been wrestling against this avalanche of guilt."

"You haven't been honest with yourself, have you?"

"No," I say.

He comes close and removes the cuffs from my wrists and lets me remove the cuffs from my ankles. He takes my hand and guides me across the room. The flashlight lands on Fox. He's hanging upside-down from a chain. His face is bloodied and his lips are spread by the dental gag into a butterfly shape. His eyes are open, and he moans softly like he doesn't have the energy to mount any serious defense.

Mr. Brock hands me a wooden paddle from a canoe. I like its heft. The way it feels heavy in my hands.

"I know what you need," says Mr. Brock.

"All this time…" I say, my voice trailing off.

"You thought it was guilt that was hollowing you out."

"Yes. But that wasn't it at all. I've really just been missing the way it makes me feel. Nothing compares."

I smile and swing the paddle.

EVERYPLACE, NOPLACE

by JoAnn Chaney

I F YOU THINK ABOUT IT, airports are strange places. Hubs of activity where crowds disappear to faraway locations and then magically reappear. There are hidden passages and tunnels and moving sidewalks, and sometimes there are unmarked planes that're boarded by silent individuals dressed in pressed suits and crisp blouses and dark sunglasses, and those flights are never listed on the departure or arrival boards, and they leave in the middle of the night and no one is ever sure where they go, or why.

Denver International Airport is especially strange. There are all sorts of conspiracy theories surrounding the place—it was built by Nazis; the Illuminati are headquartered there; the artwork throughout tells of the end of the world. DIA is occasionally called the Gateway to the West, but it's not only to the west.

DIA is a gateway to Everyplace. But it is also a gateway to Noplace. And gateways are both entrances and exits. This is important to remember. They run two ways. In and out. This won't make sense to many of you, but some will understand. You wish you didn't, but you do.

The Detective haunts the airport at all hours of the day, but perhaps that's to be expected when three murder victims are found on the property in the span of two weeks. He breezes through security and rides the tram and walks through the concourses without a second glance from the staff. It'd come down that he was to be left alone to conduct his investigation, and when the employees at Denver International Airport are given an order, they execute it flawlessly and without question.

Dead bodies showing up in an airport isn't good for business, and the police insisted on sending out the Detective, even when the CEO assured them her own security team had it under control. In the end, the CEO had to accept the Detective's presence. If she'd flat-out refused the police, there would've been questions and more probing, and the last thing the CEO wants is more attention pointed at her.

But only one man. I want to keep this quiet, the CEO said. She wasn't thrilled to be backed into a corner, but there was no way around it. Solved quickly and neatly. It's bad for our bottom line, I'm sure you understand.

The fourth victim is found inside the bowels of a carousel in the baggage claim area. A good hiding spot, under all the grinding machinery and rotating conveyor belts, but it was necessary to disassemble the entire thing to reach him. Half of the baggage claim is curtained off for privacy as they work, but the drapes can't hide the smell of the man's rotting corpse, and the complaints from the other side of the fabric are clear as day.

"Cause of death?" the Detective asks. He and the coroner are standing too close together, but no one notices or comments. Or cares. The only eyes watching are those of the stone gargoyles placed throughout, to overlook and protect the luggage, and they certainly don't care if two consenting adults are spending their time outside of work fucking each other.

The coroner's name is Susan. Susie, he calls her. Baby. She doesn't like that. She doesn't feel like their relationship—is that what you'd call it?—warrants any cutesy nicknames.

"The back of his skull is crushed, so I'd guess that's what did it," Susie

says drily.

"The impact point is about the size of a horse's hoof?"

"What?" she said. "No. It's more like the size of a sledgehammer."

"But it could've been caused by a horse kicking? That's a possibility?"

Susie sighs. He's asked this question before. Several times.

"When was the last time you got a full night's sleep?" Susie asks. "Or ate a good meal?"

But the Detective isn't listening.

The Detective is a stereotype brought to life. He is a weary cop, jaded and bitter and angry. He drinks and smokes too much, doesn't get enough to eat, doesn't spend enough time in the sun. He is gaunt and hollow-eyed, more like a character from a Tim Burton film than a real person. He is a haunted man, an unhappy man. A brilliant investigator, but full of strange ideas and weird theories. No one is ever sure if they should take him seriously, so they chalk it up to the usual: he's off his meds; he's drinking too much; not enough sleep. But his numbers speak for themselves: despite his crazy-talk, he's closed more cases than any other detective on the force.

Still, he can't get a partner to work with him. He's just too damn spooky.

Susie recognized these things and still decided to go to bed with him, partly because she was lonely, but also because she saw a spark in him. It's the same song so many women through the ages have cried: if only he'd change, he'd be perfect for me.

Spoiler alert: the Detective isn't going to change.

The Detective can often be seen sitting outside the airport, smoking near the sculpture of a giant stallion reared up on its hind legs. Blucifer, the locals call it. The blue demon stallion with the glowing red eyes that watches over the airport. He guards travelers against outside forces, some say. Monsters that stalk and hunt the innocent.

But some claim Blucifer is the actual monster.

The Detective talks to Blucifer when he's out there, sitting on the cropped grass at the foot of the statue. He's not just speaking, but holding actual conversations, even pausing when a response would be appropriate. The two of them—man and fiberglass horse—have struck up quite the friendship. The Detective speaks more candidly to the statue than he ever did to either of his wives.

But now the Detective isn't having a conversation with Blucifer. He's come straight from the side of the fourth victim, and he's angry. Standing at the base, screaming up at the underside of the horse's jowls. He's so upset his face has gone an alarming shade of reddish-purple, the corners of his mouth are crusted in dried foam spittle.

"I know it's you killing these people!" the Detective shouts. Traffic on the nearby road has slowed to a crawl. Everyone likes a show. "I don't know why, but you'll be sorry!"

Blucifer's bright red eyes stay focused on the mountains to the west. He doesn't react. Of course he doesn't. He's a sculpture. Only that, and nothing more.

You wouldn't be wrong if you called the Detective insane.

It's a bizarre case.

None of the four victims has any family the Detective is able to contact. They have names, they have identification and tickets—but they don't seem to actually exist otherwise. No one knows them. Their home addresses don't exist, their names don't show up on any sort of search. Their IDs are fakes.

There were no witnesses to any of the murders, no motives for why four

random travelers had been killed. But like any other airport, DIA has an extensive surveillance system. State-of-the-art, top-of-the-line. Security is able to see and record anything that happens on the property—at least, that's how it'd always been. It'd always worked perfectly.

Until now.

Now, when the Detective goes to look at the footage of the room where a victim was found, or the hall leading into that room to see who'd gone in and out, the recording would be mysteriously gone. Not erased or even damaged, you see, but just gone. As if it'd never existed in the first place. For example, with the latest victim, the recording of the baggage claim area suddenly stops at 11:11 in the evening, there is the tiniest hiccup, and the video starts up again, exactly eleven minutes and eleven seconds later. The same exact amount is missing each time. Eleven-eleven. It is as if that period of reality has literally been cut away, eleven-minutes-and-eleven-seconds of film spliced from the middle and the loose ends melded back together seamlessly.

Well, almost seamlessly. Nothing that has been torn asunder can be put back together without the slightest flaw.

"The murders always happen at 11:11," the Detective tells Susie. "And the CCTV cuts out for exactly eleven minutes and eleven seconds."

"What's the significance of the numbers?"

"Philosophers thought numbers had different vibrational properties. Some believe it's a signal from the angels that something important is about to happen," he says. "Or it could be an indication that the universe is expending great energy in opening a—" he trails off into silence.

"Opening a what?"

When he looks at her again, his eyes are awash in a strange light. She shudders away from the sight of it. It's the Detective's body standing in front of her, but he's not actually in there. She shakes off the goosebumps, feeling silly.

"A gateway," he says dreamily. "As if a gateway is being opened."

He repeats the words to himself all night. They feel like the correct words, like he's onto something, like he's slid the key into the lock but hasn't turned it yet. He's almost there. But almost doesn't close cases. Almost doesn't solve murders.

Sanity and insanity, like so many other parts of life, are two sides of the same coin. You don't get one without the other as a bonus prize.

So, you wouldn't be wrong if you called the Detective sane.

No one knows exactly when the Detective became convinced it was Blucifer committing these murders. Perhaps it was when several shards of paint were found stuck on the first victim's pants, and it was exactly the same shade of blue that the horse was painted. Or it might've been when victims two and three were found together in one of the back hallways, and he saw the bruises left on their bodies, deep purple and blue marks that were vaguely hoof-shaped.

But it doesn't much matter how the Detective reached his conclusion, only that he got there at all.

After the fourth victim is found, the Denver PD sends out more officers to join the investigation. The `Detective is offended by this. He works best alone, always has. But his captain won't waver. Four dead in a few weeks is four too many. They need to figure the case out before they start looking

like incompetent idiots.

"We don't need any more help on that front," Cap says.

The Detective hates having so many other officers around, but it does have benefits. More manpower means there are more eyes to watch, more mouths to ask questions. And every warm body available is present at 11:11, waiting and watching. They stay scattered through the airport, keeping their eyes open and ears to the ground.

For a week, no one sees anything out of the ordinary. But on the seventh day, the day meant for rest, things go haywire.

The Detective hasn't been sleeping much lately. Or, honestly, at all. It's a combination of stress and anxiety and caffeine that keeps him up (as well as whatever uppers he's taking to keep himself running) and he swears to anyone who'll listen that he'll get some rest when he solves this case.

But on the seventh night, at around ten-thirty, the Detective finds that he's unable to keep his eyes open a moment longer. He sits down on the floor of concourse B, near gate 38, his legs sticking out in front of him, and promptly falls asleep. He'd promised himself he'd only close his eyes for a few minutes and take a nap so short it couldn't even be called a nap, but a nip. But this is like drowning, getting sucked under deep, murky water. There's no escape from that sort of sleep, not until it lets you come up for air.

The Detective wakes up when someone grabs his arm and yanks him up. His feet kick something away with a metallic clatter—a sledgehammer. The head of it is gigantic.

"I fucking knew it," the man says. It takes a minute, but then the Detective recognizes him—it's one of the officers who'd been sent in to help. His name is Frank, and his breath smells like salami. All the men the Detective has ever met named Frank smell like salami. "We all figured it was you, and now we know it."

The Detective is confused, until Frank hauls him further down the concourse. Near gate 11 there's a dead woman face down on the carpet. There's plenty of blood, and bits of bone and brain on the floor around her. The back of the woman's skull has been beaten in so thoroughly it resembles raw ground beef.

"I didn't do anything," the Detective says. He's still barely awake and can't believe what he's seeing. What is happening? "I was asleep."

"Is that right?" Frank sneers. "You're in charge of this investigation, it was your job to watch this concourse, and you fell asleep? You expect me to believe that? I know you killed her."

"I don't—"

"Shut the fuck up, man. It's your right. Because anything you say can be used against you in a court of law—"

It quickly becomes clear the sledgehammer was not used in the murder. It is clean, unused. The hammer is made from a metal not found on Earth and etched with scrollwork and a language no one has ever seen before, which raises questions no one knows how to answer.

The Detective is released after a few hours. He's obviously not the killer, but he's also not fit to run the investigation. A man who falls asleep on the job shouldn't be on the job to begin with.

Take some time off, Cap says. Get some rest.

"I examined the female they brought in earlier," Susie tells the Detective. It's late, nearly ten at night, and they're at her apartment but not in bed. They're in the kitchen, drinking black coffee and talking. They're better as friends than lovers, and they both know it. "She had—nevermind."

"Tell me."

"You were taken off the case."

The Detective gives her a hard look until her cheeks redden.

"She had a tail."

"What?"

"I've never seen anything like it," she stammers. "It made her look like she was half human and half lizard."

The key is turning; pins falling; tumblers sliding into place. The door is opening. The gateway, you might say.

"Or maybe she wasn't human at all," he says. "Is she still at the morgue?"

"Yes."

"Take me?" the Detective asks. When Susie balks, he continues. "It's important. And if I don't find anything, I'll let it go. I promise."

But the woman is gone. All four of the victims are. Not gone-gone, exactly—there are the melted sludge remains of them on the tables, black and green and orange chunks. The smell that rises from the tables is putrid and ungodly, and when the Detective leans in he sees there are holes being burned right through the metal, as if the remains were corrosive acid.

"I've never seen anything like this," Susie says. She looks perplexed, but not frightened. The fear will come later. "What happened?"

"We've got to get to the airport," the Detective says. His gaze is hungry, somehow, and it frightens her. "We've got to go now."

The Detective is going over a hundred up Peña Boulevard, racing toward the airport, and almost crashes when he brings the car to a screeching halt. He then throws it into reverse and flips around, driving down the wrong side of the road. But at this time of night there's no traffic.

"What's wrong?" Susie cries. She is hanging onto the door handle so tightly her knuckles have gone white.

"He's gone," the Detective says. He pulls off the road and up onto a grass embankment, and at first Susie doesn't know what he means. But then she sees, and understands.

There is only a fiberglass platform on the ground in front of the car. Only this, and nothing more. Because Blucifer is gone.

"I knew it was Blucifer, but I thought they were innocent victims. Bystanders," the Detective says as he drives. His eyes are lit up in a manic glow. "But I see now, this whole time, he's been protecting the airport. The numbers, that sledgehammer, the way the bodies disappeared. I understand now. Those—things, whatever they are, are trying to get in disguised as humans, and he's been getting rid of them. Like squashing nasty bugs you find in your house."

The Detective and Susie walk into an airport that is completely silent and still, as if a spell has been cast over the place.

That may very well be the case.

The sliding glass doors hiss open for them willingly enough, but there are no employees to greet them, no travelers walking by.

"This is bad," the Detective says. He is very nearly in a panic. "Can't you feel it?"

Yes, Susie can. There's a buzzing that lifts the hairs on her arms and the back of her neck, and the creeping feeling of someone sneaking up behind her. She wants to run screaming back to the car and never come back to this place, but she's too scared to leave the Detective's side. Somewhere in the distance is the beating of a horse's running hooves.

"What's happening?" she whispers, but he doesn't answer.

There is the soft shushing of footsteps behind her, and she turns to see a woman rushing at her, hefting a hammer above her head, ready to bring it down on Susie's skull. This woman is in a business suit and sensible heels, but her mouth is stuck in a snarl and her eyes are black and cold. Lizard-like.

Not normal human beings, she thinks, stumbling back. Not human at all.

There's the roar of a gun firing, and the lizard-woman falls back. Dead. The Detective's department issue was taken away when he was relieved of duty, but he always has his personal weapon.

"Let's go," he says, holding out his hand to Susie. He seems more focused than she's ever seen him, more in control. Like the man he was always meant to be. "We have to help."

In a choice between fight and flight, Susie had always assumed she was a runner. But a person's true character is revealed in moments of great pressure, and it turns out she is a fighter. The Detective was surprised when she ignored his hand and pried the sledgehammer from the dead—thing that'd tried to brain her.

"Are you sure?" he asks.

She nods. She's afraid to say anything, because if she opens her mouth she might vomit. And then she might run.

Together, the two head toward the sound of the running horse, and when they find Blucifer, Susie is shocked by the sight of the gigantic sculpture come to life, his eyes raining hot fire and his hooves furiously kicking and stomping the dozens of figures running around him. They are climbing up his legs and throwing weapons—there are so many. Too many. There are screams and shrieks coming from the crowd in a language Susie has never heard before, the sounds of which pierce her eardrums painfully.

Blucifer sees the Detective and Susie and pauses, and tilts his head as he looks them over. It feels as though everything hangs in the balance in that moment, and it would be bad if the horse found them wanting.

But he does not. The blue stallion seems to nod slightly, then throws his head back in a scream that Susie will never forget. The Detective takes this as the signal to raise his gun and begin firing, and Susie hefts the hammer onto her shoulder and runs head-on into the melee, her own war-cry mingling with Blucifer's.

But try as she might, Susie isn't a warrior. She is a doctor who spends her days cutting into the dead and analyzing their remains. She is good with a computer and a scalpel, not a sledgehammer, although she does manage to smash several of their heads wide open. But when one of the things runs at her, foaming at the mouth and out for blood, she is lucky to be merely knocked unconscious instead of killed.

When Susie wakes up, she's sitting in a well-appointed office, in front of a large mahogany desk. The desk plaque tells her the pleasant looking woman sitting behind it is Kim Day, the CEO of DIA.

"Good morning," Kim says. "Glad to see you're among the living."

"What's going on?" Susie asks. "Where's the Detective—?"

Kim sighs and leans back in her chair, the leather squeaking under her.

"I'm afraid he was gravely injured," she says. "But I do want to thank you for what you did. Because of you and the Detective, this place is safe. At least for a while."

"This place? The airport?"

Kim shrugs.

"Yes, the airport. And Denver. The entire country." She gestures widely. "This planet. This reality. The two of you helped fight back some-

thing that's been trying to break through into our world for a long time."

"I don't understand."

Kim smiles. A trifle sadly, it seems.

"You won't, and I don't have the capacity or time to explain it all," she says. "This place has been under my watch for a long time, and things have been quiet. The gateways seemed to have been forgotten, abandoned. I became complacent, I suppose, and over the years I've dismissed all my guards, until it was only Blucifer and myself left. They were waiting, though."

"Who are they?"

Kim shakes her head.

"They are evil, and they are fighting to get here. To take over. To see every one of us dead. I called for help when I realized they were managing to sneak in, and I didn't think anyone had heard. But then you and the Detective showed up, and the tide turned in our favor. Blucifer could've lost the battle last night, but he didn't. Because of you. And the Detective."

Susie jumps.

"Where is he?"

"I've sent him to Noplace," Kim says vaguely. "Or maybe it's Every-place. I can't keep it straight these days. He's gone to recover from his wounds. But he'll be back. We'll see him again."

"I don't understand," Susie says. Frustrated.

"You will," Kim says. "It'll take time. Just know that you've become a part of this. You should go home, and rest. I'll be in touch. You and the Detective will be of great use to us."

"Us?" Susie asks wildly. "You talk like you're not human yourself."

Kim smiles again, and there's a blip, a bit like the skip on the surveillance footage where it was pieced back together. In the moment of that blip, the attractive blonde sitting behind the desk disappears and is replaced by a glowing figure made more of fire than flesh, but as quickly it is gone, and Susie is alone in the office. It would seem that the time for questions and explanations is over.

Susie drives home, and sees that Blucifer is back in his place, staring fiercely at the mountains. She doesn't sleep that night, or much any night after. She wonders where the Detective is. She wonders about Noplace, and Everyplace.

And she begins the process of understanding.

FLICKER

by Jason Heller

T HE HORSE WASN'T THERE.

Everything else about the scene was the same. The screen flickered black and white. A man and woman dressed in crisp, pressed clothes stood on a crowded city street as cars built in the 1940s drove by. The lips of the man and woman moved, but no sound came out of their mouths.

I had the movie on mute. It didn't matter what they were saying.

Everything in the movie was the same as it was when I watched it before. Only this time, the glowing blue horse was gone.

The television hung from Meg's bedroom wall. She sat on her bed, legs crossed, leaning forward. I stood next to the bed with the remote in my outstretched hand.

"Tell me when the horse is supposed to appear," she said.

I thumbed the rewind button and squinted at the screen. "Um. Yeah. It should have happened already."

"Lindsey. Are you serious?" she said, throwing up her hands. "This is your dumbest theory ever. You know, if you wanted to come over, all you had to do was ask. No supernatural conspiracy necessary."

I ignored her. Sometimes she was just too goddamn logical. "One more time," I said, pressing play.

Again, the scene.

Again, no horse.

Meg went on. "You really expect me to believe this? This movie was filmed in 1942. I looked it up on IMDb. It was produced in black and white. No Technicolor. No hand-colored frames. And no one ever went back and colorized it. How could there be a glowing blue horse walking around in that monochromatic background?"

I swung my arm back, ready to throw the remote against the wall. Meg grabbed my wrist.

"Don't even."

I dropped the remote on the bed. Her grip softened, but she didn't let go.

"Not to dredge up the past…"

"But this is why we broke up," I finished.

Meg didn't answer.

"This isn't just one of my theories," I said, my eyes still glued to the screen. "I swear. I turned this movie on cable the other day, and there was that fucking horse. Bright blue behind those black-and-white actors. Then it came on again a couple days later, so I recorded it on my old VCR. When I played it back at home, the horse was still there."

"The horse with the red eyes," Meg said with that same old flatness in her voice.

I finally tore my gaze away from the TV and caught the look on Meg's face.

"I know how it sounds."

She finally let go of my wrist. "Honey, I get it. These past few months have been tough for you. I know it hasn't been easy to see me move on. But Jennifer and I are happy, and you've just got to accept that. I still want us to be friends. What you're doing right now, though…it scares me, Linds."

I walked over and unplugged my VCR from Meg's TV. The frozen 1940s image disappeared with a blip. "Well, I wouldn't want to scare you. But you know what? Maybe you're not the only one who's scared."

She got up from the bed and hugged me. She smelled like she always used to. Spice and shampoo.

"I love your mind," she whispered into my hair. "The way you see the

world. The angles you approach everything from. It's why you wound up in film school and I wound up in a bank. I used to think we balanced each other out. You're creative, a dreamer. I'm the practical one. But sometimes you just..."

I pulled away from her and laid my finger over her lips. Then I wrapped the cables around my VCR, stuck it under my arm, and stared her in the eyes until she turned away.

When I got home, I plugged in the VCR. I played the scene again. There was the horse. Prancing down the street behind the black-and-white couple. Unnoticed by the crowd of extras. Gleaming like blue neon against a grayscale cityscape.

Its eyes burning red as blood.

Only this time, something changed.

Halfway across the screen, the horse stopped trotting. It stood still, its breath steaming. The crowd on the sidewalk split and swarmed past the animal, as if it were a tree that had suddenly sprouted from the middle of the cement.

Then the horse raised its majestic head. Its mane billowed in the air, like it was seaweed waving under water.

It turned toward the camera.

It looked straight at me. Eyes weeping flame. Lava flowing in rivulets along its muzzle.

It nodded.

Something stung my cheek. I reached up and wiped it from my face.

It took me a moment to realize there was a teardrop on my fingertip, crystalline and glistening, a prism.

When I looked up, the horse was gone.

Nothing I learned in film theory or cinematography class prepared me for this.

The TV woke me in the middle of the night. It turned itself on. The play of light bathed the back of my eyelids until I opened them.

There, on the screen, was the scene.

There, again, was the horse.

The VCR wasn't even plugged in.

I couldn't say how long I stared at it. The scene was on a loop, and if I ever dreamed, I'd have wondered if I were dreaming. But I've never been able to dream, not even when I was a little girl.

Meg always said that's why I was a dreamer in my waking life. Every brain needs to dream, to process, to reshape, to escape. And if that couldn't happen while I was sleeping, all that pent-up dream-stuff still had to come out. Like a lake flowing into a river that finds its way to the sea.

What was that sea, though? Where did my dream-stuff need to go? What did it have to rejoin?

The horse on the screen kept trotting. From nowhere, to nowhere. The edges of the screen were its origin and terminus. It blinked in and out of existence, over and over, somehow more real in its artifice.

After about the thirtieth loop I got out of bed, made a cup of coffee, took out my meager box of tools, and got to work.

I don't know how long Meg was knocking at the door before I heard her. "Linds! Lindsey? Open up. Please. I know you're home. Come on. It's me. Please."

How long had I been working on the television? It was all a blur. My depth of field swam in and out as I stumbled toward the door. I squinted into the peephole, but the warped fisheye image of Meg standing in the

hallway of my apartment building did little to settle my nerves.

"People think that cables grow in their homes," I said. I hoped that would explain everything.

"What?" asked Meg.

"Is it morning yet?"

"Morning? It's evening. Are you sure you're okay? I'm worried, Linds." Her voice trembled. I tried to picture each fluctuation in pitch as an individual frame. I tried to understand.

I placed my hand against the door. The skin of my palm, transparent as glass, seeped through the wood.

"Go, Meg. Forget about me. In television, everything is fine."

I never liked watching movies on TV. Formats squished into pathetic dimensions. Definition filtered through pixels. Aspect ratios warped. No matter how sophisticated television technology got, I could never lose myself in a film on the small screen. It never looked right. It never felt right.

The cable that dangled from my left eye socket was being stubborn. Pushing it deep into my retina was easy enough. The socket was soft. But with one eye seeing in a new way, my depth perception was in a state of flux.

Finally, like threading a needle, I managed to get the other end of the cable fed through the intestines of the TV. After I soldered it in place, I breathed a sigh of relief and moved on.

It took most of the day. Or was it days? Knocks rattled the door. Rings lit up my phone.

Can you imagine that some people actually watch movies on their phones? I shook my head in disbelief at the notion, my bare skull scarcely able to rotate within the intricate visor of wires that encircled it.

Scraps of scalp lay on the floor. They were no longer needed. Just useless insulation.

Finally, my fingers slick with blood, I was done.

I pressed the buttons that I had carved into my forearm.

My lone eyelid fluttered.

The screen flickered.

But it wasn't the screen on the television. That was long dead. It had been dead for decades. Why hadn't people realized it yet?

The greatest films don't take place on a projected surface. They take place inside us.

The horse. It was back.

I could see it. Flickering. Imagination made meat. Flesh built out of brain-stuff.

I wept. Tears and mucus and claret foamed around the cable that penetrated my eye. The foam coursed down my cheek. Crystalline and glistening, a prism.

I saw myself from both outside and inside, simultaneously.

What had Meg told me? "I love your mind. The way you see the world. The angles you approach everything from."

I was no longer in my room. I was no longer in my body. I was not pure. The television tolerates only purity.

Can my new eyes give me new sight? Can we splice our own perception? Am I different somehow?

The question is bled of consequence as the horse, blue and swollen with snowy static, prances alongside me. I'm on the street. With the crowd and the cars. I glance around and notice the man and woman in the crisp, pressed clothes. Only now I'm seeing them from the back. All I can discern is their silhouettes. They have no human features. They're wooden, flat, pancaked. Like the facades of buildings on a movie set.

The horse halts. It snorts sparks. It bows its head in supplication.

My heart unspools.

Gripping a fistful of flaming mane, I hoist myself up on its back.

Its flanks flow beneath my thighs.

As we gallop together toward the black void at the edge of the screen, I take one last look at a sky I know I'll never see again.

It's full of scratchy clouds, like smudges on a window. It's brighter at the edges, as if illuminated from behind.

For a second, I think I see Meg's face. Enormous, like the face of the moon. I think of her hair, spice and shampoo.

But I blink, and she's gone. The sky's gone too. Just a trick of the light.

NINE TENTHS OF THE LAW

by Molly Tanzer

D ONNA HAD PICKED UP JARED'S FAVORITE—Romano's to go, he liked the rosemary bread and the penne rustica—and was just putting it in the oven to keep warm when they brought him in. *They* being EMTs, after pounding urgently on the door, and *brought him in* meaning he was on a stretcher. He had an IV in his arm and his eyes were bandaged with thick layers of gauze.

Donna felt a flash of annoyance as the EMTs wheeled him toward their bedroom, sending their cat Skimbleshanks hissing and skittering nervously out of the way. She had planned to propose they separate that night, over the tiramisu she'd put in the fridge. Then Jared moaned, and she chided herself. She was still his wife…for now, at least. She ought to be beside herself with worry, not annoyed over having to put off an awkward conversation.

"What happened?" she asked, hovering in the doorway while they got him into his pajamas and between the sheets, fumbling in the darkness of the room. Jared seemed pretty out of it. Doped up on painkillers, maybe? "Why didn't someone call me?"

"Workplace accident," the woman replied, answering only the first of Donna's questions. "He'll be fine, he just needs to rest. Please don't turn on those lights. His eyes are very sensitive right now."

Jared worked in administration at Denver International Airport. "What sort of workplace accident?"

"Someone will be by to talk to you," the woman assured her, her eyes flickering to the other EMT, a buff young man with tattoos and one of those man-buns.

"What sort of someone?" Donna did not have to fake the concern in her voice, as it was due to the oddness of the situation rather than her husband's condition.

As if on cue, there was a knock at the front door. Donna left the EMTs to let in a man in a gray suit. His hair was short; his shoulders, broad. Donna thought he looked vaguely military, but the pin on his lapel was the new DIA logo, the white peaks of the airport's distinctive roof against a dark blue background.

"Mrs. Crane?"

For now. She pushed away the thought and nodded.

"My name is Mr. Smoot. I'm sorry to meet you under these circumstances, but it's a pleasure." He did not try to shake her hand. "How is he?"

"He's in bed," she said. She suddenly smelled the food and rushed into the kitchen to turn down the oven temperature. Mr. Smoot followed her. "That's all I know at this point," she said, over her shoulder. "What happened to him?"

"Nothing a few days of rest won't cure."

She frowned. "That he needs rest is all anyone's told me."

"There's not much to tell. Just a workplace accident." Donna was becoming annoyed; given how everyone was putting her off she suspected something might really be wrong. Her face must have betrayed this, as Mr. Smoot set his briefcase on the table and opened it, withdrawing a single sheet of paper from one of the files. He handed it to her—it was a photocopy of an incident report.

She began to skim it as Mr. Smoot spoke; he and the document said basically the same thing: "He was riding in the employee train. They were testing a new sort of lighting system down there, and a bulb flared and burst. He was looking in the wrong place at the wrong time. We had him rushed to the hospital. They did a quick surgery—with a laser, nothing to

worry about. Really, he will be fine. He'll have to wear the bandages for a few days. When they come off he'll have two black eyes, but that should be it."

"I see." Donna set the paper on the table. She was relieved to finally have an answer and understood why they'd wanted a DIA rep to tell her. Damage control; lawsuit avoidance. "I'm glad it's not serious."

Mr. Smoot smiled. "We are, too. Now, as to the logistics, you work as a dental hygienist, correct?"

Donna frowned. "Um, yes." Creepy that he knew, but it must be in Jared's file somewhere…? And yet, every time a new acquaintance learned her husband worked at Denver International Airport, they inevitably asked about one or more of the *X-Files* style rumors that floated around the place like cottonwood fluff in the springtime. Was DIA where they'd take the President in the event of a global crisis? Did its murals predict the Rapture? Were the delays and budget increases that had plagued its construction due to the secret alien research facility beneath the tunnels? Was it true that Blucifer, the cobalt-blue, flame-eyed horse statue that terrorized the entrance of the airport, had killed his creator?

The truth was out there…except it wasn't. Well, except for the Blucifer thing. That was true. The statue had fallen on the sculptor's leg, severing his artery. But as for the rest of it, no way. She'd taken the tour. It was just an airport.

"We'll make sure you get all the paid time off you need to take care of your husband. Or, would you prefer a nurse be assigned? One will stop by, of course, to check in on him until the bandages come off, but without being able to see he'll need someone here to help him. We'll of course cover any and all costs of home health care if you choose the second option, but we thought you might like a little mini-break."

"Sure…" Donna may have gotten her GED, but she was no dummy. This was *definitely* lawsuit avoidance. "Thanks."

"Excellent. Well, I'm sure you'd prefer to be in there with him than out here with me." Mr. Smoot sniffed the air. "Smells like you had dinner ready for him…so sorry."

"It's just takeout," she assured him. "Would you…like some?" Jared wasn't going to want the penne rustica that she'd driven twenty minutes into Aurora to get. Someone ought to enjoy it, and Mr. Smoot wasn't bad looking, actually. It might be nice to have dinner with someone different, just for a change. What might they talk about? The possibilities were endless! "I got wine. He probably can't have any of it."

"I'm sure once the painkillers wear off he'll be hungry. Thank you though, very kind of you to offer."

The EMT showed up in the kitchen doorway. "Mrs. Crane, he's as comfortable as we can make him, and awake. He's asking for you. And we'd like to go over some aftercare."

"Thank you," she said automatically.

"I should get going," said Mr. Smoot, closing his briefcase. "Here's my card," he said, handing her one. "Call me if you need *anything*."

"Okay," she agreed.

Just as they'd promised, all Jared needed was rest and darkness. A little help getting to the bathroom and back, or to the kitchen table for meals. After five days, the bandages came off, and for better or for worse he was back to his usual self.

Donna forced herself to put off bringing up a possible separation until at least his black eyes faded; tried to focus on the positive within their relationship. Jared had a good job, as did she. They lived in a nice house a reasonable commute away from the airport and the dental office where she worked, and had nice friends whom they saw regularly.

Turning these facts and others into a sort of litany, Donna began to doubt herself. Her life was good, so why did she feel so on edge all the time? Her feelings of dissatisfaction made no sense. Why did she feel

relief instead of regret when Jared called to say he'd be working late? She shouldn't feel that flash of annoyance when she heard his key in the lock; shouldn't find it so irritating when she asked how his day was and he said, literally every afternoon or evening, "Good. Busy." Shouldn't resent the way he never asked about *her* day, or his perpetually preoccupied, predictable "Oh?" when she prompted him with a "I had a long day" or similar. That and a million other things ought not to make her nerves sing with tension and her heart flutter with frustration and resentment.

But they did.

Jared was *exactly* the same after he recovered. That's what confirmed for Donna that the oddness surrounding his accident was simply DIA attempting to avoid going to court. Jared worked the same amount, said the same damn things, ate with the same hand. Nothing was different about him. Sadly.

At least so she thought…

Just like every other part of their marriage, sex had become a routine. To be fair, *that* monotony was pleasant enough, not like his responses to her attempts at conversation. Always shy about such matters, Jared would turn off his light and pretend to sleep, waiting for her to tire of reading. Once she turned off her lamp, he would grope for her under the covers in the darkness of their bedroom, first finding a breast, then drifting down to her sex, which he would caress until she was wet enough to accommodate him. Usually she came, either while he was inside her, or after, squeezing her thighs together after he rolled off.

About a week after the accident, when the purple bruises around his eyes had faded to mustard yellow and a soft, pea soup green, Jared reached for her. She was ready. As far as she was concerned, Jared's ability to sexually satisfy her, however inadvertently, was the only thing he had going for him. Responding more eagerly than usual to his touch, she was pleased when instead of anxiously stroking her over her panties he pulled them aside and slid a finger gently but deeply inside her—and gasped in surprise when he inserted a second.

All too soon he withdrew them both, to snap on his bedside light. She blinked, and when her eyes adjusted, she saw he was sucking his fingers as he gazed at her exposed body. She shuddered, half-alarmed, half-aroused, and covered her breasts with her hands, unaccountably shy. He pulled them away almost roughly.

"I want to see," he said.

His voice was the same, but something was different. His eyes. They glinted queerly in the light, like Skimbleshanks' did when he was hiding under the bed. Were they a slightly different color now? Or was it just the low wattage of the bedside lamp and the sickly bruises?

She didn't think long on it. How could she, while he was peeling down her undies and pushing her knees apart to inspect her sex? She was unable to interpret his expression—all she could come up with was *wonder*, but that wasn't possible, not after ten years. And yet, how else could she explain the way his eyes widened and breath quickened as he spread her open before tasting her, which he'd never previously been particularly inclined to do. His attentions inspired her to respond with equal enthusiasm and soon she was suckling his hard cock. His delight inspired her, and she actually whined a little when he took it away from her—but her complaints turned to moans when he plunged it inside her and proceeded apace with more than his usual vigor.

He came before her, with an unexpected yelp much different from his usual relieved exhalation of breath; more aroused than she could ever remember being, she came as he slowed his thrusting. He said nothing after, just smiled and pushed her sweaty bangs away from her forehead before turning off the light. She was left in darkness, confused but far too happy to worry much about it as she drifted off.

The next morning she felt like a housewife in an old movie when she

caught herself humming as she toasted her English muffin. Amazing, the power of excellent sex…she was actually in a good mood. Sliding into the chair beside him instead of across from him, she grinned at him.

"Have a nice time last night?"

"Hm?" he looked up from the paper. His awful bruised eyes no longer shone with that same intense, interested light.

"Last night," she said, faltering.

"Oh," he said vaguely. "Yes."

Donna no longer had any appetite for her cooling English muffin, margarine coagulating in all the nooks and crannies. Feeling disappointed—even a bit betrayed—she said nothing as he folded the paper, gave her a quick peck on the cheek, and left for work without putting his cereal bowl in the sink, as usual.

Things went back to normal, and Donna cooled down enough that when Jared next feigned sleep she didn't keep reading until he really fell asleep, as she sometimes did when feeling particularly resentful. Indeed, she put her book down early, as she was curious to see if she'd be treated to another display of genuine interest in her needs and her body. Hell, if the shift proved permanent, she might be able to deal with their marriage. For a little while longer, at least.

He reached for her in the darkness, to her mild disappointment. As tired as she had become of her husband's face, she had enjoyed watching him grimace and wince during their lovemaking last time. His lip had curled and his eyes had closed when he came; it had almost looked like it pained him, which had been very hot to watch. So, while she usually kept quiet during sex, that night she asked, "Want me to turn the light on?" as he fiddled with her nipple.

"What?" Jared's surprise was genuine.

"The light," she said. "Like last time."

He paused, then reached over and snapped it on. *"Definitely,"* he said, as his eyes gleamed.

While she was tempted to pay more attention to the fact that he was already hard, she placed a hand on his chest.

"What's going on?" She said it calmly.

Jared froze. She waited.

"What do you mean?" he asked.

"Something's going on, and I want to know what it is. And I want to know badly enough that I'm putting off...*things*...which, let me tell you, is difficult after last time."

Jared laughed. "You did seem to like it. I did too."

"Oh, *now* you want to talk about it?"

"I wanted to talk about it before, but..." He looked worried for a moment. "I couldn't."

"Why not?"

"Because..." He shrugged. "Because I'm not your husband."

This shocked her less than she thought it should. Then again, she was tired of her husband. Whoever he was now, he had the advantage of not being Jared.

"All right," she said. "Who are you, then?"

"That's hard to explain..."

"Try."

Jared—well, *Not*-Jared—nodded. "I thought it was strange, when I found out, that you don't know. But your husband, he isn't an..." Not-Jared squinted, as if thinking hard, *"administrator.* I mean, he *is*, but not for the airport. For what's under the airport."

She felt a frisson of fear and pleasure. The truth *had* been out there! All those times she'd scoffed at friends or strangers... "What's under the airport?"

"A research facility. Around twenty of your Earth years ago we made contact with you. Ever since, we—our two species—have been working

to facilitate an *experimental collaborative co-consciousness.* Jared is hosting my mind in his body."

Donna held up a hand. "Our two species? What sort of species are you?" It—it was now an *it* to her mind—opened its mouth, but before it responded, she added, "And what is your name?"

"My name is," it sounded like *Glreerak*, and when Donna repeated it, Not-Jared—Glreerak—smiled and nodded. "Close enough. My world is—"

"You're an alien." Donna, again, felt minimal surprise.

"I am. But we are not so different. Neither of our species has achieved faster than light travel, and yet we wished to know more of who else might be living in our galaxy. My people are naturally able to separate our consciousness from our physical forms, so we developed the technology to send out a psychic beacon. You—humanity—were the first to respond."

Donna finally felt upset. "And Jared? He knew? All this time?"

"Yes. He has been the...*accountant* for the program since before you were married, but his selection as my host was more recent. They ran tests on everyone who worked there, from the top scientists to the janitors, and he was the most naturally receptive to the process." Glreerak stared at her. "This dismays you."

"He never told me."

"He could not. He was forbidden. But," it was studying her face, "perhaps he ought to have trusted you? You are...*married.* It is the sort of relationship where confidences are exchanged, according to my under-standing." Donna nodded. She felt furious, miserable. "We have a similar pair-bonding—my species, I mean—where intimacy is encouraged."

Donna dashed a tear from her eye. It felt ridiculous, crying about such a small thing, when she had been ready to leave Jared anyway. "Are you...

pair-bonded?" she asked.

Glreerak nodded. "I am."

"But the other night…"

It shrugged. "I am not in my own body. And I have been instructed by my government to find out as much as I can about human ways and lives. My mate knows sex is a part of that."

Donna looked sidelong at it; met its eyes that were not her husband's eyes. Jared wasn't unattractive. She'd been very eager for his attentions when they began dating, set up by a mutual friend. Then, his reticence had seemed manly, his steady, government job a sign of maturity.

"So, does that mean you want to…"

"Definitely," it replied. "I am supposed to learn all I can about you, after all."

"But for now," it said, once it had her writhing, three fingers inside her, "let's just keep this, ah, *educational session* between us?"

"Of course," she gasped.

Jared's eyes healed up enough that he agreed to go to a party at a friend's house. It was a nice time, for a bit, at least. Donna was with her girlfriends in the grass, giggling over a joint and drinking Mang-o-Ritas when her husband broke off from the pack of men standing around the grill to take her aside. He was grumpy after two scotch and sodas, and wanted to go home.

It was just so goddamn typical. She felt cute in her nice dress, the weather was finally good after several late spring snows, and she hadn't seen Vicky or Marissa in a while. Of course he would be a pill.

"Just a bit longer," she said, feeling like a child pleading with her parents to be allowed to stay in the pool.

"I didn't want to come anyway," he snapped. "We've stayed long enough."

"But…"

"Donna, I have to work tomorrow." She felt her expression sour at his condescending words in that exasperated tone. Work! Indeed he did, at his

secret job, living his secret life. Well, she had to work, too, at her decidedly not-clandestine dentist's office, her back aching as she picked things out of people's teeth.

"Please?" she asked.

He shook his head, but then paused; looked back at her. "Well… all right," he said, with a slow smile that was not Jared's smile. "We haven't been out in so long. You go spend time with your friends. I'll get another drink."

It was Glreerak speaking. She was sure of it. The alien was talking to her, here, in front of all these people. It was actually kind of a turn-on, the secret. Maybe she *did* want to go home…

"We can't stay *too* late," it cautioned her, waggling its finger. "But a bit longer. You're having a nice time. Later, you can thank me," it said, and winked.

They stayed until the sun set. Donna couldn't remember the last time she felt so happy, alternating between chatting with her friends and sneaking kisses with Glreerak. When she climbed into the passenger's side, she favored Jared—she was pretty sure he was Jared again—with a smile. He didn't see it, however, sitting there with the key in the ignition.

"It got so late," he said, sounding confused. "How did it get so late? I was ready to go hours ago."

Donna froze. Of course, Jared didn't recall when the alien took over. It had seemed so harmless in bed. But in public, among friends …

Then she recalled his tone, earlier, when he'd insisted they leave. Recalled that he had kept secrets from her—secrets bigger than how a pleasant afternoon had been passed.

"You had another drink," she said as casually as she could, buckling her seatbelt as cover. "Maybe you got a little drunker than you realized.

Sure you're okay to drive?"

"I feel totally sober," he said. "Huh." He waited for another moment, then turned the key. "Better keep it to two next time, I suppose."

Donna said nothing. Eventually, her heart slowed down.

Before going into the induced sleep that allowed its mind to live within Jared's, Glreerak dwelt beneath the waves, in vast city of coral skyscrapers grown and maintained by bioarchitects to harvest and emit the faint light of the planet's sun. Millions lived in that phosphorescently illuminated gloaming, lived and worked and loved and died in ways similar and different to humans in their cities on Earth.

Glreerak lived with its mate in a flat high above the ocean floor. It was comfortable—luxurious even, with a good view of the surrounding towers and parks and even the farmland beyond the city limits. They had been assigned such a wonderful home because while Glreerak's mate was one of the scientists working on the project to make contact with Earth, Glreerak held a much higher-status job: sanitation.

As with all civilizations, waste removal was an issue. Burying garbage beneath the ocean bed poisoned the food supply; allowing it to drift away created problems for other cities. So, there was only one place it could go.

While all of Glreerak's people were telepathic, only the most powerful communicators were able to pass the rigorous tests to become sanitation workers. Those who did were trained to develop their mental aptitude from a young age, until they were able to throw their minds into the bodies of simpler creatures, such as the mammal-like bipeds that lived on land. Teams of sanitation workers could combine their efforts to mobilize whole packs of them to haul waste out of the sea and inland, away from rivers and other tributaries, to minimize seepage back into the water. Glreerak was particularly talented; in fact, it could control these creatures for miles, and had seen more of its planet's land masses than any other, such as the astonishing—

"Wait," said Donna.

"What's that?" said Glreerak.

It had been an intense evening. Donna had been overwhelmed by the menu at Linger, a trendy eatery with a spectacular view of Denver that Jared had never been willing to brave due to its world cuisine-inspired menu. Indeed, Jared would have hated it—would hate it tomorrow, given

how spicy everything had been. Then again, maybe he wouldn't notice anything even as fundamental as altered digestion. He'd been withdrawn and preoccupied of late, even for him, and had become nervous as well, startling at loud noises, rubbing his eyes.

To be fair, Linger's menu had been a little weird for Donna, too, but she'd done all right with red wine, an order of sweet potato waffle fries, and the kofta, which turned out to essentially be meatballs dressed up for a night out.

Glreerak had liked everything, and the drinks along with the view of the city skyline had made it a bit homesick for its watery world.

"You can control other creatures with your mind?"

Glreerak didn't answer; it just sipped on its cocktail, some weird thing called "Streets of Puebla" that Donna hadn't liked *at all.*

"Well," it said after swallowing, "yes. My telepathic prowess is why they chose me."

Whatever she'd eaten for dinner felt like a cold and leaden lump inside her.

"So you knew."

"Knew what?"

"That you'd be able to control…*us.*"

"No!" Glreerak pursed its lips. "We wondered—*hypothesized*, as my mate would say. But we didn't *know*. I mean, it was a week before I felt comfortable enough to try, just to see. And it was you who inspired me, Donna. Your body was so soft—you seemed so receptive to pleasure. I had to see you! The shape of you, all of you. The way you responded to him, I couldn't let my time on Earth go by without taking advantage of the endless possibilities you suggested to me…"

Was it wooing her with sweet talk to distract her from the idea of a mass invasion? Were Glreerak's people testing the waters, so to speak, to turn humanity into their next generation of garbage-hauling slaves?

"You know, Donna," it said, reaching its hand across the table to take hers, "when your husband takes his turn living in *my head*, we will be revealing our planet's secrets to your species."

More than thoughts of their lovemaking, this distracted Donna from her worries of a future invasion. "What?"

"Eventually he will return with me. I am to spend a year with him, then he will spend a year with me." Glreerak looked upset. "I know he has been concerned about how to tell you—how to explain his absence. I thought you should know, though."

"He agreed to all this without..." Donna shook her head. She was so unimportant to him. What a fool she had been!

"Are you upset about the idea of losing him for so long?"

Donna looked up from her wine, saw the gleam of the ocular implants as it tilted its head at her like a quizzical puppy. She was upset—but she was upset about losing Glreerak; jealous that Jared, who had all the sense of wonder of a sack of potatoes would get to live with it on its planet. Would get to see how it made love to its mate.

She laughed. It was the only thing she could do, really. "Well, maybe he'll come back with a few new tricks to try on me after watching you with your mate."

"Perhaps. At home, I would be the one to be fertilized."

Donna blinked at it. "You're a woman?"

"No, *you're* a woman. I'm barely female! It's rather a bit more compli-cated, at home. If we were interested in reproducing, my mate would fertilize me. Once the egg developed to its solid jelly form, I would pass it back to be incubated in my partner's pouch. Eventually we would give it over to the city, where it would be implanted into a host along with the rest of the eggs around its stage. Once fully mature, it would hatch, and eat its way out of—well," it trailed off, seeing her face. "The point is, when we fuck for pleasure, it's a bit different."

"Sounds like it will definitely broaden his mind." Donna smiled. "Glreerak..."

"Yes?"

"Even if we only have a year, we have a year. Together. Let's make it a fun one."

"It has been already!"

"Sure, the past few weeks have been great, but still—you didn't come all the way to Earth just to go to work under DIA every day and live in Aurora."

"Well, a month from now, Jared's going on a tour of world heritage sites…" Glreerak paused. "Don't be upset…you were to come on that one. Mr. Smoot has been arranging it with your job. It was to be a surprise. That's why I didn't tell you, either. You know I would have, don't you, Donna?"

"Well then let's at least go away for a weekend. To the mountains, maybe. Together. Just the two of us, I mean. When we go abroad, I'm sure we'll have all kinds of handlers and such. If you—if Jared could get a half-day some Friday…"

Glreerak nodded, smiling in that way Jared never smiled at her. "Sounds delightful," it agreed. "I'll ask for the…" its eyes went a bit dim as they did when it was searching through Jared's mind for the correct turn of phrase, *"time off."*

"Good." She reached for the small menu beside her elbow. "But first, how about dessert?"

She decided on Steamboat Springs. It was inexpensive now that the snowpack was mostly gone, she knew no one who lived in the area, and there was a legendary hot spring up there, Strawberry Park, that was supposed to be gorgeous. Plus, the drive up would show Glreerak the mountains, where the aspens were still the pale gold-green of springtime against the dark pines.

It was exhilarating. The whole drive, Donna felt like she was going on a dirty weekend, even though it was her husband in the passenger's seat. Well, sort of.

Glreerak was pleased with everything—pointed out gorgeous vistas, gasped as they crested various passes. Jared would only have remarked on the traffic; worried whether they should have made dinner reservations.

Saturday, they took a picnic lunch up to the springs, sandwiches and chips and a can of the kale-flavored soda that Donna had only ever seen Glreerak buy. By late in the afternoon, they'd had enough of dipping in the various pools, heating up and cooling down by turns. But that was fine, they had urgent business in the hotel room.

Donna's googling had told her Café Diva was a hot spot even in the warmer weather, but when they walked in the door, she saw something she didn't like one bit. Vicky and her husband Mark were there, and before Donna could suggest they ought to go elsewhere to avoid being spotted, they were.

"Donna!" cried Vicky. "I didn't know you and Jared would be here this weekend. You sly dogs, are you on a lovers' getaway?"

"Haha," said Donna, just like that—not a laugh, but a statement. "Yeah we are, you caught us."

"We are too! Come on, join us for dinner! It'll be fun, you can go back to your place after." She winked outrageously at Donna. "We've only just ordered starters."

"Oh, we wouldn't want to…"

"To what? Have fun? Come on, you won't be bothering us."

Donna looked to Glreerak. It shrugged.

They actually had a really nice dinner. Glreerak did well with Vicky and Mark, even if sometimes it had to think, scanning through Jared's brain, before responding. Donna ordered a second bottle of wine to keep them from noticing too much. It seemed to work.

Back at the hotel, Donna collapsed onto the bed.

"That was close," she said. "I'm so glad we're free of them. I could barely eat, I was so worried."

Glreerak pushed her skirt up over her thighs. "Your species' constant need for nourishment isn't unpleasant, but it's a shame we have to leave the hotel to do it."

"We can order room service tomorrow morning."

"Good. No more distractions from what *really* matters."

It was the longest amount of time they'd spent together without letting Jared surface. Donna felt bad—a little bit, at least—but she hadn't wanted to argue with her husband about the drive, where to stay, what to do, where to eat. She'd wanted to enjoy some time with Glreerak without distractions, just for once.

When they cruised back into town that Sunday, after grabbing a late lunch in Denver, she felt a bit low to have to return to her marriage; her life. Even the idea of their upcoming around-the-world trip couldn't cheer her. Glreerak had said they'd see the Library of Celsus—the Parthenon—the Pyramids—the Great Wall—the Tower of London—Machu Picchu… but she'd be seeing it all with Jared. She would know Glreerak was there, just beyond Jared's eyes, but they wouldn't be *together*. Not really.

They'd agreed on a cover story: A stomach virus had knocked Jared out all weekend. As Donna unpacked the last of their things, Glreerak changed into pajamas and got into bed.

"Wow, it must have really knocked me out," remarked Jared, as Donna brought him a glass of watered-down Gatorade. "Well, I'm feeling better now."

"I'm so glad," said Donna. "You were really miserable. Probably best you don't remember it."

"Would you bring me my laptop? I ought to see if any work emails came in while I was so out of it…"

Yeah, maybe some new alien species made contact with the secret research facility where you work, she thought, but all she said was, "Sure."

She took a long shower; took her time drying off. She'd brought her pajamas with her into the bathroom—it was silly, but she felt less comfortable changing in front of Jared of late. When she re-emerged, he was in bed, laptop open. He was staring intently at the screen.

"Hungry at all?" she asked, putting a little hopefulness into her voice, as if urging him.

He said nothing; didn't look up at her.

"Well...let me know if you need anything," she said. "I'm going to watch a little teevee."

"No," he said. *"Wait."*

When he looked up at her, finally, his expression was not a friendly one. "More Gatorade?" she asked.

"I don't want any goddamn Gatorade," he said, throwing off the covers and advancing on her. Donna shrank against the wall. Jared was really upset; he didn't usually swear...

"What's wrong?"

"What's wrong? What's wrong is that I was in Steamboat Springs this weekend," he said. "Apparently I had a lovely dinner with Vicky and Mark in some restaurant up there. But how could that be, if my wife assures me I was sick in bed?"

Donna didn't know what to do. She hadn't anticipated this; hadn't thought she would ever be caught. Oh, she'd been such a fool!

"Nothing to say?"

She shrugged; shook her head.

"How long have you known?"

"Known...about Glreerak?"

"Who?"

Donna felt faint. "Your...your experimental collaborative co-consciousness."

Jared's eyes went wide. He grabbed his phone; dialed quickly. "I need someone here, *now*. To bring me in," he said. "Yes. *Yes*. Yes!" He hung up the phone.

"Bring you in?"

"You think I'm going to drive, knowing it could take me over at any

moment?" he snarled, almost yanking out a dresser drawer in his haste to grab a shirt. "Oh god, what am I going to tell them? None of us knew it even had a name, much less that it could make a puppet of me without my consent or my knowledge! None of us…except *you*."

"I can explain…"

"Oh, please do!" he said, struggling into a pair of sweatpants. "I'm eager to hear you *explain* going out of town for a weekend with it." His eyes snapped back to hers. "You fucked it, didn't you? You fucking fucked it!"

Donna wished Glreerak could intervene, but it had told her it was more difficult to take over Jared when he was emotionally agitated. She would just have to deal with this on her own. "Well…" she began.

"Never mind! I don't want to hear it, actually. I'm leaving," he said unnecessarily, "and I don't know when I'll be back."

"What's going to happen?" she asked.

"It's not up to me," he snapped. "But I have my doubts they'll be pleased. This was not part of our agreement! Jesus, they can take us over! No wonder they were so eager for this partnership…this is not good, this is really not good. Where *are* they?" he said, stomping out of the bedroom.

Donna felt a chill as she followed him into the living room, and not in regards to Jared's fears of planetary domination. "Can't we talk about this?" she said, pleading with him.

"Talk? Talk about what?"

"Are they going to terminate the…the co-habitation?"

"Probably! Donna, I was supposed to be reporting anything strange. This is new technology—new law—new everything!" He shook his head. "I'm such an idiot. I knew something was wrong, but I believed your excuses. How stupid of me, to trust my own wife!"

Now Donna was furious; all her rage came bubbling up like lava, hot and toxic. "Trust! You want to talk about trust? If Glreerak hadn't told me, how would I have known? You never even told me where you worked, what you did!"

"It's top secret!"

"Top secret!" She scoffed at him. "*You* reached for *me* that first night, you know. Did it excite you, the idea of it watching us?"

He blushed. She'd never seen him blush, not in a decade of marriage. "It was here to learn about us! That includes how married couples...um, *behave* with each other!"

"I guess it learned a hell of a lot, didn't it? Mission accomplished." Something occurred to Donna, contemplating the way she and Jared had behaved with one another, before Glreerak. She really didn't want to go back to that. Couldn't go back to that. "Maybe...maybe you won't have to terminate the relationship. Maybe there's a way..."

"What?" Jared's face crumpled. "A *way?* You're more worried about losing your lover than my mental health! It was taking me over, Donna! It pushed me out of my own mind, my own body! My own marriage!"

"No. We pushed ourselves out of that."

There was a knock at the door. Donna answered it. There stood Mr. Smoot; behind him were several military men brandishing weapons. Mr. Smoot was the only one who appeared unarmed, but given everything, it wouldn't surprise her if he had something concealed on his person.

"Come in," she said, as if this were the most typical of social calls.

"I'm afraid I can't," said he, equally pleasant. "Jared? Is that you?"

"Yes, it's *me*," he said, not exactly elbowing his way past Donna, but not waiting for her to move out of the doorway, either. "Let's go."

They walked to the black car parked in the driveway, Donna barefoot and following at a bit of a distance. She felt embarrassed to be seen with her damp hair and worn cotton pajamas, but she couldn't help but tag along. She would likely never speak to Glreerak again. She had no idea if she would ever see Jared, either. He had to come back at some point... didn't he?

Who could say? He'd never told her anything about any of it.

There was no time to ask. Mr. Smoot got in the driver's side, and Jared

slammed the car door shut in her face as she approached. He had clearly not calmed down at all, but maybe Glreerak would peek through, one last time. She looked into her husband's eyes, hoping to see the familiar gleam…but as Mr. Smoot put the car in reverse, late afternoon sunlight glinted off the passenger window. It was impossible for Donna to tell who it was who mouthed "good bye."

THE AVENGER

by Travis Heermann

Bob Smith dreamed, but not the kind anyone had ever dreamed before.

In his dream, he was thirty feet tall, galloping wild and free across a bleak, windswept landscape. In the ruddy brown sky, the sun was a dim, sharp disk, more like the moon. Endless dust and the desiccated corpses of trees stretched as far as he could see.

The absence of life made him terribly sad.

He ran and ran across the eternal landscape, hooves pounding up great clouds of powdery dust behind them. Alongside the silhouettes of mountains he could name from childhood, he galloped tirelessly to the north and to the south, searching for any sign of life.

Loneliness drove him on and on.

But there was only dust and desolation, endless shades of lifeless ocher and brown.

Then, joy of joys, he spotted a new color on the horizon, a dark strip of green that became a pine grove. Clustered around a dirty, brown lake, gnarled trees clung to life by the tips of their needles. But even as he paused to enjoy the first sight of life he could remember, a sound on the horizon caught his ear, a hissing wind carrying harmonics too high for the human ear to hear.

But here in his dream, he was not human.

His erect ears turned toward the sound. In his reflection in the water, he was a giant stallion of blue steel. His mane and tail were carbon fiber, his eyes ruby lamps, his breath scalding steam. Within him pulsed a fusion heart.

The noise rose amid a great dust storm. The feet of untold thousands of creatures raised the cloud behind them. But they were no creatures he recognized.

They hopped and ran in bounding strides on two thick, chitinous legs. Their faces had only two features: bulbous eyes like faceted, golden soft-balls, and a fang-studded mouth that opened in three directions. Tattered rags wrapped their bodies like dirty kaftans. From one side stretched a long, insectoid arm tipped by a huge pincer; from the other side, two shorter ones tipped in dexterous, jointed tentacles. Some carried things in their small appendages like machetes or hatchets, others carried nets.

They fell upon the pine grove like locusts, chopping, hewing, chewing. Their sudden arrival among the trees frightened a few strange, four-winged bats. The newcomers leaped high into the air and snagged the desperately chirping bats with nets. None escaped. The moment the creatures returned their prizes to the ground, more crowded around to dismember and devour the bats, wings still flapping as they disappeared into the creatures' gullets.

Others tore into the trees with their blades. Some could not wait, leaping and climbing up trunks to chew into the thinner branches and needles.

More splashed through the muddy lake, dredging up wriggling, slimy things and devouring them whole.

At the sight of such ravenous, unthinking consumption, Bob Smith reared, thrashing his front hooves, screaming his rage. He charged through the lake and stomped the insectoid creatures into the muck, their carapaces crunching underfoot.

They leaped upon him, but their pincers and weapons could not pene-trate his steel hide. He shook them off, bit them into pieces between his sharp, titanium teeth, crushed them with his hooves, and fought his way to the cluster chewing through the pine forest. They would not flee from him. They knew this pine grove was their last source of food within a thousand

miles. All else, gone.

He stomped and kicked and bit until there was nothing left of them. A handful tried to hide, but his nose was too sensitive.

When they were all dead, he snorted in triumph, blowing clouds of phosphorescent steam from his nostrils.

Then he lay down amid the trees, careful not to harm the world's last growth, to rest.

And it was good.

Bob Smith awoke in his bed, heart aching with loneliness, as if he were the last man on earth.

Janet snored softly beside him. Streetlight filtered through the blinds, painting stripes on the ceiling. The closed windows and hum of the air-conditioning kept the songs of crickets at bay.

Rolling out of bed with a groan, he shuffled to the bathroom. Tears blurred his eyes. He couldn't remember a time when he'd felt so lonely. In the harsh light of the master bathroom, it was hard to ignore the reflection in the vanity mirror, the doughy lump he'd become, but he managed.

Somehow, the dream had made him hungry, so after he squeezed a scant trickle of urine past a swollen prostate, he shuffled downstairs to the kitchen, wondering where in the hell that dream had come from.

The sight of the kitchen garbage can—overflowing again—provoked an annoyed sigh. Hadn't the cleaners been here yesterday? Janet had been on an Amazon shopping spree lately. Empty shipping boxes, styrofoam, and plastic packing materials were piled chest high. The whole family had been going a little hog-wild lately. Tyler's video game habit was turning him into a brainless husk. Brittany's Sweet Sixteen was coming up, and Janet had ordered enough party decorations for a football stadium.

He slumped onto a stool at the kitchen island and chewed through a bowl of cereal that tasted like sugared cardboard. It did, however, crunch in a most satisfying way, thanks no doubt to chemical sealants that resisted the milk's moisture.

Scribbled onto the magnetized refrigerator whiteboard was 'Black Friday Shopping List'. He hated Black Friday. Every year, it got crazier. Internet videos of people getting in fist fights over video game consoles and toys disheartened him in ways he was not prepared to fathom.

How many pounds would he gain over the holidays this year?

Don't think about the Mega-Wonder Super-Slicer campaign, or how that upstart punk Walker is trying to horn you out of a job, or how best to flirt with Elsa, the new receptionist. Don't think about how, if the social media numbers aren't good enough, you'll find yourself unemployed by Christmas, eighteen years of service to the company be damned. Don't think about how much the payments are for Janet's new Escalade, or that you still haven't paid off your Hummer. Don't think about how the Bluetooth Hairbrush, Smartweb Salt Dispenser, and Umbrella Drone campaigns were all abysmal failures on your watch. Don't think about the impossibility of selling a 4,700-square-foot house now that the bubble had burst. Don't think about how your 401(k) just took a fifty-three percent shit.

If he thought about all those things at once, he might go out to the garage and suck on the business end of his 12-gauge.

He hadn't been hunting in ten years. No one ever invited him hunting, and there was no one he cared to ask. He could count the number of shells he'd fired through it on two hands. He didn't need to hunt to bring home food for his family. It might have been fun to kill something, but, it turned out, he couldn't hit the broad side of an aircraft carrier.

Thinking back about the dream, he realized how little the wanton violence had shocked him. He'd never been in a fight in his life, never intentionally hurt anyone. He avoided direct conflict as a general rule. He was the go-along-to-get-along guy. Yet, the slaughter of the insectoid creatures felt so real, and he had reveled in it.

So weird.

He put his cereal bowl in the sink and shambled back to bed.

In a few hours, he would have to go to work and show that overachiever Walker that Bob Smith was not to be trifled with. Maybe Elsa would smile at him today.

Bob Smith dreamed.

He galloped north, his long legs and tireless fusion engine covering endless miles of wasteland at glorious speed. His previous journey had been hot and dry, smelling like a cage full of giant cockroaches. But this time, it was dark, cold, and full of ash. Lightning trickled across the sky in crimson fingers miles long. There was no sun, no moon, only a dim twilight, made visible by his ruby eyes.

Across endless frozen desert he ran. Nowhere did he see a shred of vegetation. A few lakes were frozen all the way to the bottom. Brittle, powdery rime covered the land.

When he saw the husk of a fallen city in the distance, he ran to it, looking for inhabitants to assuage his unfathomable loneliness. The crumbling buildings resembled nothing he'd ever seen before, the wrong dimensions for humans. Many were rounded like igloos or hives, and covered in sparkling hoarfrost that would have been pretty if not for their emptiness. Walkways crossed between elegant skyscrapers. This world was even more dead than the last.

Before grand, abandoned buildings, he found statues presumably depicting the previous inhabitants. They were stout, low-slung creatures with domed heads and stubby limbs, beady eyes and broad, flabby mouths.

Any evidence of language on the monuments had been scoured away by snow and sand. For days and nights he walked the city streets, trying to make sense of what had happened. It was just outside the city, however, where he found his answer.

At the lip of the crater, hundreds of feet across, gamma rays and beta particles sleeted over his steel skin, tripping his radiation warning. The crater's shape was unmistakable, even under layers of snow and ash.

On the horizon, another city. He ran to it, but found it just as empty, and in this instance, the enemy's aim had been better. Most of the city lay in rubble; the rest, a radioactive crater.

He howled his rage to incessant cascades of sheet lightning coursing through the clouds.

For more endless days and nights he ran from city to city, following remnants of their once stately roads, a connect-the-dots of devastation.

After all that searching, coming full circle to where he started, he chanced upon a bunker buried in the roots of a mountain. He knew the mountain, Cheyenne Mountain. But on this version of the mountain, enormous craters and sheets of slagged rock covered the slopes.

Then out of the mountain's bowels came a ragged line of armored vehicles, each moving on six insectoid legs, crawling over the landscape, undeterred by boulders and debris. He did not know what drove the vehicles—maybe they were robots—but they trained their magnetic cannons on him.

From his ruby eyes, fueled by his fusion core, he sent twin lasers powerful enough to scrawl his name on the surface of the moon—had it been visible anywhere through the dense cloud cover. His lasers slashed through the vehicles as if they were paper. A few of them managed to get off shots from their magnetic cannons before he cut them to pieces, but their heavy-metal projectiles caromed off his steel skin.

Leaving their smoking wreckage behind him, he clopped into the mouth of the tunnel, into the subterranean darkness. More spider-tanks emerged, but he cut them down. Smaller entities boiled forth, either robots or beings so cybernetically enhanced that little tissue remained. How many hundreds he turned to drifting cinders he did not remember, but when he emerged from the underground complex again, nothing moving

remained inside.

Again, tremendous sorrow washed over him at this, another dead world.

This was not his world, but one of many versions of the land he knew. These strange beings had held promise, but they blew themselves to bits and in the process destroyed all life on the surface of the planet.

Perhaps, eons from now, life would re-emerge from the deepest reaches of the frozen oceans, from what heat sources remained, squirming and chipping and clawing its way back to the surface world. But also perhaps, the deep thermal vents would go cold, and all life on the planet would just...stop.

Across trackless glacier and frozen desert, he ran and ran.

Until a blaring noise ripped him free of his lonely, desperate quest.

Bob slapped his snooze button, seized the alarm clock, and threw it across the room. It stopped short in mid-flight at the limit of its electrical cord and crashed to the floor. Bits of broken plastic bounced and skittered.

Good riddance. He could always buy a new one.

Janet was already up and gone. She loved to hit the garage sales early. Given that Tyler typically stayed up until four in the morning playing video games, he would probably sleep until mid-afternoon. Brittany would grace the world with her presence around the crack of eleven.

Bob went out to the garage and fired up the riding mower. Most of his neighbors hired lawn services, but he could mow three acres of grass in just a couple of hours with this baby. It let him think he was working, getting his hands dirty, even though he seldom got off the mower.

The lush emerald carpet squished under his tires. Screw the city and their "watering restrictions." His was the best-looking lawn in the entire subdivision.

The endless concentric circuits slowly shrunk, giving him opportunity to revel in his success at getting Walker fired. Some carefully planted kiddie porn and an anonymous call to HR had done the job nicely. One should not keep one's porn on a company network. Seeing Walker marched out of the building carrying his box full of personal items assuaged Bob's annoyance at Elsa's threat to call HR on him. Uppity bitch. Probably a dyke.

Then a loud crunch resonated in the blade enclosure. One of the sprinkler heads had failed to retract and he'd just decapitated it. He cursed himself for not paying attention, then cursed the irrigation company for using crappy equipment. This was the second time.

Before he could get back to the control box in the garage, however, the next watering cycle started, soaking him. By the time he got it shut off and returned to survey the damage, he was wading through ankle-deep water.

So he called the irrigation company, demanded they send a repairman right away, and sat down with last week's Sunday newspaper. He threw the thick sheaf of useless circulars into the garbage, frowned at the endless war and how they should have just nuked those terrorists years ago, and read the comics.

Bob Smith was a horse god.

At his feet were clustered dozens of...humans? Not exactly. Their brows and limbs were thicker, their jaws and teeth more protuberant. But they wore loincloths, vests, and homespun shifts. They carried clubs and flint-tipped weapons and wore feathers in their hair and brightly colored piercings and crude jewelry of semi-precious stones.

And they knelt before him, the giant stallion, and it was good. He basked in their adoration. No one had ever worshiped him before.

More of them came, other bands, and they began to argue among themselves, harsh grunts and sharp gesticulations. They pointed at him. One of them struck the other with his fist. A hooting, howling melee

erupted. Men and women, both fought with primal ferocity to protect their band, their children. Clubs and fists and stones dashed out brains and crushed bones until one group remained triumphant. The young of the defeated band cowered, their protectors dead or disabled.

The victorious leader seized a wounded adversary by the hair—half-conscious and squirming—and dragged her to the feet of the great stallion.

Head bowed, arms outstretched, he knelt in supplication. Then he drew a flint knife and stabbed the injured woman in the chest. She screamed and went slack. He began to cut. The sound of their rending flesh and cracking ribs was nothing the horse had ever heard before. He looked down in fascination, until finally, the man's blood-smeared hands raised her heart in offering.

What need had a horse god for a heart? He snorted a cloud of glowing steam, and they all ooohed and prostrated themselves.

The leader grinned with joy, seized another captive, and offered another heart. Then another. And another. The horse god watched placidly. His supplicants sang songs of exaltation.

But then another band arrived, awed by the magnificent horse god, and wished to take part in the proceedings. But another argument erupted, another vicious melee, and the previously victorious group was laid low.

The new victors, seeing the mound of corpses at the horse god's feet, adopted the practice, and sacrificed their enemies who still lived. And it was good. But there was no food. The presence of so many bands had driven off all the game and stripped the land of berries and wild onions. So they ate the corpses.

Another band appeared, saw what was happening, and fell upon the cannibals with spears and arrows. The superior weaponry dispatched the man-eaters with breathtaking ease. The new band stood victorious, seized the conquered women, killed the children of the previous sires, and filled the women's bellies with their own offspring.

Around the horse god grew a settlement. More bands were driven off or else took over the settlement for themselves. More offerings were brought to the horse god, animals and people slaughtered at his feet, baskets of grain, beautiful shells and stones. Over the centuries, he came to recline upon a pile of riches and blood. Until there were some who arose to denounce him as a false god.

He had never done anything to help them, they said. People brought endless sacrifices, entreating him to bring rain for crops, to make them fertile, to stave off disease. And he did nothing, they said.

The priests had the heretics arrested, tortured, and killed at the horse god's feet to show their loyalty.

And it was good.

Bob Smith awoke in time for church, tied his necktie, shrugged into his Sunday best. The kids whined. Janet clucked at them. Finally, after breakfast, off they drove in the shiny black Escalade.

In the pew, he hunched, head bowed. He mouthed the hymns. The minister droned. The collection plate came, full of bleached skulls and discreet envelopes and lint-fuzzed coins still warm from children's pockets, and something broke inside him so sharply it drove him bolt upright.

He turned his face toward the cavernous ceiling, but instead saw his self-made prison for the first time, a rut so deep he could no longer see the sky, much less find a horizon to run toward or a forest glade that hadn't been razed by human locusts.

Janet whispered to ask if he was all right, but her face was different, her brow thicker. Or maybe he saw her small, chitinous hand reaching toward him, one appendage too many on that side. He slapped that ugly little tentacled thing away. She gasped and gaped at him. The kids stared. His neighbors' beady eyes glared from under too-thick brows.

After the final benediction, he avoided the minister's greeting queue,

mumbled something about his stomach, and pretended to go off to the restroom.

On the way home, he drove in iron-jawed silence. No one spoke, but their golden softball eyes were on him.

The horse god dreamed he was a man.

He broke himself free of his base and dropped to all fours for the first time in a long time. Over passing eons, his stature had shrunk as his fusion core consumed him, atom by atom, just enough to keep him alive.

Twin ribbons of highway swarmed with cars like beetles, bumper to bumper, all but at a standstill yet all in a hurry, on a schedule. Their noxious exhaust poisoned the air.

White-rimmed eyes gleamed with shock through car windows as he walked down the scrub-crusted hill toward the highway. It was night, but his ruby eyes could see like daylight. He stretched his long-dormant steel muscles, reared, and brought them down onto the roof of the closest SUV, cutting short screams, crushing it. In a creaking, molecular draft, he drew the vehicle's metal into himself. His muscles bulged. His legs lengthened. His fusion core burned hotter. His twin lasers sliced cars and trucks and inhabitants to smoking ribbons.

He strode among the cars, stomping, kicking, blasting—and drawing it all into himself.

In the distance lay the gleaming jewels of the city. Between him and there, an endless ribbon of helpless food.

By the time he reached the sprawling subdivision, he stood two hundred feet tall. The wake of death and destruction behind him was only the beginning. He would not stop until the earth was cleansed of these locusts. He would destroy, and he would consume, and he would grow, and nothing would be able to stop him. When it was finished, he would wait for the next form of life to emerge from muck or burrow and ascend to sentience.

He looked down on the familiar house, its familiar yard. With both front hooves, he flattened his house like a cereal box.

And it was good.

THE DEVOURER

by Sean Eads and Joshua Viola

I SCORN MOST TECHNOLOGY, but there's a mobile phone that's always in my possession. The phone itself has gone through several iterations, advancing with the times, but the number has never changed. In the year after Denver International Airport opened and I got hired as an earnest and very thorough baggage handler, it was a Motorola StarTAC. Now it's a Samsung Galaxy S20. Learning the number meant final initiation into the League. Most who knew it are now dead.

The number has been used six times since 1995. The first five calls alerted me to failure after failure. The sixth came fifteen minutes ago and seemed a spam text at first glance, but a nagging intuition forced me to open it. I found an image, a monstrous, crowned creature mounted on a blue steed with flaming red eyes, galloping across the cosmos.

Below the photo were these words—

> *A dying star is a beautiful and petulant thing,*
> *lashing out at the great, unfeeling chill of the Universe.*
> *Behold the Devourer of Stars.*

"Aiden?"

Gillespie had arrived at my office, his youthful face flushed from rushing across the vast length of the airport to reach me in the administrative building. He was supposed to be at the Southwest ticket counter. I hadn't summoned him, but he must have sensed my psychic distress.

I motioned him inside. He came forward with his head cocked to the right, his eyebrows knitted. Not yet thirty, he had more courage and brashness than so many people I'd trained and brought into the League over the centuries. He would have been in the upper echelon of our noble order. Instead, now, he was the whole of the League other than myself.

"I'm sorry to abandon my post," Gil said, his Southern accent defeating any sense of urgency. "I felt a chill in my mind, like you were in trouble."

"You felt my terror."

His lips pressed tight. Even now his loyalty was so great he couldn't abide the idea of me being afraid despite my admission.

I held up the phone to him.

"What does it mean?" he said.

"It means that McGann has passed the Scepter of Mordescar through the interdimensional portal."

"That can't be true! No one knew where it was. Even you couldn't locate it."

"Any lost thing can be found given enough time, Gil. All shadows yield their secrets with patience. *Sol omnibus lucet*—even its greatest enemies. I've been such a fool."

"*You* have?"

"To let the League dwindle to the two of us."

I realized the remark stung Gil and added, "That's no criticism of your capabilities. If I had a hundred more like you, the League would know an ascendancy unseen in a thousand years. You easily pass muster."

"Thank you, Aiden."

If only all possible recruits could have been as good. As the League's founder, only I identified potential recruits, sought them out and revealed its mysteries. Somewhere along the way, I'd become too rigid in my requirements, telling myself the need was too great to risk watering down the ranks with substandard recruits. Vacancies went unfilled and became gaping holes in our security. McGann meanwhile swelled his ranks with lackeys and halfwits, prizing obedience over talent.

The strategy had paid off. The last object required to let his vile god pass into our universe had been secured and taken through the portal. The message on my phone was nothing less than gloating. He did not taunt without reason.

"I'm sure I would have felt the Scepter's presence long before it was brought into the airport. I wonder how it was disguised."

"It hardly matters now."

A familiar, hated voice chimed from the doorway. "You're so right, my brother. It does not matter. Nothing does now."

McGann pushed my office door open. Like myself, he looked to be no more than forty, though you could find accurate depictions of him in the Flammarion engraving and in many German woodcuts of esoteric knowledge.

"Bold or foolish of you to leave the door open," he said.

"I have far better defenses than a flimsy door."

"I would be disappointed if you didn't," he said, stepping inside.

Gil took an aggressive stance, adopting a posture almost akin to the martial arts. Globes of light encircled his fists and made him appear to have torches for hands. His eyes blazed yellow.

McGann clapped in delight. "Loyal pup! But this is a family dispute. You don't belong here."

"I will protect my teacher!"

"Would you burn the entire building to the ground to have a go at me, young one?"

"Take him at his word, McGann," I said. "No one's spoiling for a fight more than a young Mississippi mystic."

McGann's eyes shot back and forth between us. He smiled. "Be at peace. As I said, this is a family dispute. I only came to review a lengthy past, as one does when the time for obituaries is at hand."

"You gave up any claims to be my brother the day you forsook our god."

"The only obituary getting written here is yours," Gil said.

Gil's face showed a furious desire for battle that needed to be checked—for the moment. I pressed down against his right forearm and he relented. The light ebbed into his pores.

As it did, a commotion sounded from the hallway outside my office. I saw many people gathering there, dressed in their various disguises as airport workers. A passerby might wonder what had brought together such an assortment of baggage handlers, janitors, ramp agents, shuttle drivers and one air traffic controller together outside the office of the airport's chief security officer. All McGann's henchmen, all dedicated to smuggling a series of powerful relics into the airport and the interdimensional portal it had been built upon.

McGann smiled and turned away, walking toward his minions with his hands outstretched in victory. Gil nudged me and whispered, "His back's to us. I've got no problems fighting dirty. You sure you don't want me to try and take out as many as I can?"

Before I could answer, something beyond my office's spacious window caught my eye. Looking west toward the mountains, I saw cars coming and going from the terminal, following a path that wrapped around a 32-foot-tall statue of a blue mustang rearing back in a dark fury, with eyes that glittered brimstone-red. *Blucifer.* DIA's towering mascot, strange and perplexing to the untutored eye, always seemed like an unnatural creation to me. Perhaps it was the positioning of the horse's forelegs, suggestive of the predatory grasp of a praying mantis.

The statue stood almost two miles away from my office and yet its size felt undiminished. Just now, the statue seemed to quiver. An unmistakable ripple passed through its fiberglass body, like earthworms thrashing beneath the thinnest layer of soil.

I brought up my phone until the screen was even with the window. I looked back and forth between the image in the text message and the quickening statue.

"Great and dear friends," McGann shouted, beckoning his people

toward him. "My long struggle nears its end. It will conclude thanks to your dedication. The Devourer is coming!"

And Blucifer will be its steed, I thought. The full weight of my failure bore down upon my shoulders. I shouted and threw the phone with enough force to shatter the window's thick glass. The drone of plane engines filled my office. I heard it as an inhuman roar across the sky.

Gil raised his hands, ready to unleash a blazing fury. "For the eternal sun!"

Once again, I stopped him, forcing his arms down. McGann and his followers offered us ridicule, but there was no point in dying when cleverness still had some currency.

"You've been trying to free the Devourer for a millennia, and my League has countered every effort."

"Your so-called League is down to yourself and an adolescent admirer," McGann said. I clenched Gil's shoulders to keep him in check when everyone laughed.

"Yours is a legacy of failure," I said. "We both know the Scepter was the last object the Devourer needed to come into this universe to feast. Appetites of that nature never savor anything, nor do gluttons delay. Yet look outside. The sun, the great intelligence and influence, *my* god, still holds court with unvanquished splendor. You say the Devourer consumes stars, but I say it is nothing more than a shadow the sunlight will destroy!"

Extended blasts of bravado and blasphemy make a powerful cannonade against those whose faith isn't as strong as it seems. The effect on McGann's followers proved immediate. The glee turned into puzzled looks. Questioning glances lanced at him and doubt pushed eyebrows up to maximum heights. Gil likewise seemed relieved, hopeful that I'd deceived McGann with some masterpiece of trickery, perhaps forging a fake scepter just to delude my brother into a false hope.

In truth, the only false hope resided in my chest—

Because outside the window, Blucifer's statue continued to enliven. I guessed it would become fully fleshed, wholly monstrous once the Devourer crossed dimensions and arrived to claim the blue demon for its steed.

But there might still be a few desperate minutes left to prevent that crossing from occurring.

"Tempus suorum est solis!" I shouted, and the room shook. I threw Gil to the ground and joined him there as thousands of razor-sharp sunbeams filled the room, carving up furniture and flesh with no discrimination. I crawled for the door, pulling Gil with me as McGann's disciples shrieked out their final breaths. How I yearned to hear my brother's voice among the agonized, but instead I heard the sound of shattering glass, and without looking back, I knew McGann had seized on the hole the phone had put in the window with a headfirst dive. He alone could survive such a brutal escape, although a few stragglers somehow managed to follow him.

We escaped the office. I kicked the door shut and touched the knob, allowing a bit of power to leave my fingertips and make the metal as hot as a broiler. If there remained anyone in the office still capable of trailing us, their flesh would melt into their bones like wax as soon as they touched the knob.

"What now, Aiden? Do we fight the Devourer?"

"No. Since McGann gathered everyone to gloat, that means the portal will be unguarded. Ask no questions. Just follow."

His eyes flared with righteous duty.

We ran from the office building and hurried to the terminal, sprinting through the baggage claim area no doubt looking as mad as we felt. There was a steel door in the wall with no knob or handle of any sort. The electronic keypad on the wall to the right was just for show. I touched my hand to the door and said, *"Yield."* The door swung inward and I motioned Gil to enter. I heard my name shouted from across the terminal. It was McGann, bloodied and grinning, shards of glass and small pebbles embedded in his skin like some pearl-encrusted brocade.

"I know what you seek to do. Go ahead. You have my blessing and my goodbye."

I shook my head, as close to feeling defeated by his madness as I'd ever come. Then I pulled the door behind me, stretched forth my hand and said, "I bind you in place with the last breath of my body. You do not open again until that moment comes."

Gil and I pushed ahead down a dim corridor of unfinished rock walls. Electric light gave way to ancient, imperishable torches. We moved forward, Gil now in the lead, moving down a steepening, winding path that eventually led to a place where our next footfalls plunged us down into a chasm. The descent never failed to spark a thrill of fear in me, the sense that I might fall forever, or hit the ground with enough force to pulverize every bone. But then a light appeared, blue, flickering like flame. It grew below our feet, stopping our momentum and we touched down with the delicacy of a feather on solid ground.

We stood at the edge of a room ringed with standing stones some twenty feet high, a fair approximation of Stonehenge, though in reality far older. The blue light emanated from the middle of the structures.

"If only I could have stopped them from taking the Scepter through the portal. I'm sorry I failed, Aiden."

"Any failure is mine," I said. "My brother has spent centuries dreaming of the Devourer, dreaming and scheming. It was inevitable one of his plans would reach fruition. Maybe this world's fate was sealed the moment the cornerstone for Denver International Airport was laid, and the portal between dimensions was reestablished."

"Nothing's sealed. You wouldn't be down here if that's what you thought."

I squared my shoulders. "You're right. We must try to bring back the Scepter or one of the other five objects that makes the Devourer's transit possible. If we can wrest even one of those objects free and return it to our dimension, the Devourer will be forced back and restrained on its side of the portal."

"I just wish there were a couple hundred other people to make the trip with us, the way you described the League in some of your stories. I'd have liked to fight like that, in an army."

"Perhaps," I said. "But in the end, after all the noble souls I've known, I can think of none I'd rather stand shoulder-to-shoulder with than you."

Gil raised his hands. The flames of power engulfed them, and we walked into the portal together.

A flash of light later, we found ourselves in a place so dark anyone would have thought it an empty void except for the ground beneath our feet.

Gil stepped forward, his hands held out like beacons. The light from his body expanded across the cold plane, revealing strewn boulders encrusted with icy lichen plastered against their rocky surfaces.

"Do not be frightened of the path before us, Gil. Imagine our noble god is burning and blazing in your heart, and you'll be strengthened."

"Where do we go now?"

"That way," I said, pointing and stepping ahead of him.

"I didn't realize you've been through the portal before."

"Not this one," I said. There had been five known portals the League and I had contrived to close. Leave it to my brother to discover how to open a sixth. By that time, the League had already diminished to the point where we lacked the strength to seal it. We hadn't dare attempt what I was doing now.

"But I have been to this realm a few times. Those who accompanied me are long dead. This world was different then. Not so unlike our own. There was once an uncountable number of stars in the sky."

"The Devourer ate them all?"

"Yes."

"How long did that take?"

"It is hard to say. Time does not move the same here as it does in our dimension. It's been two hundred years since I last set foot here, and even then, you could still see a few pinpoints of light."

The dim outline of a building emerged before us; a crude represen-

tation of Denver International Airport rendered in stone—though it was more accurate to say the airport was a reproduction of this desolate temple. We entered through an unsealed opening so broad ten men could have passed standing side by side.

"This almost looks like the baggage claim area at DIA," Gil said.

"Keep a notion of the airport's layout in your mind, and imagine we're going to Concourse C. That will deliver us to the Devourer's throne room. We'll find the objects we seek there."

"Unguarded?"

"Who would be here to guard anything?"

"So the Devourer has no servants? No soldiers?"

"An entity that consumes stars needs little in the way of an army."

"But it wasn't always so," Gil said.

I smiled at his intuition and insight. "What makes you say that?"

"This temple. This palace. Someone built it. There's a reason behind it." We continued down a long flight of steps, almost identical to the airport escalators that lead to the security gates. "You perceive the Devourer's single-minded hunger, its exponential growth. It begins as a simple desire for adulation, a thirst to be admired. Then mere admiration isn't enough, and worship is required. Temples must be built to its deification. But the hunger keeps growing until no amount of flesh or emotion can satisfy it. Eventually only the stars will do."

"Why the hell would anyone worship such a creature? Doesn't your brother realize he's dooming himself?"

"Insanity is a hunger as well, Gil. It feasts upon absurdity."

He seemed to accept this idea, just as so many past League members had when they finally learned McGann's true identity. It was close enough to the truth. I'd never told anyone the story of the two of us on our knees,

282 SEAN EADS AND JOSHUA VIOLA

naked, bowing our foreheads to the ground to offer our broad backs to the summer sun. How our god cooked us that day and every day, as if we were lambs thrown into fire for a burnt offering. After lying prostrate for hours, until it seemed every drop of moisture had been wrung out of us, we rose and stared into the face of the sun until we were blinded. This was a daily ritual performed more years than I could remember. Sometimes my brother believed the blindness was permanent and I had to scold him, reminding him how our god always restored our sight by nightfall, when we'd see each other as if for the first time and smile in recognition and understanding. But that morning, he broke his pose early. I saw his mouth open and his eyes were fixed on another part of the sky.

It would be many years before I realized that was the moment the Devourer made contact with my brother, and it looked through his eyes, finding our sun hanging overhead like a succulent orange it could stretch forth its hand and pluck.

We reached the throne room, another place of vast cold emptiness. In the airport, Concourse C ended at Gate 50. That was the analogous location of the Devourer's throne here.

I saw a figure occupying it as we arrived.

McGann.

"How?"

"Did you think an enchanted door would hold me? Did you think I didn't know you'd try this gambit? But the artifacts are not here."

"You wouldn't be here if that were true."

"Oh, my brother—"

"Don't call me that. This man is more brother to me than you could ever be."

Gil stepped forward to stand beside me.

"The sun has left you blind, brother. Leave this misfit and come to me. Stand at the right side of this throne."

"And do what? Dwell in the darkness?"

"The Devourer will show you darkness is its own illumination and wisdom."

The remark might have been a taunt, except for the terrible earnestness in his tone. My poor lost, deluded brother. Even now I found myself

wanting to reach out to him, wanting to save him from his madness. But then my thoughts fixed on something he'd said earlier. *The artifacts are not here.* He wasn't lying. There was supposed to be a fixed place around the throne for each of the necessary objects. A stanchion to hold the Torch of Evermore. A delicate neck of stone to wear the Amulet of Night, an obsidian jewel. The Scepter of Mordescar should have been standing upright, mounted into a depression on the throne's right armrest. The Crown of Althamar was not present either, nor the two Rubies of Twilight, the first artifacts known to have passed through the portal just after the airport's completion.

But if they weren't here, where were they?

The pondering distracted me from realizing Gil had again reached his breaking point. The young mage let loose a torrent of energy, a blast of rage that struck McGann in the chest and threatened to shatter the throne itself. Few men could have withstood the power of his attack, but my brother belonged to that rare company.

I lunged forward as he counter-attacked, determined to absorb the black energy pouring from my brother's fingertips. If Gil had retreated even a few feet, it might have worked, but he hadn't backed down and I arrived too late. Gil screamed. The grim darkness enveloped him like a skin of tar, streaming up his nose and filling his mouth. The globes of energy around his fists flared once—and faded. He fell flat on his back, arms at his sides, his fingers relaxing in the slackness of death.

I bent to close Gil's eyes, as I'd closed the lids of so many League members over the centuries. My brother laughed, and I jumped up and unleashed a thousand years of pent-up fury. My cells drank deep from the great flowing waterfall of the sun's light, and the stored power surged through me. I'd never allowed the fullness of my god's majesty to show, selfishly fearful that doing so might reduce my body to ash. That was now my intent for my brother. He met my light with a wall of darkness that had all the efficacy of dried leaves. I pressed toward him, imagining him as melting wax.

The light from my pores swept forward to reveal the long unseen throne room walls. I discovered the same engraved image repeated everywhere. Its prominence, the sheer vanity of the repetition, told me it must be the true image of the Devourer. Until the text message showing the crowned figure astride Blucifer, I'd never had an inkling of the Devourer's form. I'd refused to let my mind stray toward such dark imaginings.

What I saw engraved on the walls was not the same figure from the text message, and the jolt of realization brought my attack to a standstill. My brother staggered and swayed on his feet.

"Clever bastard," I whispered.

"You've only just realized?"

"I've never doubted your intelligence, only lamented it must be yoked to the sickness in your soul. But I would never conceive of such an elaborate ruse."

My brother gave the slightest bow, supporting himself with one hand on the arm of the throne. He was recovering fast and wouldn't need the crutch for long.

"Even my lieutenants thought they were bringing the sacred objects to the Devourer through the portal," he said. "The intensity of their beliefs fueled your own. While you kept your attention fixed on the portal, the Devourer's avatar was built and established under the very eyes of your impotent god. You cannot conceive of the fitful sleep the Devourer has endured inside that framework of fiberglass and metal while I, his devout servant, secured the objects needed to awaken him."

"Which you installed in the statue itself?"

"Starting with the Rubies of Twilight. A dangerous gambit. I thought you of all people might detect them glowing red in the statue's eyes. They are much brighter than the light bulbs they replaced. Your obliviousness almost offends me, brother. It makes me wonder if perhaps your devotion to the sun is not as strong as you claim."

My brother's hopefulness sounded genuine, and I seized upon an idea

even more desperate than coming through the portal itself.

"Eos qui adorant solem," I began.

"Get burned! *Yes!* I knew in your heart you doubted. I knew your soul had wearied and yearned to join me. This is the time, brother. Now, at the hour of triumph, let us watch the true god devour the false!"

He pulled me into an embrace. The sensation of when we worshipped together and roamed among our livestock at the summer solstice to select the very best animals for sacrifice flowed through me. Fellowship—brotherhood.

I returned the hug. "Let us go then."

We left the temple together, moving through the portal and returning to the bowels of Denver International Airport. Even this far below the surface, I felt a concussive shaking, like the steady beat of a mallet striking the earth.

"The Devourer! He prances in victory under the baleful watch of the false god!"

I grabbed my brother's arm, instinctively determined to reason with him one last time. The crazed brightness in his eyes reminded me of the futility, and I resumed my original plan.

"I'm sorry I was such a fool. Had I not opposed you, this moment could have come centuries ago."

"None of that matters," he said. "We're together."

He led me onward, and we exited into a devastated East Terminal. A portion of the high peaked ceiling had collapsed, and the signature fabric roof swung in tatters. Bloody bodies were sprawled everywhere, victims of falling debris. Thousands of people typically moved through the terminal at this time of day, but I saw perhaps two hundred survivors cowering in corners, with mothers and fathers throwing themselves over their children.

One woman stacked several suitcases around her into a makeshift pillbox and knelt inside it, praying.

A terrifying growl sounded overhead, like nothing a horse or any other animal bred of this Earth could make. I stared through the ruined ceiling, my spirits buoyed by the flash of sunlight overhead. Then Blucifer's head eclipsed it.

The statue's size appeared to have doubled, and growing larger by the minute. What were the Devourer's dimensions in its own realm? Was there a limit to how large it could become? Would it grow and grow until the Earth itself was just a bit of dust under its hooves as it grazed on galaxies?

The statue's unexpected growth sent shockwaves of fresh despair through my thoughts. My final plan couldn't begin to work now. How could I ever hope to scale such heights?

Then Blucifer's head shifted to the right, and the sun blazed forth again. The rays struck me, nourished and rallied me. For a moment, it seemed I might climb up to the Devourer's head on a staircase of sunlight. Those blazing crimson eyes glared down and my brother dropped to his knees and raised his arms in supplication. He launched into a series of babbled prayers and did not notice me moving away, quietly at first and then making a dash across the terminal to the lowest piece of torn fabric I could find.

Seizing it, I climbed, hand over hand, teeth gnashing whenever the cloth threatened to tear away completely. Like a slender, vining plant pushing itself higher and higher on a trellis of sunbeams, I reached the ceiling and inched along the precarious support structure toward the opening through which the Devourer's head now poked down into the terminal. My brother remained on his knees, his prayerful chants rising to reach me. As I got to the top of the ceiling, the Devourer dipped its massive muzzle down and opened its icy blue jaws to receive those too terrified to flee.

I flung myself onto the Devourer's neck and tried to find any place to cling to. Its skin was still transforming, a hybrid of slick fiberglass and coarse blue mane coming through blistered, weeping flesh. I grabbed a handful of bristling hair and clutched it with all my remaining strength as

the Devourer sensed me and reared back, its forelegs suddenly slashing the air, an exact replica of the statue's original pose.

"No," I said, almost snarling. For as terrifying as the Devourer's size and fury were, what I felt most was the blazing hot sunlight beating down on my back, refueling me and reminding me that I was its champion. As the Devourer bucked again and again, I scaled its neck. The Devourer's legs crashed through more parts of the airport, its hooves bulldozing concrete and steel with the ease of a child kicking down a sandcastle.

I reached its right ear. "All your strength, all your appetite, and yet you are helpless," I said. "The whole universe is at your feet—or would be, but for the want of hands!"

I leapt forward onto the expanse of the Devourer's muzzle. Its eyes blazed in bloody fury. This close, I could see the Rubies of Twilight lodged in each socket. The left ruby was enfleshed, wet and patterned with pulsing blood vessels. But the right ruby was not yet incorporated into the body. I had this single chance. With no tools to dislodge it other than my fingers and faith in my god, I threw myself into the right eye and once more let the sunlight within me burst forth. The Devourer answered with a piteous sound that echoed across the plains to the east and the mountains in the west. The snow on those distant peaks began to slide, turning the land-scape into a series of simultaneous avalanches.

The Devourer shook its head and reared back again and again as I felt along the edge of the ruby, trying to pry my fingers under any crevice. The impact of the stomping hooves threw me away from the eye and I scrambled for a new grip. It dipped its head and I slid down the length of its muzzle. A long tongue darted from the mouth and tried to swipe at my legs.

I kicked, digging in and clawing upward. The sunlight buoyed me and

I reached the eye once more. I gripped the edge of the ruby with both hands, pried and pulled.

The gemstone surrendered by fractions. I strained and cursed in languages I hadn't otherwise spoken in centuries. Then, suddenly, the ruby was free and in my grasp. The consequences of its removal came swift. The Devourer rose onto its hind legs, but its muscles stiffened. The skin changed, losing any sense of true flesh, reverting to fiberglass beneath my fingertips. Whatever bones it had returned to its original frame, too small to support the towering height the statue now reached. It toppled forward and I had no choice but to ride it down. The impact shattered the fiberglass and the head broke apart midway at the neck. The Devourer, still locked within the statue, was now hopelessly fragmented, and I lay in his ruin.

My brother's weak voice whispered my name. He hadn't tried to escape the Devourer's pounding hooves, refusing to break his prayers even as their stomping broke his bones. As I knelt beside him, it seemed he clung to life long enough to see me with clear eyes. He could no longer speak, but his gaze communicated what was important. He was free of the Devourer.

I raised my head skyward and commended his spirit to the sun.

ANOTHER COLD NIGHT IN DENVER

by Stephen Graham Jones

T HE BAND WASN'T OFFICIALLY BROKEN UP, we were just on hiatus until
Jeff came back from whoever he was shacked up with for the week—
nothing new for him. But we weren't broken up, hadn't even really done
our first gig. Officially, when asked about this around Denver, we were
still in the guerrilla marketing phase. In a documentary Jeff had seen, a
big part of being a hair band on the Sunset Strip back when had been
pounding the pavement in the bright-bright sun, and putting up flyers on
top of all the *other* hair bands' flyers.

We weren't all hair spray and tights, of course, but the promotion game
wasn't that different all these years later, and all these miles east of LA.
Just, it wasn't flyers anymore—flyers escape their staples, blow away, and
Colorado's all about staying beautiful.

The game now was stickers. Stickers don't blow away.

Using Jeff's mom's credit card on the sly, we'd had fifteen hundred of
them printed up. Little palm-sized ovals with a nice distinctive red border,
"JFC" big and bold in the middle, a combination of my name and Jeff's
and our drummer Chris's. Name-recognition is fifty percent of the game,
so why not choose a set of initials already in everybody's mouth, right?
Right.

We each got five hundred, on the guarantee that inside a week, we wouldn't have even a single one left. Granted, we each slapped the first few on our own rear windows, on guitar cases and drum kits, and we probably burned through fifty each in the tight bathrooms of all the bars we moved through. It became kind of a race, too. I tagged the grimy mirror at Three Kings only to see "JFC" at eye-level on the backside of the door, two steps later.

We were having to get creative, I mean.

I called Jeff to see when we were practicing again, but, instead of getting dumped to his flip-phone's voicemail, I got the "service disconnected" that happened to him about every six weeks, meaning, probably, that his mom had seen that printing-charge on her credit card statement.

I ran into Chris way down in Stapleton, at Gina's aunt's place, and he was too far into whatever he'd drank or swallowed or smoked to make sense of my question about Jeff, much less answer it, so I kept moving, ended up training three cigarettes in a row around the side of the house, so as to be away from the group carousing on the front porch, the crew waxing nostalgic on the back.

"JFC?" a girl's voice asked from the darkness, a moment before she inhaled on her cigarette, the glow from that cherry showing the outline of her features. A spike of fear jammed into my chest at first, because I was eighty percent sure she was Jeff's last shack-up, but then she exhaled over her shoulder, stepped in to lean against the brick with me.

"How do you—?" I started, and then remembered halfway through: I had one of the stickers on my forehead. It had been hilarious, half an hour ago.

I peeled it from my skin, careful not to tear the paper, and stuck it on a tree limb stretching out before both of us, that I'd been planning to crush my last cigarette out on.

The girl chuckled, looked down, and I knew I was just another idiot to her.

Fine.

Maybe she was looking for an idiot, right?

"Our lead singer covered his shoes in them," I offered, sort of as defense, or to be not the most ridiculous member of the band.

"To keep his shoes together?" the girl asked.

I had to grin: maybe she *did* know Jeff.

"It's a good name for a band," she said, crushing her cigarette out right beside the sticker, like grinding a full stop in after it, which I also assumed to be the end of whatever moment away from the world we were sharing here.

"'*JFC*,'" I said, trying to emphasize it the way Jeff did in practice in my dad's garage, when we were imagining a sea of insane fans fanned out before us, farther back than we could see.

"When I was in high school," she started off, and I snuck a look over, judged her to be maybe two years graduated, max, a freshman when I'd been a senior, "my boyfriend told me that there's like a shrine for band stickers."

"Men's room or women's?" I asked.

"Look straight up, you might see some blue balls," she said with a halfway shrug, pushing away from the wall, catching my eyes for a flash.

She was maybe four steps past me, rounding the front of the house but not for the party, I didn't think, but somewhere else, before it clicked for me: "The horse?"

This stopped her but she didn't turn around, quite. Just spoke loud enough I could still hear her: "Its hooves, yeah. Airport groundskeepers try to scrape it clean, there's a little fence there sometimes, so...you know. It's an adventure, too. A challenge."

"Your boyfriend?" I asked.

"His band broke up," she said, quieter, and then was walking up the pale driveway, her hands balled in her pockets against the chill in the air, her low boots not tall enough for the snowdrift she stepped into, but whatever.

After she was gone, I smoked a fourth cigarette and considered my options: front porch, back porch, or skulk through all the bars of Denver for a couple more hours, a peeled sticker palmed to slap on brass rails, or those little plastic windows on the flappy doors into kitchens, or the bumpers of all the jacked-up trucks.

Or, I could go for the grail, right? This so-called shrine.

No way would Jeff or Chris have beat me out to the airport.

I borrowed Chris's car—like he was even capable of remembering who he was passing his keys up to—gassed it up with my last seven dollars. Two hours later—two hours and three beers—that big blue horse's red eyes rolled up through the windshield.

Would it really have balls, or had the girl been joking?

Because Chris didn't need his car impounded, and because of course there was no visitor parking, I found a shallow turnout a mile back, eased over into the ditch as deep as I thought I could and still climb out.

Stepping out, I rounded to the trunk to case the lightpoles, see if any of them had cameras hanging—I'm not a terrorist, I promise I'm not a terrorist—and when it seemed safe, I walked up through the tire's sloshy tracks, and the clean snow to either side of them, clean but crusted hard on top, with a kind of brown grime, made me remember when I'd walked down Gina's aunt's driveway, my hands balled in my pockets the same as the girl's had been. I'd even turned the way she had, planning to step into the holes in the snow she'd made, but…there weren't any?

Was I remembering right?

What, had she been an elf, could she walk on *top* of the snow?

I chuckled to myself, shook my head, wondered how I'd made it this long, thinking ridiculous thoughts like this.

Next I'd be making her out to be the house party version of the vanishing hitchhiker.

I hunched my shoulders against the cold—it had to be freezing already—got a smoke going strictly for warmth, and trudged the mile or so up the ditch, that horse glaring down at me the whole time, like daring me to take even one step more.

I took one and then a thousand steps more. And that big blue horse never looked away.

Whatever its story was, I didn't know, and didn't care. Maybe it was

a memorial for some horse slaughter, or maybe some dad made it for his daughter, who had loved ponies. Or maybe it had been there when Denver was just a few ramshackle buildings. Probably it was just a bad idea somebody had, once—oh, wait. The football team, right? How could I forget them. Talking shrines, my dad had made our house *into* one for them. Was this what the horse meant? Was it supposed to intimidate rival teams on their way in from the airport, or slash its hooves at them on the way out?

I hoped not. If the horse was a bronco, then count this band sticker out, please.

But, too, I'd walked a mile through the cold, the cuffs of my jeans were wet and freezing, and my last cigarette was already gone. I was leaving our band's name on that hoof whether my dad would count me a football fan or not.

I did wonder about those red eyes, though.

Bulbs? Or, was the whole interior of that big metal statue a churning cauldron of flame?

The second, I hoped. Maybe I could warm my hands.

There was a fence, too, just on the other side of the ditch's shallow dip. Just a low one, easy to step over. And this blue horse was *giant*, man. I had to lean back to even see up it, and was close enough now I couldn't quite see the face anymore.

"And she wasn't a ghost," I said out loud to myself, just so it would really set in my mind. Sometimes I get in a rut of thinking, and the only way to break it is by talking to myself.

Why would a ghost at a party tell me about her boyfriend, right? No, if that girl had been a ghost, then…then she'd have wanted me to go with her somewhere, so I could find her killer or finish some business, or she could eat my face, I don't know.

She'd just been some random at a Gina-thing, though. She'd just been mentioning her boyfriend so maybe I wouldn't try some smooth line on her.

The snow away from the road was more virgin, with yellow tufts of grass pushing up between it. I aimed my feet for those tufts, on the idea it might be more solid there, and I kept my numb fingers busy with trying to peel the sticker, so I could slap a big metal hoof and then be gone with my bad self.

It was going to be beautiful when Jeff or Chris waded out here, saw our band's name already there.

At least one of us was committed. At least one of us believed in this band.

Maybe halfway out there, though, I realized I was walking in someone else's foot-holes, and thinned my lips in frustration. But, if this really was a shrine, I told myself, if this was really local legend I was participating in, then…Denver's full of bands, isn't it? Some other idiot, then. Not the idiots I'd been practicing with in my dad's garage.

Still, and not completely on purpose, I cased all around, I guess for that girl off at the edge of where I could see, her short boots balanced on top of the snow. It's not like you don't walk in holes when it's use them or step through crust every step, though.

Ten, twenty seconds later, the snow was misted red.

I swallowed. It was loud in my ears.

I looked up to the horse, but it was just a dumb statue.

"A rabbit," I said out loud. "A rabbit and an owl, a rabbit and a coyote."

Of course. Or maybe a prairie dog, if they ran around in the cold, but that was the same thing, pretty much.

I did go around the blood, though.

A minute after that, back in the foot-holes, my ankle turned on something at the bottom of one of them. The first thing I did was cast around for more blood, but this snow was just that same grimy white.

I nodded that this was good, this was right.

Unless—no.

Unless whoever had been walking here had been snatched up, chewed into thirty feet up in the air, so their blood would fall somewhere behind

me, if the wind had drifted it back that way.

Sometimes I hate having my brain. It comes alive the most when the lights are off, I mean.

I went to take another step, and…that was the last foot-hole?

I pulled my own foot back, stepped down into that last space, and, again, my ankle rolled over from whatever was down there. This time I fell, and, pissed off, I stabbed my hand down to snatch the guilty rock up, fling it out into the darkness.

It was a shoe.

Worse, it was a shoe covered in band stickers. As if the stickers were holding the shoe together.

This is how she knew, I said, inside.

I looked around for Jeff, as this had to be some big joke, but I was alone. So alone.

And—and his shoe, it was…too heavy?

I didn't want to, but I looked in.

His foot.

"JFC, man!" I said, shaking my head no, and only looked up when I heard the creaking: before, I'd been too close to see the horse's long face anymore.

Now, both red eyes were staring down at me.

I scrambled back, back, ran, and on the way back up the blacktop, two cars and a bus had to avoid me at the last moment, screeching and honking and flashing their lights, but I didn't care, was mostly running backward, sure I could feel giant hooves in the ground, and, no, the band wasn't officially broken up, then, but we never did get around to our first gig, either.

Some nights, though, I'll still see our sticker in the odd bathroom, peeking out from all the other stickers like a bad memory. Like an almost-was. Like a tombstone. As for the twelve- or thirteen-hundred I still had left that night, I burned them in the garage, and every time Jeff's mom calls looking for him, I don't have any idea where he is, no, sorry, ma'am.

It's the truth, I guess. As much as I can say out loud, anyway.

NUANCE IN AN EXTREME STATE

by John Wenzel

COLORADO'S PUBLIC CULTURE HAS BEEN taking an icy bath. Besides challenging the organizers of StokerCon™ 2021, the coronavirus pandemic drowned major conventions such as Denver Pop Culture Con (formerly Denver Comic Con), StarFest, DiNK, and the planned debut of the Colorado Festival of Horror.

I've been covering this widespread disruption as an arts and entertainment reporter for *The Denver Post*, where I've worked since 2001. Encouragingly, I'm also covering a lot of great writing from Colorado authors and publishing houses, including recent titles from this souvenir-anthology's publisher, Hex. Despite the chaos of the last fourteen months, Colorado authors are still charting and winning praise nationally. Kali Fajardo-Anstine's *New York Times*-approved *Sabrina & Corina*, a finalist for the National Book Award, heralds a career deeply concerned with indigenous and marginalized women, while authors like Jason Heller (a contributor here, and a Hugo-award winning editor who also writes for *NPR* and *The New Yorker*) made good-faith plans to push their 2021 novels, as if the ground beneath them wasn't sublimating from solid rock into vapor. (Heller's *Repeater* drops August 2021 from Simon & Schuster.)

What choice do they have? Faced with externally imposed binaries—subsistence or ruin; science or death-cultism—they've been mining gray areas in harsh lighting. What gives Colorado authors the edge is their shared self-invention amid our state's famous extremes. Here, we feast on poles, synthesizing them in our gut. Witness our smooth plains and sheer mountains; crystalline blue skies and choking wildfire haze; cattle ranching and voter-approved wolves; rich white folks being served by poor brown folks who can't afford to live in a ski village; and our pioneering legal cannabis alongside some of the country's most restrictive anti-smoking laws and taxes. Oil and gas helped make modern, booming Denver, as have gentrification and redlining and Chicano activism.

Even as other cultural industries have blurred or faded during the pandemic shutdown, Colorado's literary scene continues to redefine what a state of extremes can mean. My strong but subjective sense of it has been forged over two decades of reviews and features. I've been lucky enough to interview hundreds of local and national authors and journalists who've lived, worked in and passed through Colorado, but also documentary filmmakers, graphic novelists, songwriters, stand-ups, poets, game developers, and even a few horror titans (including *Halloween* director John Carpenter, and some hack named Stephen King, who apparently has a thing for Colorado?).

I'm among a handful of Colorado journalists to whom publishers mail a dozen or so galleys weekly, hoping to woo my quasi-promotional interest or coverage. I pluck the bass in a punk cover band with other Front Range culture writers (Steve Knopper and Rich Bienstock) who have published their own nationally acclaimed books on music. Drinking from the firehose of culture is a privilege and a headache, as are many aspects of my general-assignment arts beat at a daily, mainstream newspaper whose staff has been slashed to ribbons. (I'm the sole remaining arts and entertainment guy at *The Post*. When I started 20 years ago, we had dozens of critics, editors, reporters, designers, and copy editors dedicated to the cause.)

The perks are huge, if you're into them, and necessarily fleeting. I get to see free movies, concerts, stand-up shows, festivals, touring Broadway plays, and more. But I have to write about them, soberly and fairly and accurately, on a deadline. I've been paid to travel the country while reporting stories, but I return to dozens of hours of transcription and fact-checking, arguments with editors, and intense self-loathing and imposter

syndrome (in other words: journalism). During their book and stage tours, I've been lucky enough to interview celebrity authors such as President Jimmy Carter, Gloria Steinem, Neil Gaiman, James Ellroy, Yoko Ono, Dolly Parton, David Sedaris, Joan Rivers, Stan Lee, Anthony Bourdain, Michael Chabon, John Waters, and even a few people under the age of 50—all about the subjects of authorship and identity. I've sat on stage with Dan Rather, Sally Field, former Denver resident Rian Johnson (director of *The Last Jedi* and *Knives Out*), John Leguizamo, and John Cusack to explore how their recent work sharpens or subverts their legacies. Everyone wants to be remembered well, but writers' lives are in constant revision.

I've started and almost immediately stopped reading dozens of Colorado books that arrive on my desk, preferring to let them simmer longer before taking my next bite (self-published or not). I was inspired by an article, and my mentor, Ricardo Baca, to write a nonfiction book called *Mock Stars: Indie Comedy and the Dangerously Funny* (Speck Press/Fulcrum, 2008), which is not very good, but which I enjoyed immensely. I've contributed to nonfiction and satire books along the way while reviewing novels, movies, albums, and video games for national outlets such as *Rolling Stone*, *Esquire*, and *Vulture*. The doorway of any Denver-area classroom that will listen to me has also been darkened, some more than once.

All this is to say: my ass is not the origin point for my thoughts about Colorado writers. I've come to appreciate the state's literary character is rife with horror and speculative fiction, but also historical obsession and nonfiction that builds on the Rocky Mountain region's tradition of frontier and isolation drama, environmental and military intrigue, and apocalyptic/indigenous curses. Those last depictions of Colorado, fleetingly glimpsed or in a starring role, range from *Atlas Shrugged* to *The Shining*, Paolo Bacigalupi's *The Water Knife* to *The Hunger Games*. Something about this state just screams the end of society.

"Over 40 years of popular culture, a lot of people have looked at what's happening on a global scale and extrapolated these disasters that end up mirroring reality," said Boulder novelist Carrie Vaughn, whose 2017 book, *Bannerless*, won the Philip K. Dick award, in a 2020 *Denver Post* interview. "The only thing that hasn't happened yet is zombies, and I'm not going to make any bets against that."

Colorado's list of horror tropes is yellowed. Coming up with something fresh often requires an in-state perspective, lest our horror, fantasy, and sci-fi writers snap into the circular rhythm of delighting in each other's bodily odors. This is why we celebrate Colorado authors and professors such as R. Alan Brooks, whose sci-fi graphic novel *Anguish Garden* garnered both praise and racist death threats for its imaginative, Western take on white supremacy (successfully crowdfunded in 2020).

It's Colorado's stereotypical identity, as defined by outsiders and popular culture, that can't help but intrude on these nuanced takes.

"You can really visualize Colorado when you mention it, even if you've never been here," said Denver author Mario Acevedo (also a contributor to this book), who has written urban-fantasy novels starring werewolves, vampires, and zombies. "We're shorthand for 'mountains,' but also the type of people who tend to live in the mountains. Scrappy people do what it takes to survive."

What floors me is the fearless, aching process of redefinition that Colorado writers have undertaken, embodied ably by this year's souvenir anthology theme. Blucifer, as we've learned, is a glimpse into the motley, kaleidoscopic future of not only Colorado but the West. Identity is less about geography or race, despite Colorado's moon-like isolation and blood-soaked social history. Water availability and air quality are plummeting. Every other state these days boasts craft beer, legal weed, and fancy fitness routines (real or virtual). West Coast yoga-pants culture? Here in the Centennial State, we've got a red-eyed, blue-skinned motherfucking horse sculpture that killed its creator. Take that, Meow Wolf.

Blucifer's iconic, pop-art demonism is of particular interest to me. As conspiracy theories about Denver International Airport have proliferated since its 1995 debut, I've watched airport officials gradually embrace them

as marketing tools—at one point, grabbing what they described to me as "millions of dollars in free publicity." In the fall of 2016, I endured a couple weeks of security checks to take a behind-the-scenes, underground and on-the-tarmac tour of Denver International Airport for a *Denver Post* article that tried to investigate these conspiracy theories. With almost zero promotion since then, it remains at the top of my weekly pageview report among my thousands of published stories, thanks in part to Google SEO and partly to our apparently Roman appetite for shit that's obviously and hilariously fake (spoiler alert: I debunked all the theories, but airport officials are likely thrilled when they distract from all of DIA's chronic, real-life financial troubles, as they continue to do).

Watching Blucifer eternally rear up to expose his monstrous, veinous, anatomically correct torso, I can't help but think he's doing so at the crowded intersection of various early 21st-century trends. They were foreseen in some ways by his frequently misunderstood creator, Luis Jiménez, but also by the public artists that have captured Denver's imagination with big blue bears, dick-shaped piles of dicks (a.k.a. *National Velvet*) and an exponentially variegating mural and street-art culture. Aesthetically, Blucifer's popularity—in ad campaigns, but also in clickbait articles, and on album covers, bumper stickers, T-shirts, and coffee mugs—grafts the public-art branding that's been so important to Denver's tourism onto the ambling zombie of Western expansion and blithe, capitalistic frontierism. He's a nexus of what Colorado was, is, and will be.

Airport officials never mention the not-so-fun-to-talk-about-in-interviews Nazi runway conspiracy theory, in which DIA's runways are said to be arranged like a swastika when viewed from a few thousand feet up (also untrue, and owing to takeoff and wind patterns). Perhaps not all conspiracy theories are fun and harmless investment pitches? Perhaps the malignant narcissist we voted out last year wasn't a bruise, but rather a growth on our body? Colorado's history as a state is dark: Native American massacres and mining-camp slaughters; pioneer cannibalism; Japanese internment during World War II; the Ku Klux Klan ruling Denver government for a good chunk of the early 20th century; and anti-LGBTQ legislation that compelled big names like Madonna and Elton John to boycott the state in the 1990s. The toll exacted on everyone but white men (and even a few of them, as it turns out) in the building of Colorado's mineral wealth is steep, and gory.

The good news is that Colorado's literary scene, in the past dominated by writers such as Kent Haruf, Clive Cussler, and adopted son Louis L'Amour, is more diverse and interesting than ever thanks to groups such as Lighthouse Writers Workshop, all-ages art and community spaces, and an increasing number of virtual student-writing groups. Writers who create work in and about Colorado are a self-selecting class to some extent, given the regular influx of transplants (I moved out here from Ohio in 2000, about a year after college, and have never considered living anywhere else). In interviews, Colorado writers—natives, transplants, prodigal offspring have dubbed themselves army brats and cholos; ski bums turned conservationists; nervy gutter punks; street artists and memoirists; professors who love hip-hop and fly fishing; radical-queer revolutionaries; Spanish-speakers whose families have lived here since Colorado was Mexican territory; and Native American tribal elders whose art and heritage are still being abused.

Do these things exist outside of Colorado? Certainly. But there's a stunning clarity of vision here (apologies to altitude metaphors) and an adrenalized grit that extends beyond "taming" the landscape or its inhabitants. The best work I've read and experienced from Colorado writers and artists seems to start with questions like, "How can I keep the reader as tortured as I when was wrestling with this idea all night?"

It makes me want to work harder as a journalist, to recognize my privilege as a straight white guy who got into print journalism just as the internet was blowtorching our business model. As I wrote in a protest-commentary for *The Atlantic* in May 2018, I fear jobs like mine won't exist much longer, and that means one less writer to trumpet the work of the rapidly evolving

Colorado arts scene. *The Denver Post* is owned by Alden Global Capital, a hedge fund that has hacked away at not only its fat but its muscle and bone, while also treating us as an organ donor for its other schemes. Its relentless "value extraction" from *The Post*—an otherwise healthy, successful daily newspaper in an industry where that's rare—made national headlines when former op-ed editor Chuck Plunkett rebelled against our ownership in print. (And, to a much lesser extent, when I've been quoted in *The New York Times*, *Esquire*, and other outlets during our union protests, which continue to this day). I'm not exaggerating when I say I've risked my job to advocate for responsible ownership at *The Denver Post* over the last decade. I'm among dozens at *The Post*.

As social media commenters like to remind me, critics don't know shit and the media (as in, ALL media, since we secretly group-think our stories every day) is full of lies. I don't discount their anger. In 2020, everything let us down spectacularly, not the least of which were traditional news-media gatekeepers who continue to reinforce corporate hegemony, white supremacy, and mindless consumerism. But in addition to privilege and ego and a lot of factual corrections, my career has been shaped by the creative tenor of Colorado's writers and artists. Falling prey to reductive, either/or thinking is part of the problem here.

Whatever the rest of this decade looks like, its outset has laid bare the values and will of huge swaths of U.S. citizens, rather terrifyingly. Being a journalist in the 2020s is masochistic. But when all major media and publishing is consolidated on the coasts; when I'm burned out and disgusted with journalism and ready to sell my soul to public relations; when *The Denver Post* publishes its last print edition—maybe then I'll step back. Until then, getting paid to think and write about the spectrum of creative people living, working, and passing through Colorado for the last two decades has been my dream job.

As long as Colorado can host these varied perspectives—not simply the extremes, but the connections between the borders of Kansas and Utah, or even Pueblo and Boulder—I want to be here. Our growing horror scene, with fiction, film festivals, and cultural conventions, is worth celebrating when it justifies events such as StokerCon™ 2021, and guests of honor including Maurice Broaddus, Joe R. Lansdale, Seanan McGuire, Silvia Moreno-Garcia, Lisa Morton, and Colorado's own Steve Rasnic Tem.

Fortunately, this book is not quite so temporary as a weekend convention. It's allowed us to share (mostly) original fiction from fantastic Colorado writers JoAnn Chaney, Sam Knight, Angie Hodapp, Molly Tanzer, Joshua Viola and Sean Eads, Warren Hammond, Stephen Graham Jones, Travis Heermann, and the aforementioned Acevedo and Heller. I also greatly enjoyed (and felt slightly smarter after reading) essays and interviews by Carter Wilson, Hillary Dodge, the Denver Horror Collective, Alvaro Zinos-Amaro, Hex's own Dean Wyant, Bret Smith, Jeanni Smith, Carina Bissett, and Jeanne Stein. You'd think a journalist like me would have known all this stuff. No matter how long I live in Colorado, I'm still catching up.

HEX APPEAL

by Dean Wyant

I WAS WORKING IN DENVER at the Broadway Book Mall's front desk one day in early 2014, when Joshua Viola came in carrying a heavy cardboard box on his shoulder. Nothing too unusual: people come to the store all the time with books to donate or exchange. Sometimes writers approach us hoping to sell their latest publication. Josh fell into the latter category, but he was an author unlike any I'd met. I didn't realize it at the time, but this meeting was going to be life-changing. That's not an exaggeration. You see, Josh's box didn't just carry his first novel, an ultra-violent creature feature called *The Bane of Yoto*. It included *merchandise*—Yoto T-shirts, Yoto bookmarks, even Yoto action figures. I was impressed, to say the least, with both the quality of the products and Josh himself. He was friendly and personable, and I was happy to be his first customer, snapping up a couple of T-shirts. Then I had him sign one of the action figures and, of course, a copy of the novel.

We talked books for quite a while, and by the time he left the store, we swapped phone numbers and agreed to stay in touch. We've been friends ever since.

Shortly after, I invited Josh to some book events that I frequented and introduced him to many Denver writers I knew. More friendships developed.

Josh is something of a perfectionist, and has a definite eye for detail. There were aspects about the publication of *The Bane of Yoto* he wanted to improve, so when the novel's rights reverted back to him, he decided to form a publishing company with the intention of reissuing his novel according to his exact vision. He asked me if I'd be interested in joining the venture. With no idea of what I was getting into, but always looking for something new to try, I readily agreed.

We signed the business paperwork on Halloween 2014, which seemed appropriate, and Hex Publishers became a reality. Just weeks later, Hex released its first publication, a science fiction novella titled *Luna One*. For Josh, the publication was a test run to see if the press could truly publish a book that met his expectations. With amazing cover art by Aaron Lovett, the book turned out to be a little gem, but rather than moving forward with a re-release of *The Bane of Yoto*, Josh decided to try something new—an ambitious idea to publish a horror anthology. With my author connections, I was determined to help him make it happen.

We winged it with big ambition and no experience. But with the guidance of others, such as Josh's friend and writing mentor, the late, great author and former editor of *Omni Magazine*, Keith Ferrell, things started rolling. Meanwhile, I made my first story solicitation to the late Edward Bryant. Ed was both a Nebula Award-winning writer of great renown and a mentor to such authors as Dan Simmons and Connie Willis. Always generous with his time and talent, he agreed to contribute. Not long thereafter, Bram Stoker Award®-winners Melanie Tem and Steve Rasnic Tem came aboard. Sadly, Melanie passed away shortly after accepting our contract and never had a chance to write her story. We decided the book would be dedicated to her memory.

Weeks passed and we acquired other such notable names as Steve Alten (Josh's former writing coach), Stephen Graham Jones, Mario Acevedo, and Jeanne C. Stein. As one great story after another came in, Josh and I knew we were developing something very special. And in September 2015, we released the finished project, *Nightmares Unhinged: Twenty Tales of Terror*.

Publishing is always a risky endeavor, but Hex was announcing itself with an absolute winner. The first book signing was a huge success. The Tattered Cover Book Store on Colfax Avenue in Denver hosted an unex-

pectedly large crowd that came to listen to our authors read and sign books. They ran out of seating and attendees were forced to gather on two sets of stairs to listen to our stories. In fact, we sold enough copies to make the number one spot on the *Denver Post*'s bestseller list, dethroning *The Martian*, which had climbed to the top after the film was released. The anthology began to gain ground and found a broad fanbase in the horror community. Aaron Lovett's cover art proved so good that AMC licensed it for promoting their second season of *Fear the Walking Dead*.

Before long, authors were contacting Hex wanting to know more about upcoming projects. Josh and I decided early on that Hex's anthologies would be by invitation-only. With Josh and I both working demanding full-time day jobs, time wasn't available for either of us to go through scores of submissions. Instead, Josh chose to come up with thematic concepts for future anthologies and then contact writers he and his co-editors felt would be perfect matches. This strategy has worked out extremely well.

Hex released its second anthology in November 2016, with an emphasis on diversity. *Cyber World: Tales of Humanity's Tomorrow* was edited by Josh and Hugo Award-winner Jason Heller. The back cover describes the vision they shared for the contents: "Cybernetics. Neuroscience. Nano-technology. Genetic engineering. Hacktivism. Transhumanism. The world of tomorrow is already here, and the technological changes we all face have inspired a new wave of stories to address our fears, hopes, dreams, and desires as Homo sapiens evolve–or not–into their next incarnation." The results were impressive and featured an even more diverse selection of authors who contributed twenty dark cyberpunk stories with mind-bog-gling twists and turns. Throw in Josh's insistence for amazing cover art, interior motion flipbook artwork, a PlayStation 4 dynamic theme, and even a CD soundtrack by Hollywood musician Klayton of Celldweller, and it was another big hit and bestseller.

Josh went out on a limb, as usual, and arranged a reading and book signing event for *Cyber World* in New York City, with Aaron Lovett and contributing authors Matthew Kressel, E. Lily Yu, and Alyssa Wong agreeing to attend. I wasn't able to commit to the trip at the time, but just days before the event, my schedule opened up. On such short notice around the Thanksgiving holiday, it was impossible for me to get there. Or was it? I loaded up my car and drove from Colorado to New York.

And I didn't tell Josh.

I'll never forget the expression on Josh and Aaron's faces when they spotted me sitting in the Lovecraft Bar in Brooklyn, nursing a scotch at four o'clock in the afternoon on an abysmally cold, dreary and rainy day. It was gold.

Surprise!

The event was packed with an avid, excited crowd. I left that night at ten o'clock and revisited some places I hadn't seen in more than forty years (I grew up about seventy-five miles north of New York City in the Hudson Valley) and then made the long eighteen-hundred-mile drive back to Colorado.

Cyber World became Hex Publishers' first Colorado Book Award finalist. It was a huge honor for the press and all of the contributors.

2017 turned out to be an extremely busy year for Hex, with the publication of the *Georgetown Haunts and Mysteries* anthology to support the Ghost Town Writers Retreat in Georgetown, Colorado. This time, Josh partnered with award-winning writer Jeanne C. Stein to curate a small collection of horror fiction to be given to attendees at the retreat. The anthology includes such gifted storytellers as Carrie Vaughn, Warren Hammond and Stephen Graham Jones, with an afterword by Brian Keene honoring the memory of Tom Piccirilli. The nine stories in this book take place sequentially from the year 1861 through 2017. It's a fun and spooky read. As the back cover tells, "From the ghost of a hanged man at the old Cafe Prague to the apparition of a sobbing woman at the Rose Street Bed and Breakfast to a phantom Victorian dress whooshing through the halls at the Hamill House museum, Georgetown is a well-known haunt for spirits of all kinds. But some of the town's deepest, darkest secrets have never been revealed...

until now. Prepare for nine otherworldly tales of myth and mystery that extend back to the grisly gold and silver rush days of old. And be careful or you may find a ghostly visitor reading over your shoulder."

That year also saw Hex expand into novels, starting with Mario Acevedo's young adult book, *University of Doom*, a zany tale of adolescent mad science run amok, followed by a novella by Jeanne C. Stein called *Anna and the Vampire Prince*, set in the world of her best-selling Anna Strong series. A third novel, Sean Eads' *Trigger Point*, allowed Hex to venture into the realm of suspense fiction with a novel inspired by the Craigslist Killer.

In November, we published one of our most ambitious anthologies to date, *Blood Business: Crime Stories from This World and Beyond*. Visually, this publication is stunning. The original plan was to split the book into two volumes, with one focusing on crime stories set in reality, and a second geared toward crime of a supernatural variety. We weren't exactly sure how to structure the book at first, but our friend and fellow writer, Angie Hodapp, suggested formatting the anthology as a double-sided book. Read half, then turn it upside down and read the rest. We thought it was a great way to mirror the theme and contents of the collection and we were recognized with our second Colorado Book Award nomination. In addition to the wonderful presentation, *Blood Business* is a personal favorite of mine because it contains two stories I co-authored with my good friend, Mark Stevens.

And just because we could, Hex also managed to publish two comic books that year. *My Hero*, written by Stephen Graham Jones, with art by Aaron, and *Tooth & Claw*, written by Angie and Josh, also with art from Aaron, and an afterword by Carrie Vaughn. These unique comics are quick, mind-opening adventures about beating the odds and coming out on top.

2018 found Hex focusing on three primary releases. The first of these was *The Mask Shop of Doctor Blaack*, an acquisition I made from Steve Rasnic Tem. The year before, I'd spotted Steve and Ed Bryant at the annual Antiquarian Book and Paper Fair in Denver. I joined them and during our conversation, Steve mentioned he was just finishing up a middle-grade Halloween novel. Sensing an obvious opportunity, I asked for a copy of the manuscript. I breezed through it in a day, knew it was a winner and asked Josh to read it. He agreed, and Hex gladly championed this magical story about a strange Halloween shop and its even stranger proprietor.

The second project of the year was another stellar anthology, this time edited by Jason Heller and Selena Chambers. *Mechanical Animals: Tales at the Crux of Creatures and Tech* brought more new authors into the Hex family, with twenty-two stories examining biomimicry, mankind's place in the natural order, and the nature of consciousness. Both fun and thought-provoking, *Mechanical Animals* became Hex Publishers' third Colorado Book Award finalist. What a ride!

Finally, Hex wrapped up its 2018 publishing schedule with the novella, *Denver Moon: The Minds of Mars* (cover art by Kirk DouPonce) and an accompanying graphic novel, *Denver Moon: Metamorphosis* (interior by Aaron, cover by Aaron and Xander Smith), written collaboratively between Warren Hammond and Josh. Best described as a cross between *Blade Runner* and *Total Recall,* the story centers on a color-blind private investigator and her AI-enabled handgun as they investigate violent crimes on Mars. The book earned Hex a fourth nomination from the Colorado Book Awards and the graphic novel got a spot on the Bram Stoker Award® Preliminary Ballot.

A fifth Colorado Book Award nomination followed in 2019, with Josh and Warren's *Denver Moon: The Saint of Mars.* Set six months after the events of the first book, the story never lets up for a second. Action, twists and revolution are the name of the game as the titular hero and her sidekick sidearm continue working deep in the criminal underbelly of Mars.

Then 2020 happened.

Who needs horror fiction in a horrible year? Who needs tales of survivalist plagues when every trip to the grocery store feels like you're entering the Hot Zone? You might think a pandemic would stop an ordinary small

publisher, but if you've read this far, you know Hex isn't ordinary.

A year of face masks, social distancing and social changes didn't stop us from moving forward with two more exciting anthologies.

I wrote a short story called "The Visions of Perry Godwin" a while back that I submitted to publishers but had no takers. Instead of shelving it completely, I came up with an idea to do a new anthology inspired by the theme of my story. I won't go into all of the details, which you can read about in the foreword to the book, *Psi-Wars: Classified Cases of Psychic Phenomena*, but I will say I made a somewhat nervous pitch to Josh about my idea. With little coaxing, he took me up on the concept and added his own twist. *Psi-Wars* was released in May of 2020, and brought together military-themed science fiction and horror with fascinating psychic surprises from such talented writers as Gabino Iglesias, Betty Rocksteady, Gary Jonas—and who could forget the introduction by John Palisano? The art from AJ Nazzaro and Aaron is dazzling and definitely gives readers a taste of what to expect.

Hex Publishers' newest anthology, *It Came from the Multiplex: 80s Midnight Chillers,* is a collaborative effort between Josh and Bret & Jeanni Smith of the Colorado Festival of Horror. The cover art by AJ will remind you of a time of big hair and bigger scares. The gruesome interior illustrations by Xander, and the flipbook by Aaron, add an extra layer to the creep factor. This anthology expands the Hex family with exciting new authors telling vivid, B-movie tales of horror. Get the popcorn ready.

Hex Publishers has obviously been on a roll. It's certainly gone far beyond what Josh or I were imagining back in 2014. To those who've been along for the ride since the beginning, we're glad you've stuck around. If you're just discovering us, we hope you'll find a lot to like.

I'll close with a valedictory remembrance of two members of the Hex family who've passed away since our story began. We miss Ed Bryant and Keith Ferrell deeply. They were with us in the beginning, contributing both fiction and mentorship. Hex wouldn't be what it is today had they not shared their great talents with us. For that, we are forever grateful, and we will always honor their memories.

The future is unknown, but I'm certain you'll be seeing much more from Hex Publishers. My friend Josh can't stop creating. He's obsessed.

That reminds me, I have an idea for a new anthology I need to discuss with him.

HWA DENVER: OWN IT, LOVE IT, AND ROCK IT

by Jeamus Wilkes

T HE INK ISN'T QUITE DRY on mine and Maria Abrams' acceptance letters of becoming the new co-chairpersons of HWA Denver. Speaking for myself, when Horror Writers Association president John Palisano said, "yes" in response to my ideas in relaunching the HWA's presence here in Denver—ideas included in a three-page letter that I fancied as quite radical—my first thought was, *they really are serious about doing good stuff here.*

For the HWA's Mile High Chapter, 2021 marks a time of rebuilding, regrowing, reinvention, and rock-and-roll. Our first act is a name change. "Mile High City" is a centuries-old and frankly overused nickname for Denver, Colorado. Aside from its hyper-proliferation, it's not necessarily a bad one. But in times of reclamation, it's best to own something by returning to your birth name. "HWA Denver" gets back to owning the city and its cornucopia of beautiful things.

One of those beautiful things is *horror.*

Whereas the road to hell is paved with good intentions, the road out of hell is a reverse-angle revelation that some intentions might not have been so righteous. If a group is going to pick up a banner and embrace progress, an acknowledgment of past mistakes—whether they were made by you personally or not—is key in going forward. Again, you're owning it. Let's get the bad out there so we can do our best to extinguish it: disinclusion, scarcity of diversity, paranoia in perceived wrongs, and a profound lack of adaptation in times of crisis and whiplash change.

In moving forward, the key to your group's survival is doing something *good*. And to keep the good going, you must be *intrepid*. You form necessary alliances along the way that you water and grow into amazing friendships.

2021 is when HWA Denver keeps the good with a longstanding membership roster we plan to add onto significantly via inclusion, diversity, trust, peace, and adaptation. We're also keeping the good with annual events like the *Yog Soggoth Awards* (the notorious silver yo-yo given to Colorado horror authors for their art, service, and dedication), the *Red Tinsel Party* (a holiday season live reading event in partnership with local booksellers), and when public health safety becomes an attainable thing again, add new events like *Golden Ghost Story Nights* (outdoor author readings done 'round a firepit) and *Mary's Fête* (with close proximity to Mary Shelley's birthday, an outdoor end-of-August event celebrating women in horror). And that's just the beginning. Among our priorities are fostering reading and writing groups, expansion into visual arts- and poetry-based events and activities, and shared events with our sister chapter, HWA Colorado Springs (HWA COS).

The key to HWA Denver's vitality is its alliance with HWA COS. Maria and I are relying heavily on the experience, input, and mutual involvement with HWA COS's leadership and roster. If we're going to live out the wider vision of the national HWA's dedication to "promoting the interests of Horror and Dark fantasy writers," this alliance *has* to happen. And the resulting *friendship* will be an added benefit and cause for celebration.

Throw your Devil Horns up and join us. In 2021, as HWA Denver rebuilds, regrows, reinvents, and rocks!

HWA BLEEDS INTO SOUTHERN COLORADO

by Hillary Dodge

THOSE OF US IN COLORADO'S NEWEST CHAPTER of the Horror Writers Association, HWA Colorado Springs, are here to say that when it comes to horror in our state, Denver doesn't get to have all the fun anymore.

Colorado Springs could be a scary place even before James Dobson founded Focus on the Family in our city. Evergreen Cemetery has claims to being haunted, Cheyenne Cañon has spooky associations in Native American lore, and the paranormal show *Ghost Hunters* did a fascinating episode on the Briarhurst Manor in nearby Manitou Springs. Many books could be written on the dark folklore that gets passed around these parts. Which goes to show we get pretty bloody down here, too. In fact, we owe our chapter's official formation to a little event called *Bloody Valentine: A Celebration of Women in Horror*. Of course, we held it on February 14th, 2020, because while we all love chocolate, some of us prefer a much *darker* kind of heart.

Valentine's Day was the perfect fit for an event examining women's influence in the horror genre. After all, women often get overlooked and minimalized across the board, and Valentine's Day just happens to usurp the pagan festival of Lupercalia. In case you're not up to speed on ancient religious traditions, Lupercalia was traditionally celebrated at the mouth of the sacred cave where a she-wolf suckled Romulus and Remus, the mythical founders of Rome. It was a bloody and highly sexualized celebration of fertility and feminine strength.

So naturally the Church replaced it with a day honoring a martyred old guy.

We hosted *Bloody Valentine* at the Cottonwood Center for the Arts, which became a suckling cave for our chapter, the birthing place of something great. We were honoring the creative genius of some very fabulous women writers and bringing their work the attention it deserved. We had over fifty attendees and an awe-inspiring roster of female-identifying authors, poets, and creative powerhouses who participated through a mix of live and pre-recorded readings. These included Linda D. Addison, L. C. Barlow, Andrea Blythe, J. A. Campbell, Angie Hodapp, Kate Jonez, Gwendolyn Kiste, DeAnna Knippling, P. L. McMillan, Marge Simon, Angie Sylvaine, Sarah Read, Stephanie M. Wytovich, and Mercedes Murdock Yardley. The event also showcased an academic tract, featuring "Mapping the Collective Body of Frankenstein's Brides" by Carina Bissett, an excerpt from *Monster, She Wrote: The Women Who Pioneered Horror and Speculative Fiction* by Lisa Kröger and Melanie R. Anderson, and a presentation by the Ann Radcliffe Academic Conference co-chair Michele Brittany.

The success of *Bloody Valentine* and its clear impact on the local writing community galvanized the event organizers into formalizing the Colorado Springs chapter. Founding members include Carina Bissett, M.H. Boroson, Travis Heermann, Angie Hodapp, Shannon Lawrence, Joshua Viola, and myself. I knew something about the process since eleven years earlier I co-founded the Denver-based HWA Colorado Chapter with Edward Bryant and Lawrence Berry. I watched with pride as the HWA Colorado grew and introduced the Yog Soggoth Award—a silver yo-yo given to Colorado horror authors for their art, service, and dedication. The chapter also has its annual *Red Tinsel* book reading event in partnership with the Broadway Book Mall.

But don't worry, Denver, our new HWA Colorado Springs chapter embraces writers from every corner of our spooky state, with planned monthly meetings, NaNoWriMo Write Ins, and a sequel to our inaugural *Bloody Valentine* gathering. At its core, the HWA Colorado Springs Chapter serves the professional writing community of Colorado and

surrounding regions through a philosophy of inclusion and accessibility. We welcome all.

DENVER HORROR COLLECTIVE: DARKENING DENVER'S DOORS

D ENVER HORROR COLLECTIVE held its first meeting in 2017, with four local horror authors in the back room of a Denver bookstore. Since then, we've grown to over forty dues-paying members; primarily horror writers but also artists and musicians.

Our flagship project is running critique groups focused on writing short horror fiction, novels, and screenplays. What's more, we present live and online events, ranging from "Music to My Fears" (horror fiction readings set to live music), to "All Hallows Improv Scarytelling," to monthly "Dark Wisdom" webinars focusing on the craft and business of writing horror.

We're also a publishing house, starting with *Terror at 5280'*, our local horror fiction anthology released in 2019. In this #2 *Denver Post* bestseller, all tales are set in and around the Mile High City and are penned exclusively by Colorado authors like Stephen Graham Jones, Carter Wilson, Carina Bissett, Joshua Viola, Angela Sylvaine, Henry Snider, Joy Yehle, and many more seasoned and emerging dark scribes. Then, in 2020, we published *Consumed: Tales Inspired by the Wendigo*, featuring Wrath James White, Steve Rasnic Tem, Dana Fredsti, Owl Goingback and other formidable talents.

But perhaps most importantly, Denver Horror Collective is a community where we offer one another advisory, emotional, and even financial support. While writing is typically a lonely business, at DHC, that's simply not the case. Instead of competing against one another for recognition, we join forces to lift each other up in the belief that the success of one DHC member is success for us all.

The experience of most horror authors is similar to a lone wolf howling in the wilderness—at Denver Horror Collective we're a pack. So, if you write dark fiction, live in Colorado, and could use some company, check us out at *DenverHorror.com*.

Yours Darkly,
Denver Horror Collective Steering Committee

DO I WRITE HORROR?
by Carter Wilson

I've ALWAYS BEEN CURIOUS BY NATURE. Always wanted to know how things worked, or why people behaved how they did. I love looking for logic when seemingly none is present, or looking for the tiniest of clues inside the pages of a mystery novel.

It was curiosity that made me pose the following question to myself eighteen years ago on a piece of notebook paper:

Three people are murdered at the exact same time in the exact same fashion in different parts of the world. What's the connection?

Okay, it wasn't just curiosity, but also mind-numbing boredom. I was in Denver, sitting in a shitty old Ramada Hotel meeting room, taking an all-day continuing-education class for a real-estate appraisal license. Yes, I know how boring that sounds. Think about how excruciating it actually was. Because I didn't have any razor blades handy to slit my wrists, I tried to kill the last two hours of the class by posing myself a riddle and attempting to answer it. For whatever reason, the above question just popped into my head.

That's how my writing career began.

I was thirty-three and had ZERO experience writing anything other than business reports. Of course, I didn't think the answer to my riddle would span the length of an entire book, but goddamn if that isn't what happened. Three months after that class, I had a 400-page manuscript and absolutely no clue what to do with it. I was certain my story wasn't any good, and figured my writing was terrible yet I couldn't *not* try to see if I could get it published.

I didn't know a single thing about the publishing industry. Fortunately, a lot of other people did, and thanks to the Internet, I quickly found out the first thing I needed was to find an agent.

After about a year and eighty rejections, I landed one (the same agent I'm still with today), and she shopped my manuscript to publishers. It never sold. So I wrote another, fearing my agent would dump me otherwise. That book didn't sell either. Nor did the third. Finally, nine years after the day I posed myself that riddle, *Final Crossing* appeared on the shelves at Barnes & Noble.

Now, another decade has passed, and my seventh book will be out May 2021 from Poisoned Pen Press. I've been fortunate enough to land on the *USA Today* bestsellers list, win four Colorado Book Awards, and be nominated for an ITW Thriller Award. In sum, I'm starting to figure out this writing business a little. And yet after all this time, I still don't know what kind of books I write.

I'm talking about genres.

I'm mostly referred to as a thriller writer (with neat little subcategories of psychological thriller and domestic thriller). Sometimes I'm a suspense writer, and once in a while my agent will throw out the term *literary fiction* in order to politely tell me to pick up my pacing on a story. Interestingly, I'm never labeled a mystery writer, even though many of my books have an inherent mystery to them. Go figure.

And then there's horror. I've definitely been listed as a horror writer.

Do I write horror? Fuck, I don't know. Horror is slippery, perhaps more so than any other genre. A scene in a book that horrifies you might just seem mildly unpleasant to me. Or vice-versa, because if you're reading this you probably have a stronger stomach than I do. I still get freaked out by the opening scene in *JAWS*. Everything is in shades, is what I'm saying.

That first published book of mine featured a serial killer who crucified people, hoping to bring about the End of Days. Oh, and a baby may or may not have also been decapitated. It was considered more horror than

thriller, but not enough to place it anywhere other than the General Fiction category in bookstores.

In the opening scene of my second book, a seventeen-year-old girl pseudo-seduces a thirteen-year-old boy in the woods, and just as this kid thinks he's hit the lottery she caves his skull in with a rock (also: what is wrong with me?). That girl grows into a depraved adult who can only reach sexual climax when murdering someone.

Then things changed a bit with my third book. It was the first time I wrote strictly from a female POV, and I found myself more intrigued by the lack of violence than the use of it. There was no killer on the loose, just a horribly fractured marriage forcing a wife to go on the run from her husband. There was violence in the book, some of it very ugly indeed, but I used it sparsely, in my opinion, to good effect.

From that point on, my books have been very much focused on psychological struggle interlaced with physical threat. The word *creepy* appears often in reviews. But are these horror books? According to the Internet (where everything is true), horror fiction is a "genre of speculative fiction which is intended to frighten, scare, or disgust." Now, I wouldn't say any of those things are my intention. My intention is to tell a complete story, follow a character and see how they react to adversity, and understand what factors cause them to fail or succeed. If a reader gets frightened, scared, or even maybe a little disgusted on the way, well, hey, that's cool, too.

Every book I write begins with an audience of one: me. I've been told countless times that I have to consider who I'm writing for, what the readers want from me. Make sure I can appeal to the broadest possible group. I love my readers, but they're not who I'm thinking of when that first chapter forms in my head. I want to write something that excites me, draws me in. After all, I'm the one doing all the work, so if I'm not excited to sit down every day and discover what happens next, the book will either never get done or it'll suck. It takes me a year to write a fully fleshed novel; I don't want to spend that time feeling like I'm just doing template, data-entry work.

Being original is perhaps what I strive for most. Maybe that's why I've never written a series; I want every book to be a totally separate story that doesn't follow any predictable pattern (the other nice thing about writing standalone stories: you can kill who you want when you want). I'd rather be memorable than be a formulaic crowd-pleaser. One of my favorite reviews of all times goes like this:

"This is a sick, sick book and I'm not sure if it's a good sick or bad sick. Either way, the story is quite disturbing and I can't get it out of my head."

Fuck, yeah, *I'm in your head.* By the way, that person still gave me three-and-a-half stars.

Still, this industry is unforgiving. Whenever I lecture on writing, I tell the students not to quit their day jobs. Not to go into writing for the money, because there's only a scarce amount and the bulk of it goes to the top one percent. The only reason a person should write is because they want to. They *need* to. Whether that person has a fortune to their name or nothing at all, they should write every day because there was a story they needed to tell. Or, in the case of my first manuscript, a riddle to solve. Their prose could be brilliant or it could be shit, that doesn't matter. Writing fulfills them—*that's* what matters. They should chase what makes them happy, and hopefully everything else will fall into place without them trying.

As a writer, I never have a sense of a peak. There are ups and downs aplenty—that's the nature of this business. But with each book, I feel I'm continuing to get better, that my words come more easily, and my sense of character development sharpens. Think of all the professions in which you get to a certain age and you're easily replaced by a younger generation, that age when your best option is greeting Walmart customers and sanitizing their shopping carts with Clorox wipes.

Not if you're a writer.

Not if you're a *storyteller.* In the history of the world, who are the best storytellers? Most often the ones who've been doing it longest.

There's a simple truism among writers which is this: the best may

always be yet to come. My twentieth book may sell exponentially more than my fifth, or the next riddle I ask myself will be more interesting than the last.

And perhaps the best part of all is the one thing guaranteed to any writer. The thing that drives me to pick up my laptop every damn day and get some words down.

A lifetime of curiosity.

TWISTED TROPES: SIX STEPS TO BETTER IDEAS THAT WILL CATCH AN AGENT'S EYE

by Angie Hodapp

As Director of Literary Development at Nelson Literary Agency, I'm a story geek with an eye for what works and the ability to articulate various ways authors can take their writing and storytelling to the next level. I believe in the power of story to elevate, transform, and heal, and I love to be anywhere writers are gathered. So when Josh Viola asked me to write this article—advice for horror writers seeking agent representation and traditional publication—it just so happens I was reading *Writing in the Dark* by Tim Waggoner (Guide Dog Books, September 2020). What things, thought I, could I possibly tell you that Waggoner hasn't already served up with a piping-hot side of hard-won insight in his horrorcraft masterpiece? It seemed like maybe not much. If you want to write salable horror, and if you want to build a career doing it, Waggoner's got your goods. Hence…

Step 1: Read *Writing in the Dark* by Tim Waggoner.

Beyond that, I can tell you that agents and editors see plenty of submissions for tired old horror. Ideas and storylines too closely derived from existing works. Tropes that were once shiny and new, but that (in Waggoner's words) have lost their power to engage and affect readers. The top reasons agents send rejections include poor writing and poor story execution, but right up there is a bland or threadbare concept.

The trick is to build something new that casts a familiar shadow. Shoot for "the same, but different"—the *same* because industry pros want readers to recognize your work as belonging to their favorite genre, but *different* because we want your voice, style, and brand to stand out. How do you do that?

Step 2: Make an id list.

Start by listing the tropes you're drawn to, both as a writer and as a fan. The monster in the closet (basement, attic, shed, lake, etc.), the possessed doll, the evil circus, the protagonist who doesn't know they're dead. This is the beginning of your id list—a collection of fears and fascinations that the most primitive part of your brain responds to for reasons that, at this point, don't matter.

Leave nothing out. It's your id you're indulging with this exercise, so don't judge yourself for liking particular things your ego tells you you shouldn't. Keep your id list in a safe place. Add to it as years go by. Come back to it for inspiration.

Step 3: Zero in.

Identify tropes on your id list that you want to write about. For each, list what's been done, how, and by whom. Which features of that trope recur across the canon?

These features might include particular images, scenes, settings, situations, and types of characters. The lady-in-the-lake story often features images of muddy footprints and a scene in which the protagonist goes into the lake to do battle. The possessed-doll story often features a little girl, an old house, and situations where the doll turns its head, opens its eyes, or appears where it shouldn't. The evil circus often features an enigmatic or somewhat seductive ringmaster and a supporting cast of deformed, terrifying-to-behold freaks, and bad things happen to the folks who buy tickets for the show. The protagonist who doesn't know they're dead often features an emotional-reaction scene when they find out, which, if done well, is also

a surprise to the audience.

Step 4: Get personal.

Explore why each trope is personal to you. Were you introduced to it at a formative age? What memories, good or bad, coincide with that introduction? Does it speak to a real-life trauma you endured, or a situation that tops your list of the worst things that could possibly happen to you?

Go deep. Get raw. Be honest. Good fiction is a conversation between the writer and the reader, and the more real that conversation is, the more likely the reader will feel they got something worthwhile out of the experience.

Step 5: Get universal.

What is universally, or at least largely, appealing about those tropes and features? Do they appeal to others in the same ways or for the same reasons they appeal to you?

Does that matter?

The business side of writing isn't sexy or fun to think about. It's far more enjoyable to live in the creative, imaginative half of our brains. But the two forces often clash when rejections start piling up. It's not a bad idea for a writer to step back once in a while and ask, "Is there a market for what I'm writing?"

Worrying about the market when you're writing, or preparing to write, a piece of fiction can certainly impede your creativity. But at the end of the day, career authors are career authors because they get paid. They get paid because they satisfy readers. And (writing and execution aside) they satisfy readers for one of two reasons: it just so happens they naturally want to write what lots of readers want to read, or they've developed keen market awareness over time and the ability to deliver satisfying content to a certain readership.

The age-old adage "write the book you want to read" is only really useful to writers who share tastes with large pools of their genre's readers. The more niche your sensibilities are, the more niche your readership will be.

It's a balancing act, writing what you want to write and hoping to build a career doing it. Which leads us back to the importance of concept, and that agents are looking for "the same, but different." The *same* part boosts the agent's confidence that they'll be able to place your work with a publisher who will be able to successfully market it to an existing (and hopefully large) set of readers. The *different* part gives the agent hope that your work might break out—win awards, make bestseller lists, exceed sales expectations, become a film, and earn you a higher advance for your next work.

Step 6: Get twisted.

Let's get back to the fun stuff. You've listed, analyzed, pulled apart, and examined your favorite tropes. Now twist. Bend. Cut. Melt. Weld. Nail. Glue. Stitch. See what unique horrors you *and only you* can conjure.

Apply a feature of this trope to that trope. Flip a feature on its head. Combine three seemingly unrelated tropes or features in one story. Interrogate the tropes on your id list:

> *"Hey, haunted house, who says you have to be old and creaky and surrounded by gnarled trees?"*

> *"Hey, possessed doll, who says you have to be an antique? Chucky? A tribal relic? A ventriloquist's dummy? A clown?"*

> *"Hey, teen-slasher story, who says you can only take place at a sleep-away camp or slumber party?"*

"Hey, buried-alive protagonist, who says you have to be terrified or imperiled by that situation?"

"Hey, exorcism story, who says the church, Catholic or otherwise, has to be part of the solution?"

"Hey, witch story, who says you have to choose between the empowerment and vilification of the feminine?"

Once you as a writer can identify the anchors that tired old tropes might be tying to your story ideas, and once you realize you can reject them while still composing works that belong squarely to the genre—nay, that move the genre forward—you'll be well on your way to delivering the fresh, unique concepts agents and editors hunger for.

THE END:
KEITH FERRELL IN MEMORIAM

by Alec Ferrell

THE MOST HORRIFIC THING ABOUT DEATH is that there is nothing unusual about it. Everyone dies. The process begins the moment we're born. Some are ready for it, most aren't. Either way, at the end of the day (or early afternoon), death is ready and waiting, regardless of our awareness of or preparedness for it. We're all goners. Not unusual. Horrific, but not unusual.

My father, Keith Ferrell, died at 1:34 pm on Saturday, April 11, 2020.

Every time I started to write about his life and life's work for this anthology, it felt as if he died over and over again. Is it unusual to feel like I'm his killer when I sit down at the keyboard? Probably. The act of resurrecting him through words he will never read feels wrong, especially when the outcome is always the same: he's still dead. If the StokerCon™ audience were to read my first few drafts of this piece about my dad, he'd undoubtedly suffer another heart attack.

As the only child of a dead writer, there is no fair way to share the unusually beautiful and complex nature of our relationship, as I can only tell my side of the story. So, let me share some non-fiction about my old man, Keith Ferrell.

I'll spare us—and *him*—the horseshit.

Take *that*, Blucifer.

My dad was born to write.

The End were his two favorite words in all of the English language. If and when he got to those two words, whether in his own writing or through his collaborations with dozens of writers across four decades of professional storycraft and editing, he saw it as further securing his purpose on this planet.

The End didn't come to my dad without seriously hard work, although his deep talent often made it look easy. Through the process of starting with a blank page to get to those two little words, Keith Ferrell sought to illuminate, confound, shock, and whenever possible, horrify.

His relationship with horror began in the early Sixties, when my grandfather, Henry Ferrell, would return home on the weekends from traveling as a regional sales manager for a pharmaceutical company. He would gather his four kids around the television for epic horror movie marathons. Keith, his brother Edmund, and sisters Ann and Betsy, recall these as being some of their most cherished and relaxed childhood memories together.

Edmund Ferrell recalls, "Early Saturday morning we would watch Sunrise Theater. We saw *First Spaceship on Venus*, *The Crawling Eye*, *The Incredible Shrinking Man*, *Attack of the 50 Foot Woman*, *Devil Doll*, *Forbidden Planet*, *It Came From Outer Space*, *The War of the Worlds*, all of the Universal Classics, *The Giant Behemoth*, *Them*, *The Blob*, *House on Haunted Hill*, *The Tingler*, *The Fly*, *The Creature from the Black Lagoon*, *Godzilla*, *Mothra*, *Circus of Fear*, *House of Wax*...we saw it all. Sometimes with pancakes."

Keith and his siblings connected with their father through horror movies when there wasn't much time available for connection otherwise. It takes blood sometimes.

My old man (as a young man) started reading his hero, Norman Mailer, at the age of twelve or so. He moved into the family basement and began his lifelong accumulation of as much printed material as he could get his hands on. It was in this basement that he found his calling.

As far as the friends and family who knew and loved him can determine, my dad's first known published short story came out when he was sixteen years old, in the 1969 volume of his high school literary journal *Grains of Sand*. As would become his trademark, the story stands out from the other poems and prose in the collection for its unusual construction

and literary ambition. "Leon" tells the story of a young boy who not only thinks he is God, but becomes one. Undoubtedly built to shock and horrify his teachers and classmates, "Leon" begins on a normal day in a school cafeteria and ends with our dreadful protagonist destroying the universe. Over three tight double-spaced pages, a confident and confrontational young artist emerged with a powerful and unique voice. I look forward to making it available when the time is right.

Oddly enough, we didn't know about "Leon" until right before Christmas of 2020. It came in the mail to my uncle Edmund and his partner Hartsell while the three of us were enjoying a socially distanced COVID-19 Christmas hang in their new home. Inbound from Colorado (of all places) by one of Keith's schoolmates whose family grew up in Raleigh and knew the Ferrell family, it came in a plain manila envelope at the exact moment we were together. It was as if Keith, as omniscient and omnipotent as Leon himself, saw fit to vanquish our grief by sending us *Grains of Sand*, putting himself there with us from beyond the infinite. "Here's how it all started," we imagined him proudly saying to us with this unbelievably timed message from the other side. His fifty-one-year-old story solidifies his vitality. It makes him immortal. Forever young. We laughed and gasped as Edmund read the story aloud, as good art tends to make one do.

As my dad continued to grow into a conscious young man in the 1960s, he found and cherished the written word—primarily speculative fiction and science literature—both of which would define his life's journey and purpose as a man of letters. Many of his formative literary heroes—such as Harlan Ellison, Isaac Asimov, and Arthur C. Clarke—would become peers and friends later in life, a testament to his attention, hard work, and determination.

Graduating from Raleigh's Sanderson High in 1971, he attended the Residential College of the University of North Carolina at Greensboro, where he met Martha Sparrow at a Halloween party in the basement of Guilford dormitory. My dad's idea of a costume that night consisted of covering his face in wax ala *The Phantom of the Opera*. Martha overheard him mention the name "Lawrence Talbot." She got his Wolfman reference, which prompted her to strike up a conversation with this intriguing fellow, even though she had no idea what he looked like under all that wax. On their first date, they ditched a French play to go see *King Kong* instead. They fell in love, moved off campus, and started their lives together. They were married on July 20, 1974, and would stay together for almost 47 years.

In 1975, Keith was hired as store manager of News and Novels, a bookstore in Greensboro, where he developed countless friendships as well as a reputation for his keen and encyclopedic knowledge of the printed word, while writing his own works off hours. Always writing. Martha and Keith welcomed me, their only child, in February 1978.

From 1983 through 1987, my dad secured a contract through his agent Henry Morrison to publish four critically-acclaimed biographies of legendary writers for young adults through M. Evans and Company: *H.G. Wells: First Citizen of the Future*; *Ernest Hemingway: The Search for Courage*; *George Orwell: The Political Pen*; and *John Steinbeck: The Voice of the Land*. He honored his forebears by helping share their lives and work through his own words.

Keith worked his way through editorial departments for such magazines as *The Professional Upholsterer* and *COMPUTE!* in the late Eighties. In 1990, *COMPUTE!* was acquired by General Media out of New York City, and Keith was recruited as Editor-in-Chief of *Omni Magazine*, the preeminent science and technology publication of the day—a career-defining accomplishment. During his tenure at *Omni*, Keith worked with (and edited) many of the literary heroes of his youth and forged friendships across the fields of anthropology, gaming, evolutionary studies, telecommunications, and writers of all stripes. Ellen Datlow, a fiction editor you might've heard of, worked with my dad on the staff of *Omni* and remembers him as "a sweetheart, a lovely person, and passionate about science fiction." Keith stewarded *Omni* as a vehicle for the vanguard of cutting-edge science and technology, futurism, and fiction until its final issue in 1996.

Keeping in mind the special horror movie marathons of his childhood, Keith would come home to my mother and me in Greensboro, North Carolina, after his three-weeks-on monthly schedule of issue-building at the *Omni* offices in New York City (until moving the offices to our hometown), or from traveling the world to meet with advertisers and content creators for the magazine. He would always return with a stack of comics, magazines, books (many of them signed by their authors), and movies. They occasionally came with the disclaimer: don't show your mom. *2001: A Space Odyssey* (our mutual favorite), *The Shining*, *Akira*, *Tetsuo: The Iron Man*, *Blue Velvet*, *Repo Man*, *Henry: Portrait of A Serial Killer*, *Hellraiser*, Larry Cohen's *God Told Me To*, and the entirety of the ever-expanding canon of David Cronenberg, are a brief example of the films he poured into my highly pliable early teenage mind. The films and books which most parents would keep their fifth-grade kids from having access to (Clive Barker, especially), he would all but quiz me on. George A. Romero's hypodermic teenage vampire film *Martin* was one of his favorites, and remains to this day one of the horror films against which I hold all others. As we would have our own weekend pancake fests at Ol' Miner, a long-gone Greensboro breakfast restaurant, we would discuss the elements of science fiction and horror and dissect what makes a piece of work successful.

It was from these conversations that I named my first high school band "Goats Where They Shouldn't Be"—truly an element of filmic fear. Keith was kind enough to connect me with Clive Barker himself, who agreed to let me use his illustration from *The Thief of Always* of a Jack-O-Lantern hung from a noose for the cover of our first (and only) cassette.

No kid ever had a cooler father. Period.

Paraphrasing my dad, "If you aren't the same as you were before seeing a film, hearing a song, or reading a book, its creator has done their job and turned their work into real art. That's what art is supposed to do—move you to somewhere new." Going through his collection of over 80,000 books, countless VHS tapes and DVDs, and tens of thousands of magazines, SF journals, and newspaper clippings, I am convinced that he ultimately saw the art in everything ever printed. The art of his life was to absorb and cypher the work of writers and funnel it back into the world, whether *The End* came or not.

Sometimes his art was more than editors and publishers could handle, resulting in rejection. It happens, and it sure happened to him. I recall being at the bottom of the living room stairs as a child, watching in horror as he hurled a manuscript in the rage of rejection, the pages fluttering like a blizzard, covering the steps as he howled in anger. I helped him pick up the pages of *Godkill,* a to-date unpublished political thriller about fundamentalist Christian terrorists taking over a summer camp populated by children of members of the U.S. Congress. I was maybe eleven years old. Perhaps he was simply thirty years ahead of his time. It was probably the title that killed the project. Again, I aim to ensure this one has an audience.

Passing Judgment, the first and only published novel with his name alone on the cover, came out in August 1996, just as his beloved *Omni* folded. *Publisher's Weekly*: "The plotting is smooth and the characters true...Ferrell proves a natural storyteller here, with a voice all his own." Go grab a copy.

In 1997, at the age of nineteen, I moved to New York City to "rock" (Dad being a writer, I pursued music—my own natural calling), and worked as a graphic designer in the early days of the Internet, when it was called "New Media." Keith, naturally, had already pioneered this field as the editor of *Omni Online*, the first online magazine.

In 1998, Keith and Martha moved from Greensboro to thirty-six acres of farmland in Glade Hill, Virginia—originally intended as a weekend getaway—where they took care of each other the best they knew how. Always writing, he continued to publish scientific articles, short stories (some under pen names), spoke at libraries and universities, and edited and assisted many other writers' works, guiding their creation and publication with a deft two-finger typing style and keen eye. He served on the board of the Franklin County Library in Rocky Mount, VA, an institution close to his heart, where he championed literacy and open-minded exploration of

the written word to all who were willing to take the time.

With his *Omni* days behind him, Keith worked as a story developer, editor, and frequent ghostwriter, creating myriad partnerships with collaborators he would never meet in person. Being on thirty-six acres of untamed Virginia farmland with no cell service and very low bandwidth, he did his best to tend to the land as well as to his ever-present work in the world of words. As author Thomas Frey states, "I wondered for years what I needed to do to turn my mass of manuscripts and notes into a real book. It turned out that what I needed to do was hire Keith."

Hard times were plentiful and plenty of promising projects went unpublished, but he still managed to break the *New York Times* Bestsellers list, peaking at number ten in November 2013 through his collaboration with Brad Meltzer entitled *History Decoded: The 10 Greatest Conspiracies of All Time*. Though he didn't get the top byline, his invaluable contributions at long last made him a member of the *NYT* bestseller club. We shared more than a few toasts to this accomplishment.

So what about horror?

Thanks to his collaborations with Josh Viola of Hex Publishers, a friend and partner for what would become the last ten years of his life, Keith wrote several short stories squarely aimed at the heart of horror. Simultaneously literary and terrifying, "Be Seated" and "Danniker's Coffin" from the 2015 anthology *Nightmares Unhinged*, were certainly both unhinged and the stuff of nightmares. "Be Seated" offers a Poe-esque welcome to join the table at a dinner party with a Crowley-styled host, while "Danniker's Coffin" weaves a Faulknerian suicide note. In 2020's *Psi-Wars: Classified Cases of Psychic Phenomena*, Keith's story "Psnake Eyes" melds horror with science fiction, an Ellisonian tale of how the links in chain-of-command can be easily broken between leadership and its "psoldiers." Leon was definitely present when he was writing this one.

The final story my dad wrote, literally on its way to print when he died, is straight body horror. By no means is "The Cronenberg Concerto" autobiographical in terms of portraying self-mutilation as beatific ritual, but the protagonist's love of horror films and the menacing canon of Cronenberg's over-the-top gore is rivaled only by Keith Ferrell. Pick up a copy of 2020's *It Came From the Multiplex: 80s Midnight Chillers* and behold the most disturbing tale in the book for yourself.

The only reason you're reading about my dad and not reading his story in this anthology is because of that pesky little heart attack that killed him in April 2020. But he did leave behind a few notes for the story idea he was working on, scribbled in his tight cursive I always loved. It isn't much, but here's his idea:

THE LAST HORROR CON
6,000 years in the future
"There were no horrors left. What could horrify?"

It's anyone's guess as to how he would play that one out. But I suggest, if you're game, see if you can take that idea through to *The End*.

The end came for him far too soon, at the unbearably young age of 67, leaving behind literal tons of human expression and for me to sort through, saving the art—and anything with his handwriting on it or name in the header—and burning the rest. Within his ample office are stacks of manuscripts and artifacts of his published, unpublished, and unfinished work, some barely more than a fevered scrawl on an old envelope. I will be moving—and moved by—the words and work of Keith Ferrell for the rest of my life. As the man directly responsible for his legacy, if this is the first you've heard of him, it certainly won't be the last. If you were lucky enough to know him, you get it. We miss him and always will.

If you've read all the way here to the end, and have an idea that you're dying to write, remember these words, still hanging over his desk:

START FAST, START DEEP.

Start *now*. It may be closer to the end than you think.

There's no time to horse around.

HENRY KEITH FERRELL

July 7, 1953—April 11, 2020

Read much more—in his own words—at *keithferrellwriter.com*.

SELECTED WORKS OF KEITH FERRELL

It Came from the Multiplex: 80s Midnight Chillers
Edited by Joshua Viola
"The Cronenberg Concerto" by Keith Ferrell
(Hex Publishers, 2020)

Psi-Wars: Classified Cases of Psychic Phenomena
Edited by Joshua Viola
"Psnake Eyes" by Keith Ferrell
(Hex Publishers, 2020)

Cyber World: Tales of Humanity's Tomorrow
Edited by Jason Heller and Joshua Viola
"It's Only Words" by Keith Ferrell
(Hex Publishers, 2016)

Nightmares Unhinged: Twenty Tales of Terror
Edited by Joshua Viola
"Be Seated" and "Danniker's Coffin" by Keith Ferrell
"Fangs" by Keith Ferrell and Joshua Viola (as J.V. Kyle)
"Bathroom Break" by Keith Ferrell and Joshua Viola (as J.V. Kyle)
(Hex Publishers, 2015)

History Decoded: The 10 Greatest Conspiracies of All Time
By Brad Meltzer with Keith Ferrell
(Workman Publishing Company, 2013)

Millennium 3001
Edited by Martin H. Greenberg and Russell Davis
"River" by Keith Ferrell and Jack Dann
(DAW, 2006)

Asimov's Science Fiction
"A Reunion" by Keith Ferrell; December 2004

Science Year: The World Book Annual Science Supplement, 2004
"Computers" by Keith Ferrell

Black Mist and Other Japanese Futures
Edited by Orson Scott Card and Keith Ferrell
"Thirteen Views of Higher Edo" by Keith Ferrell (as Patric Helmaan)
(DAW, 1997)

Passing Judgment
(Novel; Forge, 1996)

The Official Guide to Sid Meier's Civilization
(Compute, 1992)

Harold Robbins Presents: The Treasure Seekers
By Keith Ferrell (as Michael Donovan; Pocket Books, 1988)

Harold Robbins Presents: Fast Track
By Keith Ferrell (as Michael Donovan; Pocket Books, 1987)

Harold Robbins Presents: At The Top
By Keith Ferrell (as Michael Donovan; Pocket Books, 1986)

John Steinbeck: The Voice of the Land
(Biography; M. Evans and Company, 1986)

George Orwell: The Polical Pen
(Biography; M. Evans and Company, 1985)

Ernest Hemingway: The Search for Courage
(Biography; M. Evans and Company, 1984)

H.G. Wells: First Citizen of the Future
(Biography; M. Evans and Company, 1983)

ABOUT THE CONTRIBUTORS

MARIO ACEVEDO is a national bestselling author of speculative fiction and has won an International Latino Book Award and a Colorado Book Award. His work has appeared in numerous anthologies to include *A Fistful of Dinosaurs*, *Straight Outta Deadwood*, *Blood Business*, *Psi-Wars*, *It Came from the Multiplex*, and a Western novel, *Luther, Wyoming*. Mario serves on the faculty of the Regis University Mile-High MFA program and Lighthouse Writers Workshops.

MEGHAN ARCURI writes fiction. Her short stories can be found in various anthologies, including *Borderlands 7* (Borderlands Press), *Madhouse* (Dark Regions Press), *Chiral Mad*, and *Chiral Mad 3* (Written Backwards). She is currently the Vice President of the Horror Writers Association. She lives with her family in New York's Hudson Valley. Please visit her at *meghanarcuri.com*, *facebook.com/meg.arcuri*, or on Twitter (*@MeghanArcuri*).

CARINA BISSETT is a writer, poet, and educator working primarily in the fields of dark fiction and fabulism. Her short fiction and poetry have been published in multiple journals and anthologies including *Weird Dream Society*, *Arterial Bloom*, *Gorgon: Stories of Emergence*, *Hath No Fury*, *NonBinary Review*, and the *HWA Poetry Showcase Vol. V* and *VI*. In addition to writing and research, she has worked as an editor on several projects. She teaches online workshops at The Storied Imaginarium, and she is a graduate of the Creative Writing MFA program at Stonecoast. Carina Bissett is a member of Codex, SFWA, SFPA, and HWA. Her work has been nominated for several awards including the Pushcart Prize and the Sundress Publications Best of the Net. Connect with Carina on Twitter (*@cmariebissett*) or Facebook (*facebook.com/carina.bissett.5*). You can also find her on Goodreads (Carina Bissett) and Amazon (Carina Bissett). Her website is *carinabissett.com*.

A community organizer and teacher, **MAURICE BROADDUS**'s work has appeared in *Lightspeed Magazine*, *Weird Tales*, *Apex Magazine*, *Asimov's*,

Cemetery Dance, *Black Static*, and many more. Some of his stories have been collected in *The Voices of Martyrs*. He is the author of the urban fantasy trilogy, *The Knights of Breton Court*, and the (upcoming) middle grade detective novel series, *The Usual Suspects*. He co-authored the play *Finding Home: Indiana at 200*. His novellas include *Buffalo Soldier*, *I Can Transform You*, *Orgy of Souls*, *Bleed with Me*, and *Devil's Marionette*. He is the co-editor of *Dark Faith*, *Dark Faith: Invocations*, *Streets of Shadows*, and *People of Colo(u)r Destroy Horror*. His gaming work includes writing for the Marvel Super-Heroes, *Leverage*, and *Firefly* role-playing games as well as working as a consultant on *Watch Dogs 2*. Learn more about him at *MauriceBroaddus.com*.

MICHELE BRITTANY is an independent popular culture scholar residing in Phoenix, AZ, and is the editor of *James Bond and Popular Culture: Essays on the Influence of the Fictional Superspy* and *Horror in Space: Critical Essays on a Film Genre*. The latter has been nominated for a Bram Stoker Award® for Nonfiction. Michele actively supports several popular culture organizations in a variety of capacities that include serving as the Book Review Editor for the *Journal of Graphic Novels and Comics* and is the North American New Correspondent for *Comics Forum*. She serves as Co-chair of the Ann Radcliffe Academic Conference. In addition, she is the Editorials Manager for Fanbase Press, a Los Angeles-based independent publisher. She is an active member of the Horror Writers Association and the National Coalition of Independent Scholars.

JAMES CHAMBERS received the Bram Stoker Award® for the graphic novel, *Kolchak the Night Stalker: The Forgotten Lore of Edgar Allan Poe* and is a three-time Bram Stoker Award® nominee. He is the author of the collections *On the Night Border*, described by Booklist as "a haunting exploration of the space where the real world and nightmares collide," and *Resurrection House* as well as the dark urban fantasy novella, *Three Chords of Chaos*. *Publisher's Weekly* gave his Lovecraftian collection, *The Engines of Sacrifice*, a starred review and called it "...chillingly evocative." He is also a trustee of the Horror Writers Association. His website is: *jameschambersonline.com*.

JOANN CHANEY is a graduate of University of California, Riverside's,

Palm Desert MFA program. She lives in Colorado with her family. She is also the author of *What You Don't Know*, which was named one of Book Riot's Best Mysteries of the year and longlisted for the CWA New Blood Dagger award. Visit her online at *joannchaney.com*.

The mission of **DENVER HORROR COLLECTIVE** is to facilitate, celebrate, and inspire horror writers and artists throughout the greater Denver metroplex and Front Range Colorado communities. You can reach DHC at DenverHorror.com, at Denver Horror Collective on Facebook, @ *denver_horror* on Twitter, and *@denver_horror* on Instagram or email us at *submissions@denverhorror.com*.

NICHOLAS DIAK is a pop culture scholar, specializing in Italian genre cinema (particularly Eurospy films), the sword and sandal genre (esp. neo-peplum), post-industrial music, synthwave music, and H. P. Lovecraft. He has contributed essays and reviews to various academic anthologies, journals and online magazines. He is the editor of *The New Peplum: Essays on Sword and Sandal Films and Television Programs Since the 1990s* and *Horror Literature from Gothic to Post-Modern: Critical Essays* both from McFarland. He holds an MA from the University of Washington and is a member of the Horror Writers Association. While part of the HWA, he co-created and co-chairs the Ann Radcliffe Academic Conference. His hobbies include watching films, video gaming (both retro and modern), pinup art and photography, tiki culture, cooking, cocktail making, and comic books. He lives in Phoenix, AZ, with his girlfriend Michele Brittany (also a pop culture scholar) and their two cats, Cecily and Algernon.

HILLARY DODGE is an author, librarian, food literacy consultant, and educator. Her short fiction has been published in magazines, anthologies, and podcasts including Pseudopod, Space Squid, and Hellbound Books. She also writes nonfiction on a variety of topics, including technology, medical history, and food literacy. In 2016, she and her husband quit their jobs and relocated their family of three to South America where they spent two years overlanding in Chile and Argentina while researching and writing about food, culture, and the ghosts of South

America. Connect with Hillary on Twitter (@hnraque) or Facebook (*facebook.com/hillary.raquedodge*). Her website is *www.hillarydodge.com*. You can also find her on Goodreads (Hillary Dodge).

Although **KIRK DOUPONCE** studied traditional illustration in college, he spent the first decade of his career as a graphic designer working in the publishing industry. Never losing his love of illustration, he would merge the two disciplines whenever possible. In the early 2000's, Kirk discovered ZBrush, an amazing digital sculpting program. It became his gateway drug into the world of 3D illustration. Today, Kirk's portfolio is a mixture of digital painting, photography, 3D, and typography. With these skills, Kirk has created over a thousand book covers for publishers in the US and the UK. His work has appeared in *Spectrum Fantastic Art, Communication Arts, Infected by Art, ImagineFX,* and on his mother's refrigerator. Kirk lives in Colorado, with his wife and their four children.

SEAN EADS is a writer and librarian living in Colorado. His first novel, *The Survivors,* was a finalist for the Lambda Literary Award. His third novel, *Lord Byron's Prophecy,* was a finalist for the Shirley Jackson Award and the Colorado Book Award. His short stories have appeared in various anthologies.

ALEC FERRELL is a musician and multimedia producer based out of Durham, NC. Find him *@clearlyalec, clearlymedia.net,* and *clearlyrecords.com.* He loved laying out this book and promises more Ferrell bylines in the future.

WARREN HAMMOND has authored several science fiction novels, quite a few short stories, and a graphic novel. His 2012 novel, *KOP Killer,* won the Colorado Book Award for best mystery. His latest series, Denver Moon, is co-written with Joshua Viola. He is also chief intoxicologist and co-host of the Critiki Party podcast.

Freelance writer, novelist, award-winning screenwriter, editor, poker player, poet, biker, **TRAVIS HEERMANN** is a graduate of the Odyssey Writing Workshop, an Active member of SFWA and the HWA, and the author of the *Shinjuku Shadows Trilogy*, *The Ronin Trilogy*, *The Hammer Falls*, and other novels. His more than thirty short stories appear in Baen Books' anthology *Straight Outta Deadwood*, *Apex Magazine*, *Tales to Terrify*, Cemetery Dance's *Shivers VII*, and others. As a freelance writer, he has contributed a metric ton of work to such game properties as the *Firefly* Roleplaying Game, *Legend of Five Rings*, *EVE Online*, and *BattleTech*, for which he's been nominated for a Scribe Award. He enjoys cycling, collecting martial arts styles and belts, torturing young minds with otherworldly ideas, and monsters of every flavor, especially those with a soft, creamy center.

JASON HELLER is an author and Hugo Award-winning editor who has written for *The New Yorker*, *The Atlantic*, *Rolling Stone*, *Entertainment Weekly*, *Pitchfork*, and NPR. His debut novel was the alternate history satire *Taft 2012* (Quirk Books), and his latest book is *Strange Stars: David Bowie, Pop Music, and the Decade Exploded* (Melville House), a history of science fiction's influence on 70s music and a finalist for the Locus Award and the Colorado Book Award. His upcoming books include the science fiction memoir *Extraterrestrial Summer* (Melville House) and the urban fantasy novel *Repeater* (Saga Press/Simon & Schuster). He lives in Denver and can be found at *jasonhellerauthor.com*.

ANGIE HODAPP is the Director of Literary Development at Nelson Literary Agency. She holds a BA in English and secondary education and an MA in English and communication development, and she is a graduate of the Denver Publishing Institute at the University of Denver. She has worked in publishing and professional writing and editing for the better part of the last two decades, and in addition to writing, she loves helping authors hone their craft and learn about the ever-changing business of publishing.

STEPHEN GRAHAM JONES is the author of sixteen and a half novels, six story collections, a couple of novellas, and a couple of one-shot comic books. Most recent are *Mapping the Interior*, *My Hero*, *The Only Good Indians* and *Night of the Mannequins*. Next is *My Heart Is a Chainsaw*. Stephen lives and teaches in Boulder, Colorado.

A Colorado native, **SAM KNIGHT** spent ten years in California's wine country before returning to the Rockies. When asked if he misses California, he gets a wistful look in his eyes and replies he misses the green mountains in the winter, but he is glad to be back home. As well as having worked for at least three publishing companies, Sam is author of six children's books, five short story collections, three novels, and over five dozen short stories, including two media tie-ins co-authored with Kevin J. Anderson: *Wayward Pines: Aberration* (Kindle Worlds, 2014), and "Of Monsters and Men" in *Planet of the Apes: Tales from the Forbidden Zone* (Titan, 2016). As a stay-at-home father, Sam attempts to be a full-time writer, but there are only so many hours left in a day after kids. Once upon a time, he was known to quote books the way some people quote movies, but now he claims having a family has made him forgetful, as a survival adaptation. Connect with Sam on Twitter (*@AuthorSamKnight*) or Facebook (*facebook. com/AuthorSamKnight*). You can also find him on Goodreads (Sam Knight) and Amazon (Sam Knight). His website is *www.samknight.com*.

Champion Mojo Storyteller **JOE R. LANSDALE** has written novels and stories in many genres, including Western, horror, science fiction, mystery, and suspense. He has also written for comics as well as *Batman: The Animated Series*. As of 2018, he has written 45 novels and published 30 short-story collections along with many chapbooks and comic-book adaptations. His stories have won ten Bram Stoker Awards®, a British Fantasy Award, an Edgar Award, a World Horror Convention Grand Master Award, a Sugarprize, a Grinzane Cavour Prize for Literature, a Spur Award, and a Raymond Chandler Lifetime Achievement Award. He has been inducted into The Texas Literary Hall of Fame, and several of his novels have been adapted to film.

Beyond his current career as a Creative Director of Video for TIDAL, **JONATHAN LEES** has spent over twenty years championing filmmakers through his programming work with the *New York Underground Film Festival*, *Anthology Film Archives*, *TromaDance*, and now, *Final Frame*. He moonlights as a writer of horror stories but promises that he is not a horror himself…sort of. Jonathan's new story, "Persistence," will be published in 2021 within the next volume of Michael Bailey's acclaimed *Chiral Mad* series.

JONATHAN MABERRY is a *New York Times* bestselling author, five-time Bram Stoker Award®-winner, anthology editor, and comic book writer. His vampire apocalypse book series, *V-WARS*, was a Netflix original series. He writes in multiple genres including suspense, thriller, horror, science fiction, fantasy, and action; and he writes for adults, teens and middle grade. His works include the *Joe Ledger* thrillers, *Ink*, *Glimpse*, the *Rot & Ruin* series, the *Dead of Night* series, *The Wolfman*, *X-Files Origins: Devil's Advocate*, *Mars One*, and many others. Several of his works are in development for film and TV. He is the editor of high-profile anthologies including *The X-Files*, *Aliens: Bug Hunt*, *Out of Tune*, *New Scary Stories to Tell in the Dark*, *Baker Street Irregulars*, *Nights of the Living Dead*, and others. His comics include *Black Panther: DoomWar*, *The Punisher: Naked Kills* and *Bad Blood*. His *Rot & Ruin* young adult novel was adapted into the #1 comic on Webtoon, and is being developed for film by Alcon Entertainment. He is a board member of the Horror Writers Association, the President of the International Association of Media Tie-in Writers, and the editor of *Weird Tales Magazine*. He lives in San Diego, California. Find him online at *www.jonathanmaberry.com*.

BRIAN W. MATTHEWS has published four novels and several short stories. He is an active member of the Horror Writers Association, as well as a member of the International Thriller Writers. He lives in southeast Michigan with his wife.

SEANAN MCGUIRE is the author of the Hugo, Nebula, Alex, and Locus Award-winning Wayward Children series, the October Daye series, the InCryptid series, and other works. She also writes darker fiction as Mira Grant. Seanan lives in Seattle with her cats, a vast collection of creepy dolls, horror movies, and sufficient books to qualify her as a fire hazard. She won the 2010 John W. Campbell Award for Best New Writer, and in 2013 became the first person to appear five times on the same Hugo ballot.

Mexican by birth, Canadian by inclination. **SILVIA MORENO-**

GARCIA's debut novel, *Signal to Noise*, about music and magic, won a Copper Cylinder Award. *Gods of Jade and Shadow* was the 2020 American Library Association Reading List winner in the Fantasy category and won the 2020 Sunburst Award for Excellence in Canadian Literature of the Fantastic. *Mexican Gothic* won a Pacific Northwest Book Award and made many best of the year lists. She has edited several anthologies, including *She Walks in Shadows* (World Fantasy Award winner, published in the USA as *Cthulhu's Daughters*), and others. Silvia is the publisher of Innsmouth Free Press. She co-edited the horror magazine *The Dark* with Sean Wallace from 2017 to 2020. She's a columnist for *The Washington Post* and reviews books for NPR. She has an MA in Science and Technology Studies from the University of British Columbia. Her thesis can be read online and is titled "Magna Mater: Women and Eugenic Thought in the Work of H.P. Lovecraft."

LISA MORTON is a screenwriter, author of non-fiction books, award-winning prose writer, and Halloween expert. Her work was described by the American Library Association's *Readers' Advisory Guide to Horror* as "consistently dark, unsettling, and frightening", and *Famous Monsters* called her "one of the best writers in dark fiction today". She began her career in Hollywood, co-writing the cult favorite *Meet the Hollowheads* (on which she also served as Associate Producer), but soon made a successful transition into writing short works of horror. After appearing in dozens of anthologies and magazines, including *The Mammoth Book of Dracula*, *Dark Delicacies*, *The Museum of Horrors*, and *Cemetery Dance*, in 2010 her first novel, *The Castle of Los Angeles*, was published to critical acclaim, appearing on numerous "Best of the Year" lists. Her book *The Halloween Encyclopedia* (now in an expanded second edition) was described by *Reference & Research Book News* as "the most complete reference to the holiday available," and Lisa has been interviewed on The History Channel, the Discovery Channel's series Perfecting History, and in *The Wall Street Journal* as a Halloween authority. She is a six-time winner of the Bram Stoker Award®, a recipient of the Black Quill Award, and winner of the 2012 Grand Prize from the Halloween Book Festival, and her most recent releases are the novellas *Smog* (Double Down #2) and *Summer's End* (both from JournalStone Publishing). A lifelong

Californian, she lives in North Hollywood, and can be found online at *www.lisamorton.com.*

AJ NAZZARO is a freelance illustrator and concept artist living in Denver, Colorado. He is a lifelong gamer and has worked in the trading card and video game industry for almost ten years. After working with Wizards of the Coast on the game *Kaijudo,* he began creating artwork for *Hearthstone* including thirteen expansions and over sixty cards. AJ also contributes artwork to two other Blizzard Entertainment titles, *Overwatch* and *Heroes of the Storm.*

JOHN PALISANO is the author of *Dust of The Dead, Ghost Heart, Nerves, Starlight Drive: Four Halloween Tales, All That Withers* and *Night of 1,000 Beasts.* He won the Bram Stoker Award® in short fiction in 2016 for "Happy Joe's Rest Stop". More short stories have appeared in anthologies from *Cemetery Dance, Weird Tales, Space & Time, PS Publishing, Independent Legions, DarkFuse, Crystal Lake, Terror Tales, Lovecraft eZine, Horror Library, Bizarro Pulp, Written Backwards, Dark Continents, Big Time Books, McFarland Press, Darkscribe, Dark House, Omnium Gatherum* and more. Non-fiction pieces have appeared in Blumhouse, Fangoria, Backstreets and Dark Discoveries magazines. He is currently serving as the President of the Horror Writers Association and has been featured in the *Los Angeles Times* and *Vanity Fair* magazine.

BRET SMITH retired from IBM after thirty-four years as a program manager. He's a lifelong *Star Trek* fan and loves all things pop culture. He met his wife **JEANNI SMITH** on a blind date while she was attending the University of Arizona for her BFA. They've been happily married for over thirty-five years, attending conventions together since the 1980s— their most beloved decade—including over fourteen San Diego Comic-Cons. They raised two artistic sons, Xander—a successful Hollywood artist, and Cameron—a multi-talented musician. Today, when Jeanni isn't busy working as an antiques dealer, she and Bret are focused on their responsibilities as co-founders of the Colorado Festival of Horror. To tie into their upcoming convention, they collaborated with Joshua Viola of Hex Publishers on the anthology *It Came From the Multiplex: 80s*

Midnight Chillers. They live in Longmont, Colorado, with five cats and a lot of books.

JEANNE C. STEIN is the award-winning, national bestselling author of the Urban Fantasy series, The Anna Strong Vampire Chronicles, and the Fallen Siren Series, written as S. J. Harper. She has thirteen full-length books to her credit, several novellas, and numerous short stories, including "The Wolf's Paw", reprinted in Hex Publishers' 2015 anthology, *Nightmares Unhinged*.

BECKY SPRATFORD [MLIS] is a Readers' Advisor in Illinois specializing in serving patrons ages 13 and up. She trains library staff all over the world on how to match books with readers through the local public library. She runs the critically acclaimed RA training blog "RA for All". She is under contract to provide content for EBSCO's NoveList database and writes reviews for Booklist and a horror review column for *Library Journal.* Known for her work with horror readers, Becky is the author of *The Reader's Advisory Guide to Horror*, Second Edition [ALA Editions, 2012] and recently completed the 3rd Edition. She is a proud member of the Horror Writers Association and currently serves as the Association's Secretary and organizer of their annual Librarians' Day. You can follow Becky on Twitter *@RAforAll*.

MOLLY TANZER is the author of the Diabolist's Library trilogy: *Creatures of Will and Temper*, the Locus Award-nominated *Creatures of Want and Ruin*, and *Creatures of Charm and Hunger*. She is also the author of the weird western *Vermilion*, an io9 and NPR "Best Book" of 2015, and the British Fantasy Award-nominated collection, *A Pretty Mouth*, as well as many critically acclaimed short stories. Follow her adventures at *@molly_tanzer* on Instagram or *@wickedmilkhotel* on Twitter. She lives outside of Boulder, Colorado, with her cat, Toad. If you'd like to contact Molly, feel free to drop her a line at *emollytanzer@gmail.com*.

STEVE RASNIC TEM is the author of over 400 short stories and seven novels and is a winner of the Bram Stoker Award®, British Fantasy, and

World Fantasy awards. A collection of his selected stories, *Figures Unseen*, recently came out from Valancourt Books. His stories for children and young adults have appeared in such anthologies as *A Nightmare's Dozen*, edited by Michael Stearns, *Bruce Coville's Book of Spine-Tinglers 2*, and *Scary Out There*, edited by Jonathan Maberry.

JOHN WENZEL is an award-winning reporter and critic for *The Denver Post* whose writing about comedy, film, books, music, video games and other pop-culture topics has appeared in *Rolling Stone*, *Esquire*, *The Atlantic* and *Vulture*. He hails from Dayton, Ohio, where he grew up thinking about the Wright Brothers and Guided by Voices.

JEAMUS WILKES has been working as a writer and editor since 2003, providing those services on a freelance basis whilst engaging in his own fiction, nonfiction, poetry, and publishing ventures. Jeamus' educational background includes Commercial Art & Advertising, Criminal Justice Administration, and English (with Creative Writing specialization). His fiction writing credits include "That Time Maggie Ghosted Me" (appearing in Denver Horror Collective's *Terror at 5280'* anthology), "When the Spirit Leaveth the Flesh" (appearing in Hellbound Books Publishings' *Cold Flesh* anthology), and the nonfiction essay on fiction narratology, "Unreliable Horrors" (as published in *Hello Horror* volume 3, issue 16). As of February 2021, he serves alongside Maria Abrams as co-chairperson of HWA Denver. Jeamus lives in Golden, Colorado, with his wife, stepkids, and a zoo of dogs, cats, and fish.

CARTER WILSON is the *USA Today* and #1 *Denver Post* bestselling author of seven critically acclaimed, standalone psychological thrillers, as well as numerous short stories. He is an ITW Thriller Award finalist, a four-time winner of the Colorado Book Award, and his novels have received multiple starred reviews from *Publishers Weekly*, *Booklist*, and *Library Journal*. His seventh novel, *The Dead Husband*, will be launched in May 2021 by Poisoned Pen Press. Carter lives in Erie, Colorado, in a Victorian house that is spooky but isn't haunted...yet.

DEAN WYANT is a forty-five-year resident of Colorado. He is a book-seller, book collector and avid reader. His previous co-authored short stories have appeared in *Nightmares Unhinged* and *Blood Business* by Hex Publishers and Found by RMFW Press. *Psi-Wars* marks his first solo short story publication.

ALVARO ZINOS-AMARO is a Hugo and Locus award finalist who has published some forty stories and over one hundred reviews, essays and interviews in venues like *Clarkesworld, Asimov's, Analog, Lightspeed, Tor.com, Locus, Beneath Ceaseless Skies, Nature, Strange Horizons, The Los Angeles Review of Books,* and anthologies such as *The Year's Best Science Fiction & Fantasy 2016, Cyber World, Humanity 2.0, Blood Business, This Way to the End Times, Shades Within Us, The Unquiet Dreamer, Nox Pareidolia,* and *It Came From the Multiplex.*

ABOUT THE ARTIST

AARON LOVETT has been published by AfterShock Comics, *Tor.com, The Denver Post,* and *Spectrum Fantastic Art 22 & 24.* His *Nightmares Unhinged* (Hex Publishers) cover art was licensed by AMC for their hit TV show *Fear the Walking Dead.* You can see his most recent work in *Monster Train* (Shiny Shoe and Good Shepherd Entertainment), which was a number one Global Top Seller on Steam and named Best Card Game of 2020 by *PC Gamer.* He was a finalist in Dark Horse Comics' *The Last of Us* Halloween art contest and Skydance Media's *Terminator Genisys* art contest. His art can be found in various other video games, books and comics. You can view his portfolio at *www.artstation.com/adlovett.* He paints from a dark corner in Denver, Colorado.

ABOUT THE EDITOR

JOSHUA VIOLA IS A FOUR-TIME Colorado Book Award finalist and 2021 Splatterpunk Award nominee. He is co-author of the *Denver Moon* series with Warren Hammond. Their comic book collection, *Denver Moon: Metamorphosis*, was included on the 2018 Bram Stoker Award® Preliminary Ballot. Joshua edited the *Denver Post* #1 bestselling anthology, *Nightmares Unhinged* (Hex Publishers), and co-edited *Cyber World* (with Jason Heller, Hex Publishers)—named one of the best science fiction anthologies of 2016 by Barnes & Noble.

His first novel, *The Bane of Yoto*, won the USA Best Book Awards, National Indie Excellence Awards, International Book Awards, and Independent Publishers Book Awards. His follow-up novel, *Blackstar*, was a narrative companion to Hollywood musician Celldweller's concept album of the same name. Joshua's short fiction has appeared in numerous anthologies, including *Doorbells at Dusk* (Corpus Press), *D.O.A. III – Extreme Horror* (Blood Bound Books), and alongside his literary hero, Stephen King, in *One of Us: A Tribute to Frank Michaels Errington* (Bloodshot Books). He's a regular contributor to Denver's popular arts and culture magazine, *Birdy*, and has had a few appearances on *Tor.com*.

When he isn't writing and editing, Joshua dabbles in art. In 2020, he collaborated with his husband, Aaron Lovett, on AfterShock Comics' *Miskatonic* #1 Cover Alpha Comics variant. Together, they also developed the Never Summer Industries/Breckenridge Brewery 2014 collector's edition snowboard design, and the official logo for Breckenridge Brewery's 2014 Denver Comic Con beer, "Brews Wayne." They were also finalists in Skydance Media's *Terminator Genisys* art contest. As a video game artist, Joshua worked on *Pirates of the Caribbean: Call of the Kraken* (Disney Interactive), *Smurfs' Grabber* (Capcom) and *TARGET: Terror* (Konami). He also tries to squeeze in time as the VP of a successful processing plant that supplies organic meat and vegan options for the nation's major grocers and retailers, as well as keeping Hex Publishers up and running—all in the beautiful (when it's not on fire) state of Colorado. Connect with Joshua at *JoshuaViola.com*.

ACKNOWLEDGMENTS

FICTION & POETRY

EDITORIAL CONTENT

THE HEX ARTWORK GALLERY

MORE ANTHOLOGIES
FROM HEX PUBLISHERS

Shadow Atlas: Dark Landscapes of the Americas
(Edited by Carina Bissett, Hillary Dodge and Joshua Viola)

It Came from the Multiplex: 80s Midnight Chillers
(Edited by Joshua Viola)

Psi-Wars: Classified Cases of Psychic Phenomena
(Edited by Joshua Viola)

Mechanical Animals: Tales at the Crux of Creatures and Tech
(Edited by Selena Chambers and Jason Heller)

Blood and Gasoline: High-Octane, High-Velocity Action
(Edited by Mario Acevedo)

Blood Business: Crime Stories from this World and Beyond
(Edited by Mario Acevedo and Joshua Viola)

Georgetown Haunts and Mysteries
(Edited by Jeanne C. Stein and Joshua Viola)

Cyber World: Tales of Humanity's Tomorrow
(Edited by Jason Heller and Joshua Viola)

Nightmares Unhinged: Twenty Tales of Terror
(Edited by Joshua Viola)

SOUVENIR BOOK SPONSORS

SOUVENIR ANTHOLOGY

STOKERCON™

THE **PHANTOM DENVER** EDITION 2021

birdy.

Tyler Gross, *Thrashmania*, From Issue 022 • more at *birdymagazine.com*

Join Bobby Holmes and his friends in a thrilling young adult horror series by author J.M. Kelly.

The Lost Treasure

The spirit of an ancient pirate, a fortune teller, a murder, and buried treasure. Join Bobby Holmes, his friends as they solve a deadly mystery in the bucolic town of Mountain Lake, and struggle to save their own lives.

Monster on the Moors

A werewolf, witches, and a Gypsy King. Join Bobby Holmes, his cousin Brenda Watson, and friends as they risk their lives to solve a deadly mystery in the North York Moors of England.

J.M. Kelly is the author of five books on topics ranging from Middle Grade Fiction, Adult Comedy Mystery, and Educational Leadership.

Read more about the author at jmkellyauthor.com   Books available on amazon.com

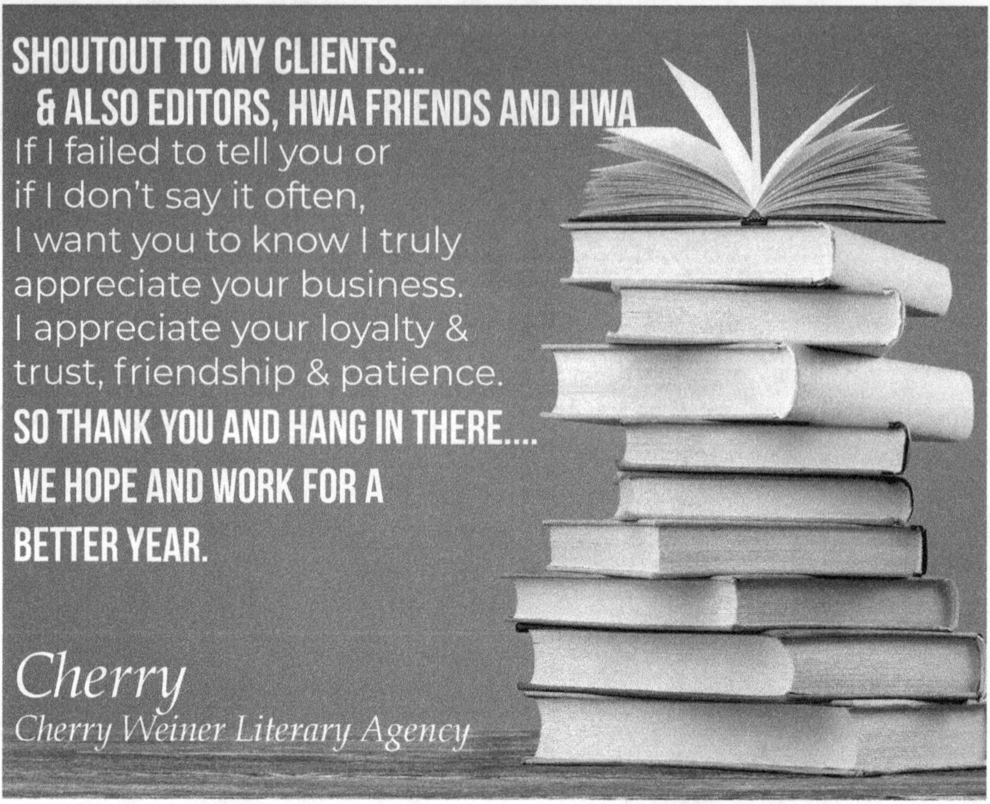
SHOUTOUT TO MY CLIENTS...
& ALSO EDITORS, HWA FRIENDS AND HWA
If I failed to tell you or
if I don't say it often,
I want you to know I truly
appreciate your business.
I appreciate your loyalty &
trust, friendship & patience.
SO THANK YOU AND HANG IN THERE....
WE HOPE AND WORK FOR A
BETTER YEAR.
Cherry
Cherry Weiner Literary Agency

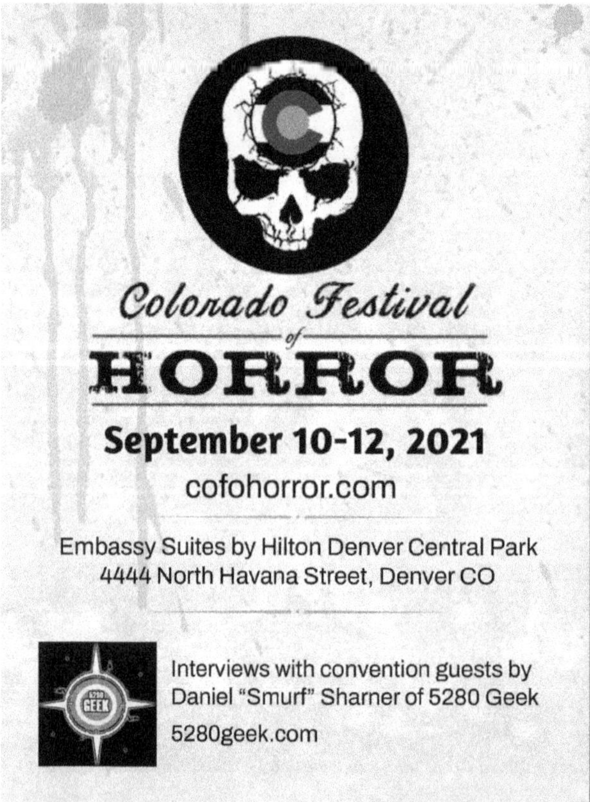
Colorado Festival of HORROR
September 10-12, 2021
cofohorror.com
Embassy Suites by Hilton Denver Central Park
4444 North Havana Street, Denver CO
5280 GEEK
Interviews with convention guests by
Daniel "Smurf" Sharner of 5280 Geek
5280geek.com

It Came from the
MULTIPLEX
80s Midnight Chillers
HEX PUBLISHERS
It Came From The Multiplex
Hex Publishers' 80s horror
movie-inspired anthology
available at the show
Convention Exclusive Cover
Multi-Author Signed Bookplate
Limited to 250 copies!

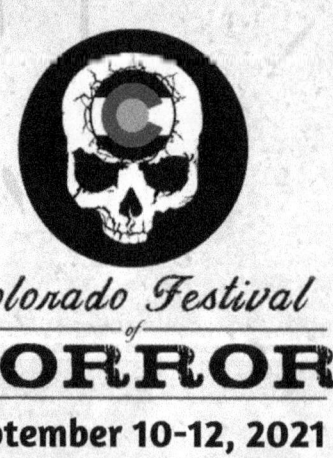

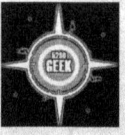

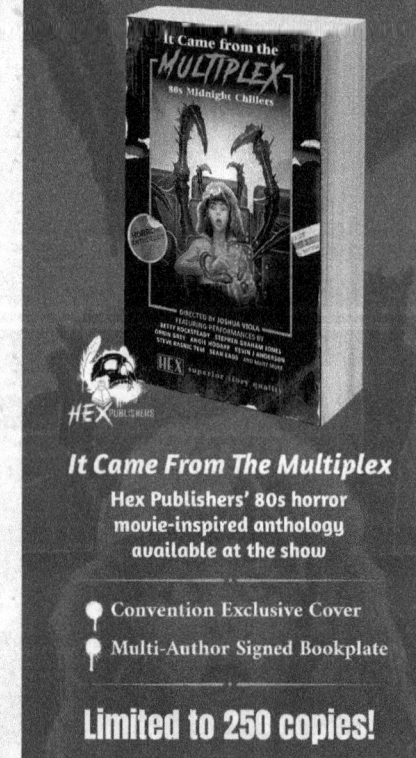

CPSIA information can be obtained
at www.ICGtesting.com
Printed in the USA
BVHW031429160521
607084BV00014B/18